DREAMS AND SECRETS BOOK THREE

THE
CHILDREN
OF
DEATH

LINN COLDIRON

Cover Design by Jules Designs
(www. coversbyjules.crd.co)
Book Layout by Linn Coldiron

The Children of Death / Linn Coldiron ~ Second Edition 2024
ISBN: 978-1-955200-31-8

10 9 8 7 6 5 4 3 2

To Lorin and Rachel for giving me the love of writing that I will never be able to rid myself of.

The Dreams and Secrets Series

Lotus In the Mountain
An Imminent Dream
The Children of Death
A Hollow Secret
The Risen Queen

A Note from the Author

In the process of creating this story, world, and characters, I've spent hundreds of hours researching the cultures involved, including learning Mandarin and living in China for a period of about a year. However, research does not replace lived experience and I, in no way, claim that the experiences of my characters represent the entirety of the Asian American community. The same goes for the indigenous tribe I created for the sake of the story and clans. I created the culture based on my own readings and understandings of Native American tribes, particularly the Shoshone tribe which much inspiration was taken. For lived experience representation, please seek out books by authors of any culture you wish to read about. There is a list of some of my favorites on my website, linncoldiron.com.

Content Warnings

While a work of fiction intended for entertainment, there are darker elements and themes in *The Children of Death*. This book contains the following content warnings: violence using fantasy magic, colonialism, slavery, genocide, suicide, curing disabilities, ableism, prejudice, racism, and homophobia.

The Children of Death dives into many deep topics taking place in a different, fantasy world. It is a collection of stories told from the point of view of immortals recalling not only their personal history, but also the history of their people. It is heavily critical of colonialism, imperialism, genocide, slavery, racial issues, ableism, and homophobia.

Creation

Chapter One

In order to start at the beginning, we must go back to the before. There are only stories of this time. Stories that live within our souls. Stories our mothers told us. Our grandmothers. Bedtime tales meant to scare us as children. These are not written stories. They are spoken, passed down from generation to generation. If you were to ask one of us now, who did not live in the time of the gods, they might tell you a different story. But every tale, no matter who speaks it, always begin the same way.

They always, without fail, begin with Death.

Death. The creature of life. Death. The being of the end. He is everything and nothing like the stories you tell of him on Earth. He is an entity, given shape and form by whoever is about to die. He is informed by culture, by personal opinions, and by the state of the world. He is sometimes she. He is sometimes they. He is sometimes nothing at all.

To the gods, he is everything. To the Vilaim, he is God. But to Death, he is but a lonely soul longing for the day when someone will bring him the peace he has never known.

In order to understand who the Iravata are, what we are doing on Earth, and how we came to be in this war, we must go back to before there were gods. Before there were immortals. Before there were Vilaim.

We must go back to the day that Death came into being. We must tell *his* story.

Chapter Two

At first, there was nothing. A vast expanse of darkness. No, not darkness. *Nothingness.* A vast expanse of nothingness consuming anything and everything. Because there was nothing. It was here, it was then, it was now, that Death blinked into existence, taking no form, no name, and no identity. He was all that existed. He was the only being wandering through this nothingness. His mind, unaware of time and space, drifted as he gained a form. A conscience. Desire.

He walked. He walked, and walked, and walked. Wandering until he could wander no more, and then he continued on. Because there was nothing else to do. There was nothing else to do but wander for millions of years.

And then, without warning, there was mist. A haze of white drifting along the nothingness. Death relished in the mist. He longed for more. For something to step on. His desires grew. Firm ground spread out from his footsteps. A light appeared in the distance. Something to give him hope. To make him feel less empty.

He longed for another like him. For while the light brought him warmth, he still wandered alone. He desired someone to speak to, to understand the thoughts forming in his ever developing mind. He could not be the only one. He was the only one.

He kept walking.

And he was lonely.

Death did not notice when the mist dissipated. His fingers brushed against the rough bark of trees. His feet sunk into the mossy earth. The world around him lit with colors, magic dancing in the sky as a forever rainbow leading him through the terrain.

Time is nothing to Death.

Death has existed since the Before. He has existed for all of time. For all of space. He is the reason life is here, and he is the reason life will disappear. He will outlast everything until the After, when life ceases to exist.

Time is nothing to Death.

He did not notice the change. If asked, he could not tell you where the trees came from. When the light in the distance grew brighter and took form. When the sky took on color. If asked, he would tell you that he blinked and one day it was so. He stared up at the sky, at the sun, and he wondered for the first time:

Who am I?

There was no answer. So, he wandered. The jungles of the South led him through swamps. Over logs. Into trees. Touching, examining, understanding everything around him. He took in the warmth of the sun. He took in the dampness of the water. The silky leaves and the sharp spine on flower stems. It was life, he realized. He was no longer alone.

And yet, he was lonely.

He wandered. North of the swamps, he came across the plains. The ground was firmer here. Solid. He did not sink. When he dug his fingers into the soil, they came up dirty and moist, but not wet. New life existed here. Golden grass rose to his waist, swaying in the wind.

Wind.

Such a beautiful and dangerous part of life. A fickle aspect of nature, sometimes giving, sometimes taking, always moving. Never sitting still long enough to see the consequences of its actions. Death breathed in the wind, and for the first time, he smiled. His lips had never had a reason to move before. He had no one to talk to. He did not require air to live. He was life itself. He was death itself. Yet, he smiled. Because the wind was fickle, and he longed to dance like the grass.

His clothing appeared without a thought, covering his body with loose folds. He wished for them to play with the wind, as the wind played with the grass, and his wish came to fruition. The first sound out of his lips, his smiling lips, was a laugh. It echoed through the fields, startling him. The wind laughed along with him, and he lifted his arms to greet it.

It was not enough.

He needed more. He needed to *be* the grass. But he could not be the grass. And so, he touched his head and pulled down, creating a length of hair as long as his body until it touched the ground.

The wind giggled, pleased with its new toy, and kicked up the locks. Death joined in with a joyous sound of his own.

Was this a friend? Was wind what he was looking for?

No. Because wind is fickle. Wind does not care about the desires of an entity. Nature did not belong to Death. Wind did not yield to his commands. The grass did not wilt when he walked. The trees grew regardless of his touch. Nature existed in a plane of its own, governed by a Greater God unknown to Death.

So, still, Death was lonely.

His wanderings took him far from the plains and into the mountains clambering over one another toward the sky. At first, he hesitated. Now that he was *aware*, now that he knew of the land before him, of the nature out of his control, a hint of fear burned a hole in the space where his stomach might be.

The mountains exploded in front of him, their jagged and unforgiving sides a deterrence to his exploration. Any wrong step and he could fall to his death.

Except he was death. He was life.

He continued on, one step at a time over thousands of years. The rocks fought him, angry and vengeful, but soon he befriended them, as he had the wind. He created shoes, wanting to protect his feet from the pins and needles poking at his soft skin.

He could not die.

He could not feel hunger or thirst.

He did not experience exhaustion.

But he did feel pain.

And so he found ways around the pain. He created his shoes. He thickened his clothes to protect against the sharpness of the trees. He hardened his soul against the harsh snows, against the wind that aimed to kill. He prepared himself for whatever might come next.

As the mountains receded back into the ground, they turned soft. Sand. Dunes. Slippery and difficult to walk upon. But at the end of those, at the end of his frustration and his anger, he found an expanse of water stretching forever. It touched the setting sun, swallowing the white ball of energy as though it were nothing but a piece of fruit dropping into a pool of water.

Death paused here. He paused and sat, staring out at the surf as the tide came in and took him to a new wave of bliss.

He did not need to breath, and so he sat at the bottom of the sea, watching the plant life grow and change and live and die. He did not need to eat, or drink, and so he remained there for a million years, calmed by the natural ebb and flow of the water. He could not die, and so he did not fear when the water rose higher and higher, taking him further and further to the core of the world.

He merely waited. Waited for the tide to bring him back to the surface. And he took it all in.

Took it all in and wondered if he would ever have a domain. Nature did not belong to him. When he returned the surface, he searched each plant and rock for company. He spoke to them in a tongue long forgotten to existence.

They never responded.

They never moved.

They grew, and they lived, and they died, all out of his control.

He appreciated all of them. Every single plant. Every single rock. Every single swamp. Every single ocean.

Still, he was lonely.

He did not notice when life began. He had walked for days. Months. Years. The sun gathered with it stars and moons which dotted the night sky like an expanse of white sand had been thrown against a blackened stone. The world around him buzzed. Hummed.

Everywhere he went, he left behind a piece of himself.

A piece of life.

And he did not notice at first. He was too busy immersed in nature to notice the little creatures wandering in the wake of his footsteps. He did not notice that every now and then, a million and one times a day, his soul was pulled in different directions, off to do its job.

He did not realize he had a job.

Then, one day he sat on a rock, back where his journey had begun in the wilds of the jungle, and a creature crawled on his leg. For while all creatures feared death, they did not fear Death. He was nothing more than a thing to crawl on. An object that would cause them no harm.

He opened his eyes and stared at the little creature. It looked nothing like him. He imagined, when he found his purpose, that the creatures would look as he imagined himself. Two legs. Two arms. Hands and feet. A head. Long hair that he tied back with vines.

This creature was little. Small enough to fit into the palm of his hands with beady black eyes and four legs. Its tongue shot out and tasted his clothes. Its skin, the color of moss, shimmered in the light. He reached out and touched the head. It was not smooth like his own body. It did not have hair, but something else. Scales. A creature with four legs and scales.

Four legs, scales, and the thumping of a heart.

The creature made a noise and ran away, disappearing beneath the underbrush, and he realized that he was no longer alone in a world of plants and stones. For the first time he paid attention to the world around him—really paid attention—and found that it buzzed with life.

Creatures dangling from the trees, taking to the skies, diving beneath the foam on the waves, sinking into the mud of the swamps, and roaming the world untouched and unafraid. Large, small, fast, slow…it did not matter what traits they had. They existed, and he loved them.

He fell in love with his Creatures.

But they did not love him.

They did not speak his language. He understood them, and he coaxed them into his lap, but they only saw him as another creature, different from them. For they all looked different. They all ran with their own kind, and he was not one of them.

And then, one day, he realized that the tugging at his soul that he felt a million times a day was not something abnormal. It was not something to ignore.

It was him doing his job.

He was Death. A creature of life and ruin. And when the Creatures met their end—when they were caught by a predator, taken ill by the viruses, or fell in an unfortunate accident—he appeared at their side unwillingly and ferried them from life to nothing.

He was Death.

He had a purpose. While he did not exert command over the plants, he did over the Creatures, and he continued to wander on his never ending journey. He saw all. He witnessed the births, the courtships, and the deaths.

He was omniscient.

He was absent.

This was his domain, but not his world. He was in charge, but never allowed to interfere. He walked among the Creatures, letting the cycle of life play out and always remaining stable in his role. The sun rose, the moons set, and the stars blinked in and out. There were nights when he would sit in a field, staring up at the dotted heavens and wondered what else there could be.

As time passed, he watched his Creatures grow and change. He watched them as some died out forever. As new ones took their place. Ever changing, ever growing, ever moving on as if life itself was nothing more than a circle with no friction. Never ending. Never stopping.

And through it all, he was lonely.

Then, one day, as he sat among his Creatures, watching them live and die, he wondered to himself. His mind wandered to the depth of the world. To everything he had seen. To the ocean. To the mountains. To the Creatures. And he wondered…and wondered… and wondered….

Why am I alone? Why is there no one like me? Why do I only take away? Why can I not create?

On that day, he broke the rules. He did not wait for life to come about on its own. No. He decided, despite not knowing the consequences, that he was going to create life. Consciously and purposefully, create life. He did not know who created these rules. No one had ever spoken them to him. They lived deep in his soul, guiding his every move. But on that day, he ignored them.

On that day, he did not take away life, but gave it. A Creature who looked like him.

On that day he made a friend.

Born of dust, water, and the nectar of the flowers living atop the ponds, she rose from the ground with the color of tree bark and eyes the color of the ocean. Her skin was pale, a perfect mixture of pink and white, just like the flower from which she was created. Like him, she had four limbs: two legs and two arms. Two feet and two hands. Two bright eyes.

The ability to speak his words.

He named her Seshen, after the flower from which she drew her life.

When he greeted her, voice hoarse after millions of years of non-use, she smiled at him and said, "Hello."

Chapter Three

Exhilaration overtook him. Finally, after all these years, he had a companion. Nothing matched her beauty. Graceful. Gentle. Kind. Eager to learn. The two of them traveled together, and she saw all the things that he saw. She asked questions, and he answered them. She taught him things he had never considered.

Together they discovered what she could eat. What she could drink. He could sense the things that could kill her, and so he guided her. He let her live a life he wished he could live: a life with mistakes and imperfections.

To him, she was perfect.

One day, though, he noticed that she did not always smile. When she was with him, her smile was infectious. It brought out a joy in him that he had never thought he would experience, but when she was alone, when she thought he was not looking, she stared out at the ocean from atop her favorite rock with longing in her soul.

He had been alone for so long that any company pleased him, but for her, it was different. She had inherited his desire for companionship. Death was her friend. She had called him that many times, introducing him to the word, but he was not like her. If he bled, he did not die. If he ate poison he did not suffer.

She was different.

He was different.

He could not bring to her the companionship he knew she sought.

Seeing her look longingly out at the sea destroyed him in the depths of his soul. He wanted to bring her happiness, to bring her joy, to make her feel half of what she brought to him.

So, once more, he broke the rules. No one had punished him for creating Seshen, and no one would punish him for bringing more. Using the flowers of her creation, he added life into others. Others in her image. Brown hair. Blue eyes. Lithe. Pale skin. He gave them language. Curiosity. Determination. He brought them to her, and watched as light returned to her beautiful eyes.

As laughter returned to her beautiful lips.

She taught them all that he had taught her. What foods to eat. How to build structures. She was their matriarch.

She was their queen.

A male of her kind courted her and she returned the love. They bonded and had children. The children aged. The community grew. There were more children. Rules and customs. Together they created a culture with music and dancing and stories of the man who had created them.

Of Death, who had backed away.

Only Seshen knew him. She tried to convince him to join them. To exist within their world, but he stayed away. She had brought him so much joy, and he was happy to give her what he could not supply by himself. After all, he could not be next to her at all times. He had a job to do.

He would wander the earth, letting her live her life with her people as they raised her to the status of leader. Then elder.

And then, on a day where the rain poured from the sky and soaked the ground with life, Death was pulled back to the little community where his creations lived. He knew before he arrived why. He did not have to ask questions.

She waited for him. Sitting there with her beautiful eyes and a young face, waiting for him to ferry her to the other side.

Because, like everything in the world, at some point she had to die. He knew this. It is why he brought her happiness. Why he filled her short life with a lover. With children. With purpose.

When she died, he held her hand and walked her all the way to the gates of the world beyond. A world he could not enter. She smiled at him and whispered that he would be all right before she vanished into the light, forever lost to him.

With the village, he watched them mourn her death. She was the oldest of them. The first of their kind. She was the one who taught them right from wrong. Who showed them how to live and build happiness. She was kind and gentle and always curious.

She was their queen.

And their queen had died.

Their lives would move on, he realized. The world would forget her existence once everyone there had died. She would become nothing more than a story to be told at bedtime. The story of Seshen. The woman who gave them their namesake.

For the Seshen people would continue on without her. And they would continue on without Death. They had figured out how to live, and he would be there when they died.

Once more, he was lonely.

He turned his back on the Seshen village and vowed to himself that he would never return. He would not watch the people forget her. He would not let himself feel the pain. Tears streaked his face, an unfamiliar sensation, and he hated every moment of it.

He walked away with the need to fill the void that Seshen had left the moment she vanished into the light, and decided that he was going to start over.

Lan was different than Seshen. He had her curiosity, but not her finesse. While she walked on air, he jumped from log to log, strong muscles giving him an advantage over the other creatures of the jungles. His body was broad with eyes and skin as dark as the flower Death had used to create him. His hair was short and curly, not growing the way Seshen's had.

He spoke little. He did not make simple conversation with Death, instead asking deep questions about the meaning of his creation. He was intelligent. Possibly more so than Seshen, but he did not flaunt it. It was his way of showing dominance. And indeed, he competed with Death at every turn.

The flower Death had used to create him was known for its ability to survive in the deepest caverns of the jungle. It could fight off the Creatures that wished to eat it. It could weather the harsh rains. The grueling heat. The competition.

Lan was no different.

This time, Death did not want to make the same mistakes as he did with Seshen. He did not bring Lan with him on his journeys. He led him to believe that the jungle was the entire world, and taught him only the barest minimum. He wanted to see if Lan could survive the way Seshen would not have been able to without him.

And Lan did.

So Death created more like him. A hardy group of creations who quickly developed their own culture. They worshiped the jungle as if it were a god, created tools, and built structures within the trunks of thick trees.

Soon, they left the ground, ascending to the canopies where they raised their children to be free like birds.

Death joined them. He shifted his appearance to match their own, giving up his long hair and lithe body. He took the form of a male, like Lan, and became a member of their society. He learned their language. Ate their food. Danced their dances. Told their stories. He made friends and acquaintances and he gained a sense of peace.

Pieces of him continued to return to the village of Seshen, but he paid as little attention to them as he did the Creatures. They were nothing to him without her.

But, as before, time passed. Time passed and Death did not age as everyone around him did. Whispers spread. They asked him questions about his existence. They began to worship him as a god.

Lan was not the first of the tribe to die, but he was the first funeral Death attended. He stood at the edge as they burned their leader's body and he wondered, strongly, if it was wise to stay any longer. The children looked at him with fear in their eyes. They had heard stories, of those who had gotten close to death and survived, of a man who looked like them, come to take their soul to the light.

He had helped spread those stories.

For he was Death, and he needed them to fear him so they would continue to live.

As Lan's body burned, Death turned and walked away, disappearing in the jungle, never to be heard of again.

Death longed to fill the void in his heart. His metaphorical heart. For Death did not have a heart to beat in his chest. He did not have blood to flow through his veins. He existed outside of time and space, but also within time and space. He was, is, forever will be, a Greater God.

No matter how much he wants to, he cannot escape from the Creatures. The ones he created, and the ones he did not. He cannot give up his responsibility, because what once lived must someday die. That is the cycle of life.

He knew this. With each passing cycle of the sun, every time the moons rose into the beautiful night sky painted with stars, he gained more knowledge of his purpose in life. He was to take away. He was part of an important process. A vital piece of the cycle of reality that needed to be completed by someone.

And that someone, that something, was him.

He was so lonely.

So he continued to create. He wandered through the world he had once explored and plucked new and different flowers from different terrains. He built new tribes. Watched them live. Watched them die.

Some could not adapt. Some vanquished within a generation. Sometimes by the weather. Sometimes by each other. Not all of them had the intelligence of Lan, or the grace of Seshen. Some ignored the curiosity and replaced it with greed.

He left those ones early. He did not want to see his creations fight amongst each other, destroying themselves in the process. He wanted them to live. To survive. To exist always and forever.

But while many disappeared, others flourished. While some fought amongst each other, stealing with greed and hatred in their hearts, others worked together to brave against the cold and the nasty terrains that Death had gifted them.

Nine.

Nine tribes survived their first generation. Then their second. Then their third and fourth. They were going to make it, Death would decide, and then he would leave and wander, his soul forever tugged in every direction.

One day, he returned to Seshen's tribe. They had grown, expanding over several cities now. Their queen—for they will forever be a matriarchy—welcomed him into her home with warm arms. They did not know who he was. They did not know his relation to their namesake, nor to the end of their lives.

He returned to them as a friend, in their image.

But like always, he had to leave.

He visited all nine of his creations, always in their image, always with their tongue, always knowing their customs and their ways. Some heralded him as a god. Others saw him as an omen.

The strange man who always knew too much.

All he wanted was to be one of them. He longed to be their friend. To live and die among them. He had seen life. He had seen millions of years, and nothing ever changed for him. He could never fully integrate into the societies. Whenever he grew close to a creation, they grew old and died.

Every tribe had a different way to honor their dead. Burial. Sent off to sea. Burned. Set into the swamps. It didn't matter what it was. Each time it was meant for the one who had died. Some belief, some core aspect of their culture, told them to make sure that Death could ferry the soul into the good afterlife.

Death did not know how to tell them there was but one afterlife. And no matter what, he would always find the soul of the one who had passed.

For he was Death.

And Death saw all.

He saw them flourish and grow into cities with thousands of creations living their life. Laughing children. Cared for elderly. Loving couples.

He stepped back after a time. He stopped visiting them. He stopped going to their homes and becoming their friend. He could not stop his job, but he could stop interfering. Helping them survive. He was nothing more than a hindrance to them. A confusion that they did not need in this already mystifying world.

Instead he watched.

And he learned.

He called them by the names of their firsts.

Seshen, a city in the plains, caring and true. They were the first and the strongest. Curious and careful. They worshiped their queen and kept true to the values of their matriarch.

Lan, the people of the forest, quick and strong. Their minds worked like no other, and they managed to survive the dangers of the forest without losing many.

Narumi, a grouping of villages near the ocean, hardworking, generous, and always striving to understand the difference between right and wrong.

Jous, a small clan isolated in the mountains, cunning and sturdy. With the ability to cultivate the land with so little nutrients, they celebrated everything that came to them, and refused to let the cold, harsh mountain winters destroy the fire in their souls.

Harashim, a group spread out among islands in the sea, thoughtful and brave. Nothing frightened them. Even the harshest hurricanes did not stop them from enjoying life to the fullest.

Tep, frozen in the icy caves of the North where little sun shone, were clever and thoughtful. They told the most vivid of the stories, painting the walls of their homes with tales of their ancestors.

Siman, a tribe who never quite grew, and spent their free time weaving the grasses around them into beautiful tapestries and clothing. Vibrant. Alive. Simple.

Raan remained sickly and weak, surviving despite all of Death's preconceived notions.

And finally, Nimbon, a city of thieves, treachery, and violence.

Death watched over them.

Death was lonely.

And then the wars began.

Chapter Four

It all began the day that the Seshens needed more land. Their home by the ocean was too small. The farmlands were not enough to feed their people anymore. Their queen—a descendant of the first Seshen—declared that they would go past the hills and claim more land. A solution she had not realized would come with a problem.

For, you see, Death's creations did not know of each other. To them, the world was small. They were the only. They did not know that on the other side of the hills was not empty land, but the land of others like them. Others with flaming red hair and peaceful villages.

Death had not thought about what would happen when his creations met. He had not considered that maybe something terrible would happen. When the Seshen first set out to cross the hills, when they broke through a barrier Death had not realized he had created, they came across the Siman villages.

Death remembered Siman. He had not been outstanding. He had not been the smartest creation. He had not been the most vile. He had smiled and lived a life of good luck and fortune. Easily accessible food. A love of his life. Children.

He came to die young, but loved, and his progeny continued on surviving for years, weaving and farming, all just a little too trusting and peaceful.

The Seshen were not.

Death had seen what happened when new Creatures came across each other. Fear. Uncertainty. Destruction.

He had not thought, for one second, that his beautiful creations would follow the same path. They were like him. They were built in his image and created to be his companions. They were smarter and more cunning than the Creatures. They stood apart.

He had not expected his first creations to attack the peaceful artisans. He had not expected them to treat them with fear and hesitance. They did not look the same, and for that reason, they were treated as animals. Rounded up like cattle and enslaved.

The Seshen brought the Siman back to their cities and presented them before their queen. Death watched. He watched, not sure what to do, or if he should interfere, as the queen allowed the dehumanization of the Siman.

Seshen's citizens were dubbed Vilaim—precious. Siman's people were dubbed Tulu—vermin.

It was this moment that everything changed. The Seshen did not respect the lives of the Siman, and the Siman were too passive, too peaceful, to fight back. They did not want to cause trouble. They did their best to survive in their new conditions, giving up their homes and their lands to the Seshen knights.

Death watched.

Death did not interfere.

He wanted to see how this would go. How things would turn out. How the world he had created would play out if he only did his job. He could have gone down and told the Seshen queen that she was out of line. He could have interfered. Instead he watched for a generation as the Seshen continued to abuse the Siman.

He watched. He waited.

And the Seshen found that, once more, they needed more land. This time, instead of looking only for land, they decided to look for more Tulu. More people who looked like them, but did not look like them. It was a decision by the queen. By the descendant of Seshen.

And Death watched.

He watched as they went north, along the sea, in search of better ports. Of more fishing spots. He watched knowing full well who they were going to find.

And he watched as the war began.

He remembered Narumi. A beautiful woman with flowing black hair and skin with a golden undertone. She always held her head high, asking questions of Death that he could not answer. She sought to understand morality. To understand the difference between right and wrong. Of all his creations, after Seshen, Narumi was his favorite. The feisty child who gave their parent a headache but had too much charisma to dislike.

The Narumi took on her headstrong attitude. Living further north than the Seshen, they encountered a different world. One of harsh weather and dangerous Creatures. They built their culture around the ability to defend themselves. Their harshness. Their boisterous conversations and massive feasts. Everything about them screamed that they were too dangerous to be trifled with.

But the Seshen did not know this. The Seshen did not understand the signs, for their military had been built in a different climate. Their past foe had been a peaceful people with no military at all.

The day they attacked the Narumi, they had thought that they would conquer more Tulu.

Only to find that the Narumi were not vermin. Indeed, though they looked different, with different hair and different eyes, the Narumi held themselves high and attacked the Seshen back, pushing them back and fighting with a ferocity that scared the knights of the queen.

The Seshen fled.

That night the Narumi celebrated their victory over their foes, thinking them just like any other Creature, until one young man came forward and asked why they had so much in common with one another. He asked, and he spoke out alone, if they should be celebrating the deaths of those who looked like them.

Most of the Narumi ignored him, but a few broke out in whispers. Whispers that got back to the leader of the villages and towns. They did not call him a king, but he filled that role with great pride. An elected leader who gave his people hope and prosperity. He heard the whispers and he became curious. These brown haired, blue-eyed monsters were not to be trusted. Not after the attack. But…but their existence meant that the Narumi were no longer alone.

Or maybe they had never been alone.

It was always told, in Narumi history, that a man walked among them who did not belong. Back in the days of their first settlers. The Narumi leader sat and he thought, wondering about what the rest of the world might hold for him and his people, and he ordered his bravest warriors to kneel before him.

"Go," he ordered. "Explore. Bring back news of the world outside of our home. Tell me everything you find."

Their husbands and wives waved goodbye, holding children at

their hips and tears in their eyes. The men and women set out, not sure what they would find. Not sure if they should be going at all, and began their search for others like them.

They traveled east for days. Weeks. Months. Hoping, wishing, that they would find what their leader had requested of them. But they found nothing. Death remembered the creations who lived between the jungles and the ocean. They had barely lasted a generation, falling victim to their own greed and violence.

He did not remember their name.

Just as the Narumi warriors planned to give up, to head back home and say that they had failed, they came across a jungle. They had never experienced the jungle before. They had never known a world filled with trees and moss and Creatures so rare and beautiful that they could not help but stop and stare in wonder.

They stopped for the night and made camp, wondering if this was a place where they could find medicine or new sources of food. It was far, but there was nothing saying they could not migrate. So far, there were none others like them, and they were determined, pushed forward by a strong will, to understand this new world. To bring back some good news to their leader. They may not have found others, but they found a brand new world to explore and understand.

They were ecstatic.

And seven nights into their stay, they came across a civilization.

Death remembered Lan. How could he not? His second creation. His challenging, intelligent, flower.

That night, as the Narumi observed the dark skinned men and women, the Lan danced. Unaware of the Narumi, they celebrated the kill of a dangerous predator who had been hunting them for months. A dangerous Creature the size of a mountain who crouched on four legs. The meat from the Creature would feed them for months. The fur would cloth the new children and the elderly. The bones made into new weapons.

They celebrated.

They danced.

Unaware they were being watched.

And watch the Narumi did. These strange men and women, children running, screaming, copying the dancing of their mothers and fathers, with a large fire blistering into the sky.

They watched and they waited for the Lan to notice them hiding between the trees. They knew, and they were aware, that even if they looked different, these creations were no different than the rest of them.

Their children, while thicker and darker than their children at home, were no different. They laughed: a beautiful sound. They still played: a beautiful sight.

Their men and women, while thicker and darker than their husbands and wives at home, were no different. They danced: a beautiful sight. They hugged and kissed: a beautiful sight.

The Narumi understood what the Seshen never could. That these creations were not to be killed or kidnapped. The lands were not theirs for the taking. Creations already lived here. Creations who may not have looked like them, who may not have spoken the same language, knew these lands better than the Narumi ever would.

Vilaim, they called themselves. Vilaim, they called the Lan. Precious, they decided. All of them were precious.

The Narumi warriors revealed themselves.

A small child noticed them at first. Curious as her namesake, the Lan child did not scream. There was no fear in her eyes. Merely curiosity. Merely confusion at those who walked on two legs, who looked like them, but did not. She tugged the hand of her mother who turned. Immediately, she pushed her child behind her and called for the warriors.

With the celebration shattered, a tense standoff broke between the two Creations. Warrior against warrior. The Narumi, having experienced the blade of a fellow Creation before, prepared for the worst. But with the children crying into their mother's hips and the men shouting at them to get to safety, the warriors realized that this did not need to end in bloodshed.

The Narumi put down their spears. Their swords. They held up their hands and fell to their knees, bowing their heads, and the Lan relaxed.

When they spoke again, when the Lan asked what the Narumi were doing in their lands, the Narumi understood them. Because it was not their language, but it was a language they had known for generations. Ones taught to their children through the stories of their creator. Of the man who walked among them.

"We come in search of others like us," the head warrior said.

"Others like us?" the chief of the Lan asked.

"Yes." And so, they explained the Seshen's attack. They explained that they were from the ocean—a term the Lan knew nothing about—and they had come to befriend others.

With the explanation behind them, the Lan opened their doors to the Narumi warriors. They exchanged language. They exchanged food. Clothes. Stories. Cultures. They spoke in their languages, and the language of Death: the one that spread across all the Nine. A connection forever.

Through this, they understood. They realized. They may look different, but they had come from the same being. The one who walked among them but did not interfere. Who stayed as long as their namesake lived, and left. Who still came in the night when a soul passed on.

Their Death.

A friendship bloomed between the Lan and the Narumi. Through the years, they brought each other gifts. They began to trade. They began to form a bond that would last for generations.

Death watched them. Their friendship interested him. The Seshen's treatment of the Siman interested him. The hatred between the Narumi and the Seshen, interested him. His creations. His Vilaim. They had lived apart for so long, and now they were bonding. Coming together in ways he had never imagined.

He did not know why he had never imagined this. He was Death. He was an entity. All knowing. All seeing.

Or maybe…

He wondered, then, what would happen if another meeting occurred? If more of his Vilaim needed to expand their boundaries. Not all lived as far away from each other as the Narumi and the Lan.

How would things play out as history continued, he wondered? What other things did he not know? Could he not predict? Could he not see?

Death remembered Nimbon. Death remembered the wily, scrappy woman who he had thought would die out before she had her first children. But she had not. She was strong. Living in the snowy terrain with little vegetation in the cold months. He always regretted leaving her there. Creating her there. It had been difficult for him to stay with her, knowing that the rough terrain had left her and her people treacherous thieves.

Yet, they survived. Through the generations, they survived, never growing like the others, but still thriving in the barren landscape. They lived off the meat of Creatures and the roots of plants. They shouldered furs to keep out the cold and learned the art of fire early.

They were strong.

It was here that a single thief changed everything.

Thrown in jail for stealing food, Halise had never known a family. She had never known love or compassion. Her parents had died when she was little, though she had never met her father, and she never wanted to take a mate.

At first, the jail was a paradise compared to the homelessness. She had a roof over her head. Four walls to block out the harsh winds and the falling snow.

This is not so bad, she thought to herself, lying on the first bed she had had since she was little. It was perfect. It was beautiful.

Until they sentenced her to death.

Halise had always been smarter than her peers. Her mind worked in ways that the Nimbon could not keep up with. A mind they did not appreciate in a society only trying to survive. But she understood things. Which is how, despite being locked behind bars, and guarded, she managed to escape.

She managed to flee.

Despite it all, she did not want to die. She wanted to live. To thrive. To find a place where the waters were warm and fire was not needed. That was all. She had not meant for things to go so wrong in her life, but what could you do, if you were Nimbon?

There was no place for her with the other Nimbon. She had no one to love and no one to love her. But, she thought as she stole food and warm clothes for her journey west, she had decided that there must be others like them out there. Maybe some who might care for her the way she had always longed for.

She ran. She fled her home, and the only life she had ever known, and headed west, away from the ocean up into the massive mountains that erupted from the ground beneath her.

Death remembered Tep. A painter, he cared little for violence or war, but championed telling stories through his pictures. He was the first to discover paint. The first to tell the vivid stories of his experiences to the young ones. He and his progeny lived a relatively peaceful life, even though the harsh mountains had hardened them to fantasy.

It was a young Tep man who discovered Halise. Strong from his days surviving alone in the mountains, Amir scooped up the living, but unmoving body of the strange woman. As a shepherd, he spent most of his days alone, coming back to the tribe only when it was time to sell his milk, furs, and meat to the villagers. He was a quiet man, one who made many friends, but never revealed his inner soul to them.

When he found Halise, he did not know what to make of her. He knew he could not let her stay out there to die. She was but a lost sheep in need of food and warmth, and he had the ability to take care of her. She looked slightly different than the people of his tribe. Lighter blond hair. Paler skin with a tinge of pink.

He warmed her with fire and furs, and when she finally came too, when she opened her eyes, he knew she was the most perfect thing he had ever met. They were the color of summer soil on a mountain farm, wide with curiosity and confusion. A little bit of fear.

Amir soothed her, his voice deep and comforting.

She yelled at him, voice rough and broken from years of abuse.

But, finally, she calmed down and devoured the food he provided for her. She listened to him, with his strange accent and unfamiliar words, explain that he had found her almost dead in the forest. He explained that he was concerned for her health and wanted to bring her to their healer.

She did not understand. This man, this man with eyes like a stormy sky and skin a shade darker than hers, who had muscle and a thick torso, who was different, but the same, had shown her more compassion in one day than anyone had in her entire life.

Halise and Amir spent their days together. He brought her to the village and her cuts and bruises were treated with herbs. She grew stronger. He showed her the ways of his people. She learned their language. He learned hers. She told him stories of her home. He held her while she cried.

They fell in love.

Death watched them from his perch. He normally did not spend this much energy watching his creations, his Vilaim, but they were different. They were something special because they were not from the same tribe.

The Seshen and the Siman did not mix.

The Narumi and the Lan remained friends, never mixing.

These two had decided to mix. They had decided that, despite not being the same, they were in love. That they were going to marry. That they were going to have children.

He left his perch and walked, once more, among the Vilaim. They were different now. They spoke words that only took their origin in his language, and their culture had changed while he sat and watched. Their songs, their stories, and their dances grew as time passed. Their leaders perished, leaving behind legacies—both good and bad.

They were perfect in their little bubbles. Changing, but remaining the same.

He was not sure what to do about Amir and Halise. If he interfered, he would only cause more problems. If he did not....

If he did not, his perfection creations would become tainted. It started with just one. It always started with just one.

He could not let it happen.

Chapter Five

The Seshen did not explore after they clashed with the Narumi. They did not want to lose any more men to war, and they were content to live their lives with their slaves and their cities. They experienced massive growth during this time. They always kept the Siman at arm's length. They did not expect them to *become* Seshen. They did not want them to *become* Seshen.

The Siman kept their culture. They kept their language hidden beneath bedsheets and wracked with urgency. It was, to the Seshen, an excellent compromise.

To the Siman, it was hell.

But they were, in the eyes of the Seshen, Tulu. Never Vilaim. Their struggles and their issues were nothing to the Seshen. The Siman were no better than the Creatures that they hunted and kept as pets.

This went on for generations, until one day, without warning, a group of strangers appeared at the entry to the city. They came with amber eyes, dark skin, and black hair, holding out gifts and bounty for the Seshen king.

The Seshen's warriors first instinct was to kill the newcomers, yet, the gifts were enticing. A metal that shone the color of the sun, malleable and rare; a piece of cloth, similar to clothing, but splattered with unknown paste—paint, they called it; and a bottle of tiny little crystals that thrilled the taste buds of every soldier.

Maybe, they decided, the royal family would be pleased with these strangers and make deals of trade.

The royal family was not pleased with their situation. They did not trust these new people. After all, they had attacked the Siman. They had attacked the Narumi. What was stopping these new people from infiltrating the city and killing them from within? From stealing their secrets and spreading them far and wide?

But, like with the warriors, the idea of trade was too much to forgo. It was possible, however strange, that the newcomers were truly not there to cause harm, but needed the resources that the Seshen brought with them.

Was there another way? They wondered. Was it possible to exchange with others like them, rather than enslave and steal from them? It was an odd thought. For as long as the queen could remember, they had always thought of themselves as superior. And they still could be. They could trade with these strangers yet still remain in control. In power. They would do this their way and with their rules.

With a simultaneous nod, the Seshen royalty agreed to let the strangers into the castle. But they were here under condition. They were here to listen to the Seshen explain the rules of their trade, and they were not to argue. Any sign of malice, any sign of wrong doing, and they would be killed on the stop, their heads returned to their home as a warning.

The Seshen royalty did not play games. Not when it came to their livelihood. Not when it came to the safety of their people.

The royalty ceded. They sent the warriors off to bring the

strangers into the castle, all the while whispering to one another.

"Is what we are doing…."

"It is what our mothers before us have done."

"But what if…?"

"What if…?"

What if?

Death remembered Harashim. A simple man, he went about his days farming and raising Creatures to feed his simple family. He did not question life. He did not ask questions beyond what was right in front of him. He always had a smile on his face, and he was gentle and kind to others.

His people were no different. They were not interested in questioning the universe. They were a simple folk who developed their skills in blacksmithing to make better tools for farming. Everything in their lives centered around their farming. Their deity. Their family.

By this time, they knew of the others. They had sent out scouts to search for lost Creatures one day and came across a castle so magnificent that they were astounded to discover that there was any other sort of life than the one they led. The scouts found the Creatures and returned home, frightened and curious. A spark that led them to send out more scouts. To find more like them.

They never made contact.

It was not until their leader passed away that they decided to do something about their knowledge. On his death bed, old and withered with Death standing over his decaying body, he asked his grandson to explore. To search for things outside of their small little world. To understand the other creations, the other Vilaim, who existed outside of their home.

The scouts they sent out to find the castle once more were simple folk. Two men. Two women. When they approached the walls, they were awed into submission. The knights of the Seshen had threatened to kill them until they produced their gifts: salt from their lands, a painting done by a woman, and metal.

The salt was an easy sell. Simple and white, it added a tart flavor to anything that it was sprinkled upon. The knights who tried it, preparing to die, were overjoyed by the strange taste. They said it reminded them of the sea at midnight, which the Harashim did not understand, but did not question.

The painting elicited a strange reaction from the knights. They were shocked by the beauty, asking a million questions about what this was, how it looked so amazing, and if it was even real. The Harashim spoke to each other in their dialect, commenting that it was odd these creations had never experienced art before.

But it was the metal that caught the knight's attention. The men, armed with spears, stared at the sword with wide, excited eyes. Because this…this was how they were going to conquer the world.

And they allowed the Harashim into their home.

The Harashim remained quiet as they were led into the home of the royal family. They were awed by the brick walls that extended high into the sky. By the beautiful tapestries hanging on the walls. By the magnificence of the room where the royal family sat.

There were two different groups in the room. One with flowing brown hair and crystal blue eyes. The other with red hair and eyes like the rivers back home. It was clear, from the moment that the Harashim entered the room, who was in charge, and who was to serve.

A concept they did not understand, but did not question. After all, this was not their home. They were visitors. They had come to trade with and befriend the royal family. They were not here to judge.

A man and a woman sat on silver thrones wearing lavish clothes of purple and green. Atop their heads sat crowns of silver, jewels glittering in the light streaming in through the windows.

The Harashim fell to their knees, awed by the power this couple held. They faced the man, the king, and presented their gifts. They waited for him to speak, to give commands and to tell them what to do.

He did not.

She stood, standing only slightly taller than the average Harashim woman, and spoke in a clear, beautiful voice. The Harashim realized their mistake. For it was not he who rules. It was she. She ruled over Seshen. She commanded the jobs, the laws, and the culture.

She was their queen.

Death watched this.

He watched them speak. Strike a deal of trade, of commerce, of sustainability. He saw that the Seshen respected the Harashim, though kept their command. For they were too different to mix, they had decided. The two groups would work together. But they would not live together. They would trade goods, but not progeny. They would forever work together as separate cultures and separate creations.

It was good.

With the trade between the two, weapons grew stronger. They morphed from spears to swords, and from bows to crossbows. The two groups traded military strategies and fighting techniques.

Instead of a group of scouts and knights, they built an army.

Death watched this, and his curiosity grew. For what purpose would they need such strong weapons? The Creatures barely posed a threat to them with their current arsenal.

Still, he did not interfere. He watched, quietly, and did not speak.

Death remembered Raan. A man who rejected the eating of Creatures in favor of the food he could farm from the earth. A medicine man, he spent his time working with the sick and elderly, creating medicines to keep them safe from the harm of the unseen. He was peaceful and generous, spilling these traits into the rest of his people.

They did not eat meat. They did not use fur or leather for their clothes. They kept to the plants and lived a quiet, long life. Man, woman, child, elder...everyone had a role in society. Whether it was farming, sewing, weaving, teaching, singing, it did not matter. Everyone worked and contributed to society.

They were not expecting the armies of the Seshen and the Harashim.

Startled and confused, the Raan surrendered immediately. Their men were told that they were to fight for the military. The Raan explained that they were a peaceful folk. They could not fight. Many of them were sick and elderly.

The Seshen knights told them that there was a greater threat out there. Something that would cause them to lose their autonomy, and their lands. For you see, they explained, the Narumi were heartless creatures. The Narumi were out there plotting revenge against anyone who might think about existing in their lands. They told stories of the men they had lost to the Narumi army.

The Raan did not know what to do. They did not want to fight, but they did not want to die. They did not have the skills to fight, but if the Seshen were correct, and the Narumi were out for blood, then did they have much of a choice?

They were give three days to make a decision. And in those three days, the elders and the men all agreed that they would go to war. A pre-emptive strike to protect themselves and their children.

The men said goodbye to the woman and left with the Seshen and Harashim soldiers.

It was not the worst pairing, they soon learned. The Raan discovered that if they cooked and mended the soldiers' health, then they were not forced to fight. They were put to work, not as soldiers, but as nurses and doctors. They were used to mending the ill, having practice with their own people, and they found that it was, in a way, exhilarating. They felt, for the first time, that they were part of something much greater.

And thus, a friendship was born. One that would last for thousands of years.

Chapter Six

Death remembered Jous. A woman of many talents, she, like Lan, asked too many questions. But her questions differed. She did not ask about philosophy or the meaning of life, but things closer to heart. She wanted to know…everything. Where the Creatures came from. What the soil was composed of. How to build. How to cook. How to know the difference between something poisonous and something edible. She had little interest in learning to survive for survival's sake, but instead because it was interesting to her.

She passed this trait on to the others like her. A flower of a special kind who needed to know everything. And indeed, they learned much. They built huts to house their books. They named the stars and every Creature. They created a culture where knowledge was the thing most admired, caring little for hunting or farming. For fighting.

Instead they grew flowers, named them, bred them, and created new flowers. A miracle, they had initially said. Science, they had eventually said.

They were small in population. Some years, there were no

children born at all. Some years, they shrunk so small that Death wondered if they would survive. But they always did. Something would always change, and eventually they would grow again.

They had no leader. Instead they had a collection of people who were known as the most intelligent who agreed upon a set of rules for the masses. The Collective, as they called it.

It was The Collective who one day noticed the smoke rising into the sky. They had seen fires before, both their own and the natural fires that kept the forests healthy and safe, but they had never seen contained smoke rising above the trees like this.

Curiosity led them to figure out who else had learned the rules of Fire in such a way. They explored, bringing with them children and women, and came across a camp of Narumi explorers. With their pencils and paper, they watched the Narumi travelers, who were unaware they were being examined, and wrote down as many thoughts as possible.

The Jous had never encountered anyone who looked like them before. The Creatures were all predictable. But they knew, from experience, that the Vilaim were not. Sometimes, despite their desperation for knowledge, they would have a child grow into a man or woman who cared little for education. Who would rather hunt or gather. Vilaim were unpredictable. They were uncertain. They were intelligent and able to manipulate the world around them to live, no matter what the circumstance.

They remained hidden for some time. Watching. Observing. Taking notes. They drew pictures of the men and women with their long, silky black hair, their brown eyes, their tan, yet still paler than the Jous, skin. The men and women with a language so similar, yet so different, from the Jous' own language.

When the sun set, and the strangers went to sleep, the Jous explorers ran home to tell the others. Not only were there others like them, they had similar eating habits, talked about their life in a similar way, and they were masters of fire. No Creature could achieve that.

After days of this, they confronted the strangers.

The Lan and Narumi had little desire to befriend other Vilaim. They were satisfied with their connection. They were satisfied to know that if the Seshen ever returned, they'd be ready to fight and win. They would be able to protect themselves and that was enough for them.

That is, until one day, when they were traveling, thinking that there were only three Vilaim in the world, and two of them worked together. They were unstoppable.

Then they discovered an empty village.

At least, they assumed it was empty. The houses were destroyed with wild Creatures roaming through the streets, unafraid, untouched by Vilaim. A breeze howled between the buildings, creating the most ominous aura that the Lan and the Narumi had ever experienced. It was then, that they realized there were not three.

There were more. Many, many more.

And there was no telling how dangerous any of the others might have been.

The group continued walking, searching every house, hunting the creatures for food. It was not until their third night there, after they had discovered artifacts of the Vilaim who left them. They told stories of happiness. Of community and family. They spoke nothing of what led to the state of the village that they had discovered.

On the third morning, they woke to a group of individuals with spears pointing directly at their necks.

The weak, hungry Vilaim were disarmed. The Narumi, trained

soldiers, and the Lan, quick minded, tricked them into giving up their spears as they prepared for more to come attack them. These Vilaim…they had pale skin and bright red hair with eyes as blue as the clear waters near the Narumi's home. They were thin. Ravenous. Angry.

They were no threat to the expedition.

A few more Siman, as they called themselves, appeared out of the woodwork and a story unfolded:

It all began on a warm summers day. The Siman worked, excited for a new harvest, when they were attacked. Warriors with massive, fast moving Creatures, flew through the city and ripped children from mothers, mothers from husbands, and husbands from life. They rounded up every Siman that they could find and took them away, gone forever. A few survived the attacks, having been out hunting or in the fields, and when they had returned, all they had known was misery from the blue eyed devils.

The Lan were mortified by this tale and begged the Narumi to take care of the remaining Siman. But this tale meant something different to the Narumi. Because they still remembered when they were attacked. When their own blue eyed devils tried to take away their autonomy.

Anger boiled in their stomachs. They agreed, eagerly, to protect the Siman, and they vowed revenge on the Seshen. They explained their own situation to the Lan, who also seethed with rage. They had no desire to take what was not theirs. Trade was good. Working together was ideal. But to ransack an entire people and steal away their freedoms? It was something that the Lan and the Narumi could not understand.

"This is not going to end with the Siman," one Narumi soldier exclaimed.

"No, it clearly is not." A Lan explorer settled in front of their campfire with a heavy sigh. He was older than the others, but no less determined. "If we are to protect ourselves, we are going to have to protect everyone we come across. There is no saying what these Seshen will do."

"They must think highly of themselves," another Narumi soldier said.

"We must knock them down. Show them they cannot take the free will of others!"

A chorus of agreement broke out among the travelers, and among the free Siman. It had been multiple generations since the raids, but who was to say how much more damage the Seshen had done?

Two of the Narumi soldiers agreed to escort the remaining Siman back to the Narumi villages and explain the situation. Deep down, the Siman were convinced that they were not going to safety. After all, why trust these strangers when the others had been so violent? Still, it was better than suffering with not enough support to feed their children.

They left, and those who remained vowed to fight the Seshen. To free the Siman. To bring balance back to the world they lived in.

There was one problem, however: they did not know where the Seshen lived. They had explored much of the continent, but had yet to run into anyone else. They agreed, quite readily, that they should split into groups and search for the Seshen. Search for anyone else who might exist in their small, small world.

Their world that bloomed with life and death. Their world that held secret upon secret.

Their world where everything was about to fall to hell.

The Lan went one way. The Narumi went another. They vowed to find the Seshen. They vowed to meet again in Narumi by the next full moon. They vowed to understand more about their small, small world.

So, they set off. They traveled for as long as they could until the month was almost complete. They knew they had to turn around, but exhaustion kept them stuck in place. The Narumi sat around the campfire, telling stories of their childhoods, of their lives, and they laughed and relaxed, knowing their journey was going to come to an end sooner rather than later.

They had failed.

But at least they would be home soon.

Until a strange group appeared out of the trees.

The Jous did not fear the Narumi, even when the Narumi pulled spears on them. They remained calm, even when the Narumi shouted at them, frightened. The Jous spoke in quiet voices, using the hand gestures and language of the Narumi.

And the Narumi were baffled. Because even when the Jous explained who they were, and that they were curious about the origins of the Narumi, about the stories that they told, the Narumi were uncertain. There was such a thing as being too friendly, and they feared that was the case here.

But the longer the Jous spoke, the more the Narumi relaxed. They did not seem like they cared for fighting. They led them to their home and the Narumi were welcomed into their homes with warmth and food and music and dance. The Jous shared everything with the Narumi, and the Narumi explained about their mission.

The Jous were uncertain about the words the Narumi shared. They were not ones to fight, but they were also not ones to allow injustices to fall upon others with intelligences like their own. It was then that the Jous decided to do what they could to help the Narumi. They shared their gifts with them: the gift of stargazing, of math, and, best of all, cartography.

With this, the Narumi had a clearer view of their world. They saw the maps that the Jous had created and they knew, without a doubt, that the Jous would be valuable allies.

"Join us," the Narumi begged. "Help us free the Siman and bring down the evil of the Seshen."

The Jous shook their heads. "We are not warriors."

"We do not need warriors. We need...we need scholars."

The word was foreign to both groups, but an understanding was built on that day, and the Jous eagerly agreed to join the Narumi in their fight against the Seshen. They would not wield weapons. They would not kill or maim. But they would educate.

And most of all, they would learn.

Death watched. His creations banded together, and everything about him twisted and turned with an emotion he'd never felt before. For all of his existence, he had never feared anything. He had always, and forever, known that he was safe among the lands. Nothing could touch him. He was the one who brought death, and death would never befall him.

And yet, as he watched his creations, his Vilaim, prepare for war, he feared. For them, for the lives that were about to be lost over the actions of his first.

He knew he had to interfere. He had to walk among them once more.

Except...except his mind was distracted and his attention pulled away from the Seshen and the Harashim. Away from the Jous, the Narumi, and the Lan. All the way north to the snowy mountains of the Tep where Amir and Halise grew closer.

For the first time in many moons, Death walked among his

creations. He whispered into the ears of the Tep citizens, asking them their opinion of Halise. Their answers were always positive.

"She is a lovely lady."

"She has given my son a new life."

"She gives Amir so much happiness."

"Why should we not bless this wedding?"

Death grew angry.

Every day that passed, getting closer and closer to the wedding, he tried to understand these new emotions plaguing him. The ones that gave him such tingles in the tips of his fingers and toes. He rationalized with himself that this was all right. That the two of them would be good for each other.

But then he remembered Tep. He remembered Nimbon. He remembered them all back to his perfect Seshen, and he knew that they could not break that. Every second that passed brought about more determination in Death. He had to end their union once and for all. Before they created a child of mixed blood.

A new flower.

Death did not need new flowers.

On the night of their wedding, when Amir and Halise slept in different beds for the last time, he slipped into Amir's room and watched his chest rise and fall. Watched the man dream with a smile. Walked to him with his hand outstretched.

For Death did not go as one of the Tep that night.

No. That night, he went as Death.

Chapter Seven

Nimbon is a dark place. Filled with poverty, the children learn to steal before they can talk. Many do not live to see their own children grow up. The streets are dirty, the people uneducated and filled with fear and mistrust. Marriage is not a thing. Friends are the people who do not rob you in your sleep. There is nothing good about Nimbon. There is nothing warm or safe. The Nimbon did not band together. They did not have bonds. That was not how they did things.

It was from here that Halise fled.

It was to here that she returned. Bruised. Crying.

No one noticed her at first. A young woman crying in the streets was nothing new. But she was shouting something. A warning. Finally, someone took notice. She *made* them take notice. Grabbing anyone who would listen.

Because trailing behind her with blazing fire were an angry mob of Tep citizens out for her head.

On the morning of her wedding, Halise woke to a scream outside her soon-to-be husband's room. She did not hesitate. She recognized that scream. It was the scream of a mother who had just lost her child. Dread tickled her stomach and she threw off her covers, running to find what she already knew to be true.

Amir's mother had collapsed to her knees outside of his open door, openly wailing.

Her son was dead.

Halise felt something break inside her that day. She had fallen so in love with the man who had treated her with such kindness. She had wanted to live with him until they were old with many grandchildren. She wanted to *live* with him. Not steal. Not fight. Not wonder where her next meal was going to come from.

It was a chance for a new life. One where she made him happy. One where he made her feel safe and warm.

They were going to be happy.

But he was dead. No one understood how or why. It was a great mystery.

Just like she had been.

That mystery boiled into anger. Into mistrust. It started with whispers. Then with accusations. Then with an arrest. For the people of Tep had convinced themselves that Halise had poisoned Amir in the night. They said she was sent from a foreign land to disrupt their peace. She had seduced their beloved Amir, and then killed him without regret.

She pleaded with them. Begged them to believe her when she said she had no idea what had occurred. She had come here for safety, and she had found love with Amir. She had never thought she would find love in her life until she met him.

They did not believe her.

They lit their flames and ordered her death.

She ran.

Death watched from the shadows. It was the first time he had taken a soul whose time it was not. It was the first time that, when Amir asked him, 'Why?' he had no answer.

Because Death was not quite sure himself.

Once a life is taken, it cannot be returned. There were no rules, but there were rules to Death's job. Rules he had known from the moment of his appearance. That night, when he ripped Amir's soul from his body, he had broken the rules. It had pained him. Destroyed a bit of his soul. A bit of...well, in a way, his humanity.

He was Death, yes. He controlled who lived and who died. But only when it was their time.

What he had done was wrong.

And it was too late.

He watched from the shadows as Halise fled. He watched Amir's mother weep. He watched Amir's father call for the head of his almost daughter-in-law. He did not understand the emotion in his body. The way his heart—if he had a heart—ached and clenched. Was this guilt? He had seen it before, in his creations. But he, himself, had never felt it before. Did he feel guilty for killing Amir? For ruining Halise's happiness?

He was not supposed to interfere. But he had had to.

They were perfect the way they were.

He had to preserve the perfect world he had created for himself. Everyone had their place. Everyone had their duty. He wanted it to stay that way forever.

And yet, he found himself feeling something else: self-loathing. Creating was one thing, he decided. Creating was beautiful. It was magical and safe. But taking away? Especially taking away the soul of someone who was not ready to die? That was the most evil anyone could ever do.

Amir had begged him. Gotten down and begged him to return his soul to his body for one more night to say goodbye to his love.

Death could not do it.

Because once a life is taken, it cannot be returned.

Amir vanished into the realm of light on his knees. Begging. Begging until the very end. And Halise ran through the mountains, through ice and snow, until she finally found her old home. She ran into the streets, crying, screaming.

Death sat and watched everyone ignore her.

"Get off me."

Halise fell to the dirt, tears streaming down her face. The man who had shoved her continued on as if nothing had changed. As if she had not begged for his help. Why would he help her? She was just another mouth to feed. Another begging young woman giving herself up for a bed to sleep in. There was no reason for him, or for anyone, to help her.

Except she was in danger. They were all in danger. She had led the Tep right to her old home. A place where she thought she might find some friends. But they did not know about the rest of the world. They were unaware that there were others like them who looked different and held different customs.

Whenever she stopped for too long, their voices grew closer.

Whenever she tried to hide, they drove her out. No matter how far she ran, they followed.

They did not just want her dead, they wanted to be the ones to kill her.

An eye for an eye.

A tooth for a tooth.

Revenge.

When the Tep arrived at Nimbon, they found a city of thieves. Of poverty. Of liars. Of course, they decided, Halise had come from this place. This place where children wandered hungry in the streets. Where adults cared so little about one another that it was a miracle they survived at all.

Their anger grew. Halise was a product of this hell. She was not the cause but a symptom. A symptom that had gotten their beloved Amir killed. And now, now they would burn the whole city to the ground.

They came upon the citizens with fire and rage. They burned buildings, rounded up as many people as possible, and planned to kill them with mercy. Their deity of death would take them all to a better place, and no more like Halise would show their face again.

Until the Seshen army appeared.

Nothing was going the way Death had planned. If he created, he made something beautiful. But too much and they fought. If he took away, if he interfered anymore, things only worsened.

He needed things to be perfect, but he could not understand why it was not so. He did not know why the Tep decided to burn the Nimbon instead of help them. He did not understand why the Seshen enslaved the Siman instead of trading with them. He could not comprehend why everything he touched went sour.

And why, watching Halise suffer, did he sit and do nothing.

Chapter Eight

Together, the Seshen and Harashim military agreed eagerly to explore the rest of the world. There was no saying what other resources they might discover. There was no telling who they might find, but they knew they were strong enough to take on any Vilaim they might find out in the wild, wild world.

The Seshen had not forgotten about the Narumi. How could they? The Narumi had fought back and won so easily it was as though the Seshen had not had any power. They had gotten away, and the Seshen had not tried to return to their lands since. Instead, they built up their army. They spent decades trying to figure out how to get revenge.

The Raan and the Harashim had no qualms with the Narumi. All they knew was that the Seshen held a grudge against them, and would forever more.

But the Seshen soldiers...oh, they did hold that grudge. And they knew now, with the Harashim's technology and wisdom, and the Raan's knowledge of healing, that they would be able to win if they tried again. It would be easy, they decided, to fight against the

Narumi now that they had allies.

They felt invincible.

Together, the Seshen and the Harashim agreed to travel north. To the mountains they could see rising into the distance. They had always feared these mountains. They looked, by all means, unpassable. They were untouched by any creation, they had decided. Who could, after all, live up there?

But they had to go. They needed to see if there was anything in these mountains to help them win against the Narumi. They set off, saying goodbye to loved ones, and headed with pride to the mountains.

But the mountains were a struggle. They were not prepared for the harshness of the winters. The vile Creatures that lived among the trees. The poisonous food. Many died. Many begged their commanders to return home. They missed their wives. They missed their children.

They missed safety.

But the commanders were determined.

The Seshen were determined.

When they arrived on the other side of the mountains, they found themselves in a snowy wasteland. The men were tired and hungry. They were running out of food, and out of patience. Sleeping was almost impossible, and exhaustion took more lives.

They were dwindling. And on the verge of giving up.

It was not until one day when they saw smoke in the distance that things changed. They charged toward it, hoping for civilization.

Instead what they found was a town being burned to the ground.

It took only a second for the soldiers to understand what was going on. They saw one group—much healthier looking and stronger—with fires and weapons attacking the second group who cowered and did not fight back.

What they saw was an unwarranted attack.

And without even a word exchanged between the soldiers, they decided to help.

They wanted revenge.

They wanted to purge the world of the evil from which Halise had come.

The brown eyed monsters from the north needed to be destroyed, and they were the ones to do it.

The group of raiders stopped caring about Halise after the first few buildings. They were caught up in the rage and the excitement of the moment that they lost sight of the reason they were there in the first place.

And they were so lost in the moment that they did not realize another, stronger, well-armed, group had arrived.

They did not realize that they were outnumbered until the Seshen, Harashim, and Raan army were already on their tails.

The fight was bloody and violent. The SHR Army held no sympathy for the group of invaders. They killed any who got in their way, and did not stop to ask questions. They did not care why. They just wanted to win.

In a matter of minutes the fight was over. The Tep retreated, and the SHR army cried out victory.

The Nimbon were so grateful for their saviors that they bowed at their feet. In one day their world had turned upside down. They realized they were not the only ones in the world. There were others. Halise had found a terrible group, but these people, the Seshen, the Harashim, and the Raan, were wonderful Vilaim.

The next few days, the Raan went through and helped fix up all the broken and injured people of Nimbon. The Seshen and

Harashim leaders met with the Nimbon leaders and they spoke of what happened. They discussed the world and the possibility of a treaty. The men in Nimbon were too weak to be fighters, but they could teach valuable skills.

For a few days, Nimbon experienced peace. They experienced safety. They experienced trust. They did not hold Halise accountable for her actions. They took her in and decided to protect her against the Tep.

It was, for the first time, a turning point for the Nimbon. But it was, for the second time, a turning point for Halise. And it was one she did not want.

Death fled.

He did not understand.

He could not understand.

The pain.

The anger.

The guilt.

They raged through him as his own self was pulled in a million directions at once. As his own self guided the souls of violently killed Vilaim into the afterlife. He wanted to run away forever, to never face the consequences of what he had done. What he had caused between his creations.

Except, no matter what he did, his creations died. Creatures died. Part of him, however small, was called back to do his job. To take the souls of the living. No matter how far he ran he still was forced to watch the world he had so carefully crafted fall apart.

All he had wanted was for his loneliness to disappear. He had wanted friends. He had wanted someone to be his companion.

He was lonely.

And he had made things worse.

The Tep retreated, many dead, many others injured, back to their home. Halise was gone, the Nimbon people would not bother them, and yet they were angry. Angry at the strangers with wild hair and skin colors who appeared out of nowhere. Their weapons, their fighting skills, and their numbers were dangerous.

If they were not careful, the army would find them, and destroy them.

The leaders consulted with one another, trying to figure out what to do. There was a good chance that the mountains would deter any and all attempts to find the little village. But, then again, these were a group who braved the ice fields.

Would the mountains stop them?

They prepared for an attack.

The Narumi were prepared to fight. They wanted nothing more than to stop the Seshen from causing more pain and suffering. It seemed that wherever they went, they brought with them death and unhappiness.

They were not in the right. They were not better than the others, and they had no right to destroy and take whatever they pleased.

The Narumi would not stand for it, and their allies agreed.

With the help of the Jous, the Narumi and Lan learned new tracking techniques. The three groups mapped their journey, building the first cohesive plan of their world. Their documents were valuable. The Jous brought little books with them and recorded everything they could. They found new foods to eat, devised ways to catch food with better traps, and taught the Lan and Narumi how to read and write.

With their intelligence building, bonds growing stronger, the Narumi, Lan, and Jous tracked the SHR army to the North. To unfamiliar territory.

They were not scared.

They were prepared.

When they came upon a new village, they were far from surprised. There were only a few wandering the streets with hair the color of straw. They were tense, carrying makeshift weapons. Patrolling. One member of the Jous noticed that they were preparing for a battle. Something was wrong.

After a quick discussion, it was decided that since the Jous looked most like the strangers, though their skin was darker, and hair was not golden, that they should try and make peace.

Clever and quick, one Jous did just that. He slipped in and held up his hands, showing that he was unarmed. The guard he ran into, a sturdy woman with fierce blue eyes, showed aggression at first, but relaxed the slightest bit when he explained that he was a traveler with many friends who wanted to explore new parts of the world.

She said that her people were attacked by a large group of strangely colored people. She did not trust him. But he calmed her down by explaining that he knew the group of which she spoke. Their leaders were pale with brown hair and blue eyes. They were ruthless and did not ask questions.

He explained that his group was unlike them.

His group wanted to help.

He listened to her story. Met her elders. Spoke with her people. Soon, he invited others of his group. They spoke with one another, traded stories, and became almost like one.

The Narumi were not surprised to discover that these people were victims of a Seshen attack. Their anger grew. Their disgust for the other group deepened, and they wanted this to end.

They vowed to take on the Seshen and end this once and for all in the snowy banks of the North.

Chapter Nine

The battle came.

The Seshen searched for the Tep, wanting revenge for their newfound friends. Halise was their hero. An innocent young woman tortured by the monstrous Tep for something she did not commit. They hailed her and kept her safe and well fed.

The Narumi searched for the Seshen. They heard the stories of Amir and his supposed love. They saw his grave and grew to hate the name Halise. She was the vixen, the enemy. The same kind as the Seshen. How dare she manipulate such a wonderful young man, only to take his life so young?

The Lan were unsure of this battle. They had never felt the pain of the Seshen, and were not too eager to find out. Yet, their friends were certain that this was the right situation. They had to stop the Seshen before they caused more pain for the poor people of this world. They had taken down the army, and then the castle. That was how it had to be.

The Jous were pleased with their finds. They had learned so much. Their maps were close to complete. Their journals filled with information. As far as they were concerned, the coming war was a chance to learn even more. After all, they had never met the Seshen before. They wanted to learn more, even if it meant destroying the lives of others.

The Harashim did not understand the Seshen's obsession with claiming land. It did not matter. They had what they wanted: new weapons and ideas. This war was a sad side effect of clashing culture. They understood that, and all that mattered was that they were on the same side. They were on the right side of the battle, that they knew for sure.

The Tep were grateful for their saviors. They were not warriors. Why would they need to be? Their mountains were a barrier. They wanted revenge for their beautiful Amir. Halise and her people would pay, even if it meant destroying every last member of the Nimbon tribe. What did it matter anyway? They were scum. Thieves. Murderers. Disgusting.

The Raan did not want to fight. They tried to talk the Seshen out of the fight. They should leave before things got worse. The Tep were horrible for attacking the Nimbon, but there was nothing they could do. They did not want to see anyone else get hurt. The last thing they wanted was to use their skills to heal more wounds caused by violence.

The Nimbon were scared. These strangers helped them and raised them to a new level, but at what cost? They had so little they spent their lives stealing from each other. How would this end for them? What if things went wrong and they were attacked once more? The Seshen raised Halise on a pedestal, but did she deserve it?

And then the Siman. The Siman were unaware of the battle brewing over their initial capture. They did not know that some had escaped. They did not know the Narumi were willing to die for their freedom. They bowed their heads and did as they were told.

Because what else could they do?

The battle came. It was a cold day. The snow came up to their knees. The two groups stood across from each other on a large field.

For the first time, Death's creations faced each other. The Narumi and the Seshen stood at the front. Back home, no one knew this was happening. The Seshen Queen was unaware. The Narumi elders were unaware.

No one knew.

Except for Death.

Because he sat and he watched the two groups charge. Each fighting for their own vision of freedom.

He watched, and he helped the dead.

The battle ended when each group retreated. Many were dead. No one wanted to risk losing, and did not want to push further. They retreated back to the Tep and the Nimbon's homes. And then they left, sick of the cold.

The Seshen left first, bringing Halise with them. She did not want to go. But they declared that she was a hero for bringing to light the disgusting nature of their enemy. An enemy that they did not know the name of.

The Narumi brought the name of Amir back to their home. They spoke of him as if they knew him, when in fact he had been long dead before they arrived. They came back telling their tales, and spoke of the blue eyed enemy and their friends.

Yet, they did not know their names.

Back in the plains, the Narumi and the Seshen began to build their armies once more. Each group was unsure. They knew nothing about each other. Some questioned whether they should try and talk.

They were silenced by the bloodthirsty soldiers.

They were silenced into submission by their leaders.

The Queen of Seshen wanted control. She wanted to expand her kingdom and rule over it all. She wanted to instill dominance over the demons who did not look like them.

Yet, she did not know their names.

The Narumi elders wanted to beat down a violent dictator. They wanted to free the Siman and destroy all those who hurt others.

Yet, they did not know their names.

Another battle brewed.

The strange city shocked Halise. The people were so different. They were not as violent as her own, nor as welcoming as her lover's. They lived their life with trading and communication, yet they were not close.

The streets were winding and many. She got lost many times, having to ask for directions. Some were glad to help her. Others scorned her golden hair and brown eyes. She looked nothing like them.

In the castle she watched the red haired people slink silently by. They were uncertain. Scared. Slaves. She tried to talk to one once, and they ran away without a word.

These people, these strangers who had saved her and her people...were they good?

The battle grew closer.

Each side built their army. As if they knew what was coming, they marched through the plains. They did not need messages to tell each other what was happening. They did not need to communicate. They knew. They knew that a battle was coming, and that they were to fight in it.

They were to fight people they did not know.

The battle came.

Halise went to her room. She thought about Amir. The way he spoke of peace, how gentle and kind he was to her, despite her rough nature. He had complimented her in a way she did not understand.

She loved him

He had loved her.

Her room was beautiful. Fabrics with colors she did not know were possible outside of the summer flowers lined the bed and the windows. There was hot water waiting for her to bathe. Back in Nimbon, they did not have hot water, and only those with money bothered to bathe. In Tep, it was similar.

This was not her home. As uncertain as Nimbon was, and as much as the Tep hated her, they were more her home than this ever would be. This was a place where people were held as slaves. Where she was hailed as a hero for doing nothing.

And in her name, many were going to die.

She walked to the window and pushed aside the curtains.

The city was beautiful from this high up. She stared out across it.

She pushed the window open.

It creaked.

She climbed up on the window sill.

This was not her home.

And in that moment, Death understood.

Standing next to Halise's broken body, her soul standing beside him, he understood that what he had done was play with nature.

What he had done was disrupt the order of things. These creations…none of them were supposed to exist. He had created them, searching for something he could not have. No matter how hard he tried, he would never have a friend.

Everything died.

He took Halise's soul to where he had said goodbye to Amir's. He did not understand how the world after death worked for his creations, but he felt like if he brought her there that maybe they would meet once more.

As she disappeared, he apologized for taking her lover.

She did not forgive him.

Chapter Ten

The battle began.

The two sides, names unknown, charged once more, this time in their own territory. They fought. The Queen of Seshen led the attack on one side. The head elder of the Narumi on the other.

No one knew of Halise's fate. No one cared for the Siman slaves caring for the wounded Seshen alongside the Raan. Violence and blood blinded them.

It was no longer about fighting for land.

It was no longer about fighting for justice.

It was about killing the other.

The screams, the bloodshed, and the feel of life vanishing beneath a blade compelled them. Their minds disappeared. Their life became more important than anything.

Death watched.

He watched them fight.
Death watched.
He watched them kill.
Death watched.
He watched them cry.
And it was too much.

No one understood what happened. They were fighting, swords and spears clashing, bodies falling to the ground, lifeless. Then they were not fighting. They were blown back. The fighting halted.

Everyone stared.

A man they all knew, and yet had all forgotten, stood in the middle of them. To each he looked different. To the Seshen, his hair was brown, eyes blue, and skin pale. To the Narumi, his hair was black, eyes gray, and skin tan.

Through the eyes of each, he looked like one of their own.

And yet, he looked like none of them.

He stood straight, staring up to the sky.

"Who are you!" the queen cried.

"What do you want?" the elder screamed.

Death looked at both of them, image shifting as he thought of the right words. The words he wanted to say to his creations.

"I," he said in a quiet voice. "I am Death. You are all my creations. And this war will end."

Chapter Eleven

It was not his intention to start a war. It was not his intention to create strife. He had made so many mistakes, and this time he was going to fix them.

He created a society. Each of the nine groups was part of it. Each held their own role, living together, but not mixing. He forbade them from falling in love with other groups. He set up rules.

They were not to fight.

They were not to kill each other.

The Nimbon stayed poor. They were the lowest on the totem pole. He could not forgive Halise for taking her own life. He had tried to make up to her what he took away, and she refused to accept it.

For that, he punished them.

Then the Raan. They were the ones who healed, and yet they were also the ones most prone to sickness. They did not question the Seshen's rise to power. For that, he kept them close to the bottom.

The Siman came next. Victims, he looked down on them. Like the Raan, they did not fight for themselves. He saw them as weak and pathetic. They were not good enough to be at the top.

The Tep came next. They fought, yet he still could not move past Amir's love for Halise. The way the two had tried to break his rules and intermingle…it was unforgivable.

The Harashim were in the middle. They did nothing wrong, but also did not stand out. He had no opinion on them.

The Jous, clever and quick witted, landed a higher spot than the Harashim, but were equal with the Lan. Death was unsure of how to work with them, but he could not forget how important Lan was to him. His second friend. And so the Jous became fourth. The Lan third.

Then there were the last two. The Narumi and the Seshen. Two who led the war. His first thought was to punish them both. Lan would be first, and the Nimbon would not be last. Except, the Narumi were only trying to help. He could not punish them.

And the Seshen…

He stared into the eyes of the queen.

All of this started because he had created their namesake. He had created Seshen so he would have a friend. And his love of her clouded his mind. All he could think of was her gentle laugh. All he could think about was her curiosity. Her sweet smile. Her love of nature and the world.

He pictured the queen as Seshen.

He could not punish them.

He, as their deity, declared that the Seshen would be the highest ranking of them all. They would create the rules. They would decide what happened, and he would teach them to be benevolent rulers.

The Narumi tried to protest. They were silenced by their deity.

The Siman, while no longer slaves, waited hand and foot on the Seshen rulers.

Their new city, their new home, was expanded. It took over much of the plains. Everyone had their own jobs, and their own sector. Things settled. Fights broke out and were quelled.

Generations passed.

Soon the war was history, and the Vilaim settled into a pattern. The Seshen grew smaller, and soon it was an elite group who lived as royalty. The Siman stayed their servants.

No one questioned the order.

Death watched over them, making sure that no war would break out again. He did not hide this time. He made his presence known and kept his role as deity.

He would not repeat the mistakes of last time. He would make sure they knew and understood who he was, and what he could do. They built him a home atop a large hill. It was beautiful and white, standing out among everything.

He would sit in there, doing his job. He would take the lives of all those who died. The Vilaim gave him gifts as a way to plead for their safety and happiness. He watched them learn to read and write. They worked with math, built massive buildings, explored the skies, and grew.

They grew, and stayed separate.

Watching them, as the generations passed, as the war became ancient history taught to them as a warning not to anger Death, as they found love, raised families, discovered pets, and developed into a beautiful city, Death grew sullen.

He was known to them, but separate. He could not talk to them. He could not go down and be one with them. They knew who he was, and that meant they feared him. They respected him.

The Seshen were their royalty, but he was their deity.

And he was lonely.

Then one day, a young man approached him. Death sat in his temple, contemplating his role, when he heard footsteps. He expected another tribute from one of the sectors. Someone's grandparent was going to die soon, and they wanted him to spare them.

The young man was a Jous. His hair was dark, eyes gray and glinting, skin tanned from his heritage and the sun. He was lean and tall, but not lanky. He looked like the son of a farmer, though Death knew better. The Jous did not farm. They were the intellectuals.

"What do you want?" Death asked.

The young man smiled and cocked his head. "To ask a question."

Death waved a hand. Here it was. They always asked the same questions. It did not matter what generation it was, or which sector. They always wanted him to spare them.

So when the young man asked his question, Death was caught off guard. Because no one, not in the hundreds of years he had lived up here, had cared about him.

"Are you lonely?" the man asked.

Death was curious. He turned to the man and looked him over. It was no surprise that a Jous was the one breaking tradition. They were a curious bunch. Bright. Intelligent. They produced beautiful works of art and were well respected among the Vilaim.

"Why do you ask?"

"Because," the man said, stepping further inside. "Sitting here for hundreds of years, doing nothing but answer the pleading call of your citizens must be lonely. I know I would be if this was my job."

"What of it?"

"Have you ever wanted a friend?"

Yes. All he had ever wanted was a friend. Someone to stay by his side, to talk to, to be his companion when everyone else died. Death nodded.

The man smiled. "Well, would you like me to be your friend?"

Death frowned. "You will die. Everyone dies."

The man thought for a moment. Then, he said, in a very quiet voice, "What if you made me immortal?"

Interlude

Blair stared at the moon, her hands resting on the wooden railing that separated her from the ocean. The moonlight reflected off the water, waves rushing against the shore without a care in the world. A warm breeze rustled her hair and clothes, and she took in the scent of the ocean, trying to calm herself. Trying to convince herself that this time, that standing on the porch of an Iravata's house was different than last winter. She hadn't almost died at the hands of a teenager. Derek hadn't killed someone. She wasn't learning that the monsters of her childhood were real and had been in her life for as long as she could remember.

But it wasn't any different.

Because she still had almost died. Because Mia had almost died. Because everything was messed up and there was nothing she could do about it. Because the Iravata, the monsters of her childhood, were telling a tale so large and so old that Blair was certain no one on Earth had ever heard it before.

There was so much they didn't know.

Blair reached into her pocket and gripped the crumpled up

paper she'd stolen from Jae's basement. Breathing in, she pulled it out of her pocket and flattened it, eyes scanning the now familiar words. It had information she hadn't know she'd needed. That she hadn't realized she'd wanted all of her life. It was about her clan. It was about her. It was about seers and their ability to sense one another. About how there was never just *one* seer at any given time.

Her mind swam with the new information. She hadn't realized there was so much, and according to Adelia, there were still two parts of the story to get through. What else could they need to know? What else could the Iravata tell them? Why had Shubishi asked Death to make him immortal? Why had Death agreed? Where was this story leading? What…?

Blair groaned and shoved the paper back in her pocket. She was supposed to be asleep. Shion had requested that the children get rest, wanting to save the rest of the story for when Mia's eyes weren't drooping, but Blair couldn't relax enough to sleep. Not with so many questions bombarding her mind. Not when she longed for some kind of satisfactions. She wanted to know more. She *needed* to know more.

But there was more to her insomnia than the Iravata and their story. Because during it all, as they'd listened quietly, Blair had become increasingly aware that Derek would not look at her. He'd stayed close to his sister, not trying to comfort Blair or seek out her hand when her emotions got the better of her.

Ever since they'd first kissed, two fifteen-year-olds not sure what they were doing or why, she'd thought it would be them against the world. She'd thought, foolishly perhaps, that he would understand why she'd left him behind, and that once they were together again he would forgive her and the two of them would work together to understand what was going on. They'd always had a special connection. The two of them…the two of them were meant to be together.

But she'd messed up. It wasn't funny how badly she'd messed up.

And she didn't know how to handle it.

She felt him before she heard him. The necklace amplified her powers, but it was also as though she'd finally exercised a muscle she'd been neglecting for years. Something in her had snapped during this trip, and her magic was stronger now. But so was his. Or maybe…maybe it'd always been strong, and she hadn't noticed it until her own had grown. Regardless, his magic flowed onto the porch, enveloping her like a warm bath. She shuddered.

"Finally come to talk to me?" she asked, voice snippier than she meant it to be.

Derek didn't speak.

She bit her lip, but didn't turn around. "I…I'm sorry. It's been a long few days."

"Yeah." His footsteps drew closer and he appeared at her side, looking up at the moon. "It's been a very long, very exhausting, few days."

Her hands clenched the railing and she closed her eyes, unable to face him. She didn't need to be an empath to understand he was angry. It was in his voice. The way it trembled. How it was low and quiet. He didn't sound like himself. This was…this wasn't an explosive anger. It was silent. It was deep within his soul.

"Derek," she said, "I'm so sorry."

"For what?"

"For…." She gulped. "For making sure you couldn't come with."

Again, he said nothing, staring instead at the sky. Blair chanced a glance at him, but he didn't look at her. He was frowning, eyes trained to the stars.

"Derek, come on," Blair said. "I had to do it. You know that."

Still, he was silent.

"You would have gotten hurt. Or gotten one of us hurt. Or…."

She struggled with the words. She didn't want to tell him that his powers would have been too dangerous for Mia. That having his temper and his exhaustion would have only made things worse for his sister. The sister he was closer to than anyone in the world. Who he'd already messed things up for enough.

Finally, he looked at her. His green eyes shone in the moonlight and Blair found herself lost in his gentle gaze. He lifted a hand and bushed his fingers gently against her cheek. Like always, electricity tingled her skin. Her heart soared. Was he...was he actually...?

She took a chance and stepped closer to him, never breaking eye contact. His hand dropped from her cheek, down to her neck, fingers trailing softly. Then, without much warning, he wrapped his arms around her body, pulling her flush against him. His arms shook, and she pressed her face into his shoulder.

It was going to go back to normal, she told herself. He would forgive her. He had to forgive her. That's what you did when you loved someone. You protected them, and you forgave them.

But things couldn't go back to normal.

"I know why you did it," Derek said, "but I needed to be there. I needed to protect my sister, and you took that from me."

Her heart stopped, fear encapsulating it. She pressed her hands against his chest and pushed away, but his arms tightened around her. The shaking grew more intense.

"Derek, please," she whispered, blinking back tears.

"I can't do it." He relaxed his arms, letting her go. She stayed close to him, and looked up into his beautiful eyes. "I can't look at you and not remember what you did. You took away my energy. You forced me to stay with my parents."

"I—"

"I know you had to," he continued. "But I could have been there. I could have *helped* and you didn't let me. I want to forgive you, but right now I can't."

She blinked away more tears, not wanting to appear weak. Not wanting him to know how much this was breaking her heart. Even though he already knew.

"So, we're done?" she asked.

Derek hesitated. His arms dropped to his side and the two of them stared at each other, close enough that it would only take a fraction of a second for her to kiss him. For her to convince him that she was never going to take away his energy again. That he was safe with her. He was safer with her than anyone else in the world.

But then took a step back and nodded. "I just can't…."

He said nothing more. He broke their gaze and backed away from her before turning to head inside. To go to his twin. To be anywhere but with her. She watched him go, one shaking hand gripping the rail to keep her legs from giving out on her. She waited. And waited. And waited until their magic no longer mixed together.

And then she let go of the railing. She sank to her knees, pacing her face in her hands, and sobbed.

Derek could feel her grief from inside the house. It flooded his senses, overwhelming him to the point of knocking the wind out of his lungs. He placed a hand on his chest and glanced over his shoulder. Had he done the right thing? Had he made a mistake? He knew…he *knew* that Blair hadn't meant to hurt him. That she'd done it to protect him, but still. Still she'd betrayed him. She'd gone behind his back and had taken away his chance to save his sister.

Because of her, because of what she'd done, he'd lost confidence in himself. He'd lost faith that he could trust her ever again. The thought of kissing her, of touching her, made his skin crawl with the memory of how painful it had been to have his energy taken away from him.

She'd done that.

His own girlfriend...ex-girlfriend...had done that to him.

If something happened to Mia again, if something happened to *any* of them, he needed to be there. He couldn't be sidelined. So what if he was exhausted, or angry, or upset? He needed to be useful because if he wasn't then....

He didn't know how to finish that sentence. If he wasn't useful, what then? His hand went to the knife on his hip. He was its wielder. He wasn't just a bystander in all of this. To leave him behind with his parents like he was a child was insulting.

His parents.... In all of the confusion of the moment, of the story, Derek had forgotten he'd promised his parents he'd tell them everything. He pulled his phone out of his pocket and pulled up his mom's name. He considered texting her to let them know he was all right, but decided against it when he realized she would want to call. To hear his voice. To hear Mia's voice.

It wasn't a good time. Not with his mind all over the place. Not right after breaking up with Blair.

He considered, honestly, asking Eran to erase their memories of all of this. To get involved and change history, like he'd done before, and make all of this go away. Then he thought about how exhausting it was keeping all this a secret and pushed that thought aside. Screw the clan rules. Screw the Iravata. They were all keeping secrets from them anyway, manipulating them and getting what they wanted. His parents deserved to know as much as they could.

He and his friends deserved to know everything. He knew there was much to the story that the Iravata were leaving out. How could they not? They were covering millions of years of history. But he'd learned something important: where the Iravata came from and what they actually were. Creatures created by Death.

Death.

Death was real.

This shouldn't have surprised Derek. After everything that had happened in the past year, *nothing* should have surprised him anymore. Still, the idea of an entity with the power to take life…that chilled him. But what chilled him even more was the fact that one day Death might come for him. Shubishi had said that Death didn't know what happened to souls after he reaped them, but Derek was absolutely certain that reincarnations were not supposed to exist. He was not supposed to exist.

Would Death come to fix this mistake someday? Why hadn't he done so already? What weren't the Iravata telling him? Would they tell him? Did they even know the answers to any of these questions? They weren't in their home. The sky here wasn't magical and filled to the brim with colors. Did they still have some kind of connection to that world?

Shaking his head, he kept walking. It was too many questions, and too early in the story to have any sort of answer to them. He didn't know what had happened back then, and he was certain that the next part of their story would answer some of his questions, and summon a whole lot more.

He didn't come to a stop until he stood outside his sister's room. The one that Flora had led her to, asking if she wanted her bruises to be healed. Mia had, for some reason, said no, and instead had disappeared into the room to sleep.

She was not sleeping.

Her emotions jumped from texture to texture, sometimes smooth as silk, other times so sharp, Derek was shocked they didn't draw blood. Fear. Anxiety. Relief. All emotions that rang out, awake and unwell. He shuddered, placing a hand on her doorknob. Did she want to see him? She'd been quiet for most of the night, not saying a word through all of the Iravata's story. But she'd let him hold her. She'd tensed whenever he had to pull away to stretch or shift.

It was okay, he told himself. She wasn't the one who had left him behind.

He opened the door.

"Mia?"

She jolted up, twisting to face the door with wide eyes. All of her emotions combined into fear and he took a step back as it flared into his chest. Breathing out, he stepped into the room and closed the door behind him. Mia stared at him, shaking.

"It's just me," Derek said in a low voice. It was so difficult seeing her like this. Knowing that he couldn't help calm her emotions.

It took a moment for her fear to settle back into anxiety. Her shoulders relaxed and she curled into a ball on the bed, tearing her gaze from him.

"Knock next time," she whispered.

He hadn't even thought to, and wondered briefly if Jae hadn't knocked before coming into that room in the mansion. "Sorry."

"It's okay."

Her emotions said otherwise, but Derek didn't comment. Mia wore a pair of pajamas, having requested something to wear other than the clothes that Jae had given her. Flora had produced them from somewhere in the house, but Mia didn't look any more comfortable in them than she had in the clothes Cody and Blair had rescued her in.

Then again, she didn't look comfortable in general.

Derek held in a sigh before crossing the room. He sat on the edge of the bed, his back to her. "What do you think of the story so far?"

She shifted behind him. When he chanced a look, he found her laying on her back, hands resting on her stomach as she stared at the ceiling. He hesitated for a moment before joining her. Together they sat in silence, staring at the ceiling fan spin round and round. A lullaby begging the two of them to sleep.

"I think that they're hiding things," Mia said after a time. "They're always hiding things from us."

"Yeah. They are." He reached out and gripped her hand, resisting the urge to calm her emotions. He'd gotten better at not doing it over the past year. He wanted to respect her boundaries and not manipulate her, but honestly he wanted to do it for selfish reasons. Because her anxiety, her fear, were so intense that it was making it difficult for him to relax himself.

Mia gripped his hand back. "We should call Mom."

Derek glanced at her. "Should we?"

"She's probably worried." Mia's tone was flat. Emotionless. "You said...they know things now. I don't want to worry them more than I already have."

Derek knew she was right, but her tone concerned him. He sat up and stared down at her. "Are you okay?"

He knew she wasn't, but he had to ask.

Her head twisted in his direction and a chilling smile crossed her face. "I'm fine."

"I thought we said we weren't going to lie to each other anymore," he reminded her.

The smile dropped and she let go of his hand, turning her back to him. "I can't sleep."

Derek placed a hand on her shoulder and she shrugged it off.

"I can't sleep. I can't close my eyes without seeing that room. Without seeing Jae. I'm just so scared. I'm scared that if I go to sleep, I'll wake up and find that I'm not really here. That *this* is a dream."

"I can help you sleep," Derek offered.

Mia tensed, and frustration mixed with her fear.

"I know you don't like when I do it," he said, "but you need sleep. We all do. I can help."

"But it'll still be there," Mia muttered. "You can't take away what happened. Just the feelings I have. And then they'll come back, and then…." She sat up and looked at him. Her eyes had no light in them. No soul. "You can't keep taking away my fear forever."

"I'm not saying forever." He sighed. "I just…for tonight. So you can sleep."

It hurt to see her this way. To see the way she stared at him with a blank expression and no energy. How beneath it all, her emotions were a wreck, unable to decide what they wanted to do. What they could do. She wasn't a person right now. She was a shell going through the motions.

He held up a hand. "I want to help."

"Then…could you please go get Cody?" Mia muttered.

Derek flinched, glad that Mia couldn't see him react. She would ask him why. It wasn't an unreasonable request for her to want to be with the one who had saved her. Still, Cody had betrayed him, and the idea that he and Mia were closer than ever, that *they* had this bond that would never break, hurt him. He wanted Cody and Blair gone from his life. But they would always be attached because of Mia. Derek couldn't bear to separate from his twin, so he would have to see Cody and Blair forever.

"Okay." He slipped off the bed and headed toward the door. He glanced back at Mia, who still lay on her side, back to him, and then closed the door. He leaned on it, closing his eyes as he took in the drip of anxiety. Tears. Mia was crying.

In that moment, Derek hated himself more than he ever had in his entire life. He hated himself more than when he'd lied to his sister. He hated himself more than when he'd snapped at her. He hated himself more than when he'd killed Steven. Because he was worthless here. He couldn't help his sister. He hadn't been able to help her before. He hated that he was so damn worthless that he was making her cry.

But, he decided, he could go find Cody.

He pushed away from the door and walked down the hall to the room Flora had shown Cody to earlier. He didn't bother to knock.

"Mia's looking for you," Derek said to Cody.

Cody jumped, closing the book he'd been reading, and stared at Derek with a rush of adrenaline clambering onto Derek's skin.

"She's—"

"Don't ask me." Derek turned to leave.

"Wait, Derek!"

Derek paused, mostly out of habit, but didn't face Cody.

"I...."

Cody's emotions fluctuated from hesitation to guilt. "I just wanted to apologize for leaving you behind."

"I've heard it from Blair," Derek snapped. "I don't need it from you too."

Cody was silent for a second before he said, "Hate me if you want, but don't hate Blair. We did what we had to. You *know* that. She hates herself enough for what she did. She doesn't need it from you too."

Derek spun around. "Didn't realize you cared so much about Blair. What, you two finally friends now?"

Cody stared at him, defiance in his eyes. "I don't need to explain myself to you. Be pissed if you want, but you know as well as I do that you were in no state to help us. If you'd come along, we might never have saved Mia."

The words cut deep. They were everything that Derek knew, but hadn't wanted to admit. Still, he didn't want to hear them from Cody. He didn't want to hear them from Blair. He didn't want his friends thinking he was so pathetic he couldn't help his own sister when she needed him.

He'd failed her. Again.

He'd failed her.

"Go fuck yourself," Derek snapped before he turned heel and

stormed out of the room. Cody didn't call after him this time. His eyes swelled with the need to cry, but he ignored it and instead hurried to his room. He wanted to talk to someone. To *do* something good. But there was nothing he could do right now.

He sat on his bed, staring at the door. He half expected Cody or Blair to come through the door and try to comfort him, but they wouldn't. He'd made sure they wouldn't.

Then, after a moment he remembered what Mia had said about calling their mom and he pulled out his phone, dialing her number. It rang once.

"Where are you?"

His mother's voice was alive with worry.

Derek closed his eyes, relishing in the sound of his mother's voice, but he knew he couldn't tell her much. They were near a beach? Somewhere warm? Florida, maybe?

"I don't know how to explain it," Derek said.

"Are you safe? Is Mia…?"

"We're both safe. Mia is asleep right now, but she's…." She wasn't okay. None of them were okay. "We'll be home soon, okay?"

"Come home now," Intira begged. "Or tell me where you are so I can come get you."

"I can't." Derek hated the sob on the other end of the call. "I'm so sorry, Mā, but I can't tell you anything yet. I will, though. We'll tell you everything as soon as we figure out what's going on. I promise."

She only continued to cry. He sat there for a few minutes, listening to her try and get words out, but none of them were coherent. He didn't want to interrupt her. He didn't want to hang up on her and make her worry more, but the exhaustion hit him like a brick. His eyes drooped closed as the weight of today washed over him. His body needed sleep. His mind needed sleep.

"Mā," he said in as gentle of a voice as he could, "I'm really sorry, but I have to go. I…it's late and I…I'll call you tomorrow, okay?"

"I want to talk to Mia," she managed to get out.

"She's asleep."

"Tomorrow."

"Tomorrow." He sighed. "Bye."

He hung up before she could say anything else. He would call her tomorrow, and he would give the phone to Mia and everything….

No.

Nothing was going to be okay.

Still, he lay down, throwing the blankets over his body as he drifted off. He wanted to go home. He wanted to see his parents reunite with Mia. He wanted everything to go back to normal as soon as possible. But he needed to know what the Iravata were going to say. He needed to know the rest of their story. Not because he thought he deserved answers as to who Jae was, but because he deserved to know who *he* was, and he had a feeling he was about to find out.

Immortal

Chapter One

The day that Shubishi asked to become immortal is the day that a new era came into motion. It was the day that everything changed for the Vilaim. For the world. For Death.

It took days of convincing for Death to grant Shubishi's wish. He did not know the reason behind Shubishi's desire, nor did he ask. What caused him to hesitate was not Shubishi's motivation, but Death's own. He was desperate for a friend. So desperate that he did not want to wait another moment to create a being who could not die. It would only take a second. Just like creating his flowers, it would only take a moment of thought to take away his ability to die.

But was it right?

Should he interfere again? Should he upset the balance of the world as he had once before? Twice before? He had created the flowers, and he had taken Amir's life when it was not his time. Because of those things, because of his desires, he had almost lost all of his flowers. He had almost lost the only good thing he had ever done in his life. Shubishi convinced him that it was different.

"You are not taking my life without my permission," Shubishi said. "You are not upsetting the balance of the world. You are merely granting a request. A simple request. For, you see, though I will not be able to die from age or poison, when my time comes, and you will know when that time is, all you must do is reap me."

Death would know when that time was. He would know exactly when it was time for Shubishi's life to end. There was no reason, no good reason, to deny his request. It would not be for forever. It would not be the end of everything. It would just be....

Good.

Because Death would finally, *finally*, have a friend. Someone who did not die. Someone who desired to be with him. Someone he did not have to create. Shubishi came to him as a full package. Intelligent, cunning, kind. The perfect friend. He was nothing like Seshen, but did that matter?

So, he granted Shubishi's wish. It took a fraction of a second. A brush of a finger against a forehead.

It was done. Shubishi could no longer die. Death felt when it happened. He felt a shift in the world, and he saw that it was good. He saw that he was no longer alone. That he would no longer make mistakes because there was Shubishi. His friend.

It took time for the Vilaim to notice Shubishi. He mostly kept to the shadows, hiding his attention from others. Jous knew of him. He was a student. A scholar of literature and philosophy. A smart boy from a good, simple family. They were not anything special, and so he was not anything special.

But time passed, and Shubishi never aged. His mind grew. His knowledge expanded and changed and aged. But his physical body did not age. As his parents died, as his friends married and had children, they noticed that there was something different about Shubishi. Something special.

He walked with Death.

There had been some, in the past, in their history, who had walked with Death, but none for so long. None who never aged. None who spoke with such familiarity. Who outlasted queens. It was he, the simple boy from a simple family in a simple time, who had broken through a barrier.

He did not lord over them. He did not walk the streets and declare himself better than. If not for careful observers, the Vilaim may never have even noticed his existence. He kept to the shadows. To Death's shadow. He remained quiet, always studying and always eager to learn more. He observed his fellow Vilaim and learned their changing customs. He watched over the years as new traditions mixed with the old. But he did not interfere. He did not get involved in the dramas of daily life, for while they interested him, they did not pertain to him.

All the while, questions grew in the minds of the Vilaim. In particular, in the mind of the queen. For she had grown in his time: a small child who had seen him walk with Death into a young woman who wanted to know *why* he walked with Death.

She went to Death on her day of coronation and asked him, quite plainly, who Shubishi was and why he never changed. And Death replied, with gentle tones, that he was a friend. A Vilaim who had given up his mortality to keep Death company during the long years. The queen did not understand. She grew angry at his admission and retreated into her castle for immortality held no interest to her. She could not grasp the concept. She could not understand why a Vilaim would wish to live forever.

It was then she began to question Death and his rules.

She stayed quiet about her anger. She was queen. She did not want to disrupt the balance of their carefully planned world, but in her mind she thought, and to her children she taught, that the world they lived in was not all it seemed.

As Shubishi's mind grew, so did his powers. He did not realize it at first. He had spent so long studying and keeping away from the Vilaim, that he did not notice the colors.

After the queen questioned Death, Shubishi decided to leave for a time. He wanted to explore the world, as his forefathers had done. He wished to know and understand everything about the world he lived in, and so, with Death's blessing, he left the city and wandered the fields. The swamps. The mountains. He did not fear the cold. He did not fear the weather. For he was immortal, and Death watched over him at every step.

It was while he was gone that he noticed something different. He had thought, for so long, that he was merely observant. That the actions of his fellow Vilaim were predictable. The idea of powers, of magic, had never once crossed his mind. For while Death had powers, he was an entity. Vilaim were…they were different. They were his creations, his flowers, but they had no powers of their own.

Then Shubishi noticed the world around him changed. He watched the Creatures skitter about their lives, always changing, never living for long, and he realized that he was not just watching them. His eyes and his ears worked as they always had, but there was something more. A tint. A hue. A color around each of the Creatures.

He did not understand at the time what he was seeing. He knew, so well, that he would never change. Death never changed. So why would he?

But he had changed.

In a panic, he returned home, desperate to understand these colors, only to find the Vilaim were brighter than before. His mind rushed, questioning everything, until he was too exhausted to think straight. He retreated to the temple, to his home, and slept for days.

When he woke, everything was different.

Each color was unique. It took time for Shubishi to differentiate between each unique color, but he had all the time in the world. A generation passed. Two. Three. Before he finally understood what he was seeing.

Souls. He was seeing their souls.

He never mentioned this power to Death. For Death appeared happy. For Death had settled into a rhythm with his creations and Shubishi did not want to disrupt his peace. Instead he watched from afar for a time. He watched and waited for his power to grow.

As they grew, he noticed the subtle differences in the souls. Not just colors, but brightnesses. But feelings. He could see those like him. Those with powers. Because nothing ever stays the same. The world changes and those within it change as well. Nothing is stagnant. The Vilaim had not been created with powers. They had them now.

The powers were small at first. Unassuming. Like his. But as the generations passed, they grew stronger, and Shubishi realized that he no longer wanted to stay hidden from the Vilaim. Because they interested him again. He wanted to study these powers. To understand where they had come from, what they meant for the Vilaim, and more than that, how this would change things for the Vilaim as time went on.

And as the powers grew, so did his. The more he interacted with the Vilaim, the more he realized he could *do*. He could not just see, he could manipulate. He could force the souls to fluctuate. To change. Just small things. Just slight things.

But he knew he would grow ever stronger.

He knew....

Shubishi did not know where the name came from. One day, he was no one, and the next, he was revered. The Vilaim paid attention to him. They noticed the way he walked among them as if he were a friend, and how he walked with Death as if he were a friend. He was not like Death, they had decided. He was something different.

The word began as a whisper. The royals, the queen, started it. A whisper on lips at parties and functions. A whisper that spread among the rest of the Vilaim, even to the furthest reaches of Nimbon. The educated, uneducated, rich, poor, men, women, adults, and children all knew the word. They bowed their heads when he passed. They praised him when he spoke to them.

They worshiped him as they had worshiped Death.

Soon, the word was more than a whisper. It was a title. One that tickled his pride and amused Death.

The Vilaim called Shubishi, who was once one of their own, a God.

Over a generation passed with the name. A God. Shubishi had become a God, walking with the entity, Death. As time passed, Death wondered if Shubishi would grow bored with his immortality, but he did not. For the world changed and morphed and the Vilaim grew and developed their cultures. There was always so much to learn. So much history to watch from the shadows.

No, Shubishi did not grow bored with his immortality. He

relished in it. He flourished, growing stronger and wiser every day. He knew things, he had seen things, that no one else knew or had seen.

Except for Death.

Shubishi did not tell Death of his powers, but Death noticed when the change occurred. And he watched Shubishi, he watched the others, carefully. He did not tell the Vilaim what to do with their newfound powers, for they were mostly weak and went unnoticed, but he kept watch over them. He kept watch over Shubishi.

Through Shubishi's eyes, Death saw things in a new light. He felt connected to the world in which he held dominion. Shubishi explained things to him that he did not understand. Death listened and learned and grew and changed.

Everything was changing.

But the more things changed, the more they stayed the same. The Vilaim remained in their cultures. They remained separate and unequal, and Death saw that as good.

So, he let things sit, glad for a companion who understood his desire for company. Who was always willing to be his friend, no matter what.

For the first time since Seshen had died, Death was no longer lonely.

Chapter Two

Then one night it happened. A night that changed the world once more. A night that set every event in motion.

Chapter Three

The night was cool. Shubishi took note of the cool air as he walked through the Seshen gardens, fingering flowers and leaves as he passed by them. There was nothing quite as beautiful as the gardens the Seshen cultivated. They had a gift for it, being created from flowers first and foremost. He had spent many hours among the petals, among the foliage, thinking and plotting his next trip outside of the city walls. He had grown to know this place better than he knew his own room. It was here he had met with the queens of past. It was here he had had conversations with them.

It was here he smelled the smoke.

A breeze brought it to his senses, and the cool night heated.

Shubishi looked up from the flowers, startled, and tried to find the source of the smoke. The Seshen were not big on fire. That was something the Nimbon and the Tep were masters of, having come from cold. The Seshen used fire to cook, but they avoided it at all other costs. There were no bonfires. No camps. They kept their lanterns to a minimum. Even now, in the dark of the night, they did not light the path he walked upon.

They did not like fire.

He strained his eyes, searching for a possible bonfire in the Tep or Nimbon sections of the city. Had the winds shifted in such a way that the smoke carried over the walls?

No.

No, they had not.

His eyes widened and before he knew what was happening, his feet left the ground, sprinting toward the palace.

Toward the fire.

Screams shattered the silence of the night. Shubishi reached out with his power to search for the queen. To find her and make sure she survived the fire. She had to survive the fire. If she did not, then there was no saying what would happen to the Vilaim. To the Siman. She had planned to change the way that the Vilaim city worked. For you see, she had grown up hearing from her grandmother, and her great-grandmother that things were not as they seemed. That the way of Death was not necessarily the way they should live.

She had grown up hearing those words, and she had internalized them in a way no queen had done before. She had internalized them, and confided in Shubishi that she was going to free the Siman. She was going to fix the reputations of the Tep and the Nimbon. Make peace with the Narumi.

She wanted to bring everyone together.

She wanted to abolish the monarchy and create a council.

But he could not find her. Her soul was gone, vanished from the palace. From the Seshen's section. From the city. From the world.

The queen of the Seshen was…dead.

Her children were dead.

Her guards…he came across their bodies, slain not by fire, but by knife. Shubishi knew that something sinister had happened here.

There were only a few hundred Seshen left in the world. They had stopped having large amounts of children, their numbers dwindling over the years. And as Shubishi stared out across the city, flames licking at his heels, he realized that there were fewer.

And fewer. And fewer. Fewer....

He bolted. He did not know where his feet were taking him. Not away. He was not heading toward the gates of the Seshen's section, but toward the center of the city itself. The stone buildings of the Seshen's homes blazed with fire, the souls inside dying one by one. Shubishi tried not to think about the lives disappearing. He had seen many die over the years. He had no more living relatives he knew by name. He had no friends from childhood. They were gone, taken by Death like everyone else around him.

But this was different. Because this was all of them. There had not been violence like this within the Vilaim's home in his entire life, and he had lived quite a long life.

He coughed, trying his best not to inhale the smoke so he could stay focused, but it was difficult with the heat blaring around him. His head swiveled from side to side until finally he saw them. Two souls screaming for help in a house. Two living, breathing souls.

He ran toward them. Nothing else mattered but making sure that he saved at least one Seshen. To save one life tonight.

"Hello!" he called out to the house. A woman holding a small child appeared in the window. The woman was burnt, tears in her eyes from the smoke, from the fear, and the small child—who appeared unharmed—clung to her mother. Her soul shook.

"Jump down," Shubishi commanded, arms outstretched. "I will catch you."

The woman muttered something to her child. The little girl clambered onto the windowsill, letting out a wail. Her nightgown nearly tripped her. She could not have been more than five years of age.

The little girl clung to the windowsill, hesitant to jump. He could see it in her soul. She was scared of the fire, scared of the jump, and scared of him. Her mom urged her. She shifted.

A glinting knife caught Shubishi's attention. He watched, in utter horror, as it appeared in front of the woman's throat and slit it. The woman gagged, falling to the ground, and a hand outstretched, reaching for the little girl.

For the first time in his life, Shubishi did not think. He did not question his actions. He reached out to the little girl's soul and *pulled*, forcing her off the ledge just as the hand missed her. The child screamed, flailing through the air, but he ran forward and caught her before she could hit the ground. Looking up, he tried to get a sense of the assailant, but their soul was fuzzy, face obscured by a dark hooded cloak.

For the second time in his life, Shubishi did not think. He ran, holding the little girl as if she were the only thing remaining in this world. He bolted through the blazing village. He could feel no others. Just himself and the little girl. Even the stranger was obscured, possibly by his own fear.

Fear. He had not felt fear in a very, very long time.

The flight from the center of the city left him panting. He escaped the smoky, hot area and burst into the Narumi's land.

Lights were on. He heard voices. But none of them mattered.

He collapsed to his knees and pulled the little girl away from him, setting her on the grass. She would not look up, shaking, sobbing. He glanced up at the center of the community.

All he could see was fire. A sea of flames and destruction. Not a single soul left. The king, the queen, the royal children, the citizens, the Seshen people. All of them gone. Except this little girl.

"Hello," he whispered to her. With a shaking hand he touched her cheek. She flinched away. Tears moistened his palm. "Little miss, please, look at me. I will not hurt you. I am here to help."

She did not say a word, instead letting out a sob. He breathed out.

"Will you tell me your name?"

There were more voices now. They came closer, holding lanterns. The whispers ranged from what happened with the fire, to who Shubishi was talking to. He had to imagine the Narumi were filled with a range of emotions. They were never fond of the Seshen, but still valued life.

"Little miss, please tell me your name?" he said again, trying once more to touch her. She lifted her head with his hands, bright blue eyes misty from tears. They were surrounded by red skin, both from tears and from light burns. Not too injured. Nothing that would not heal in time.

The Narumi behind him were quiet. The little girl glanced over his shoulder and started hyperventilating.

"Hey, hey, shh," Shubishi whispered. He thought of what his mother would do to calm him down when he was upset as a child. The only thing that came to mind was a kiss on the forehead. So he leaned forward and did just that. "It is all right. You are safe now."

The little girl reached up and wiped the tears away with fists. Shubishi wondered if she was mute. Or possibly traumatized. He tried once more.

"What is your name?" he asked.

The little girl blinked her blue eyes, and then pushed a bit of brown hair out of her face. Her voice, quiet as the wind, came out trembling. She said one word.

"Shion."

Chapter Four

She was the last Seshen. A child of four years who had lost everything in a night of flames. At night, when she closed her eyes and allowed sleep to overcome her, images of fire consuming her dead parents woke her. She would wake and scream, tears streaming down her face.

Shubishi always came. Her screams were a summon, dragging him from bed to comfort her. He would scoop her into his arms and hold her while she cried, whispering words of comfort. He did not know how to care for a child, but was too afraid to let her go. The person who had attacked the Seshen made sure to kill them all.

She was the last Seshen.

He had to protect her.

He kept her close, during the day teaching her about the world, how to read, how to write, how to dance, and about her clan's culture. At night he found himself sleeping in her room just in case the nightmares woke her once more.

It started with every night. Then only a few nights in a week. Then a month. Within a year she slept soundly through the night.

Shubishi was not sure what to do with her. Her curiosity was only matched by her stubbornness. He found it a struggle to keep an eye on her. She would disappear and come back covered in dirt and cuts, saying she had fallen down a hill. But there was no fear in her eyes. Just frustration that she had fallen, and determination to get it right next time.

She grew.

Years passed.

At seven, he watched her sit alone on a bench, reading a book designed for great scholars, and he knew that even though she was not the daughter of the royal family, she was destined to be the queen.

Death knew this as well. He asked Shubishi, as a friend, to teach Shion the ways of the royal family. She was a Seshen. The last Seshen. It was her place, her duty, and her right to know how to be a ruler.

Shubishi was scared. They still did not know who had attacked the Seshen, but there was no telling if they would come back. If he taught Shion to be a queen, would the killer come back for her too?

Still, he did as he was told. He taught her to sit straight, pay attention, and learn about the people she would one day rule. She listened with intent, every day growing more intelligent, more bright, and calmer.

At twelve, she was almost a replica of the queen. She walked with grace, loved to learn, and held her head high no matter what. Shubishi brought her out from Death's home and let her explore the rest of the world. She spoke with the people, asked questions about their lives, and enjoyed every minute of it.

But she was alone in that sentiment.

The others watched her with contempt. They looked down at her for talking to them. Behind closed doors they said she should have perished with the rest of her family. Behind closed doors, they whispered that it was not right for her to live while the others had died. And behind closed doors, the hatred of the Seshen continued to fester, their sins never having been made right.

Shion knew the whispers. She had grown up learning to be quiet, to disappear in a crowd, wanting to learn about the people she was to one day rule. She knew that the rest of the Vilaim detested her. Even the tribes that had been friends with the Seshen during the Great war did not understand why she was treated so specially. She was not descended from the queen. She was not one of her children.

Still, Death let her live in his world. He kept her close, letting Shubishi raise her into the perfect model of the queen. And she would continue to let him. She would do as he said and not complain.

After all, she was the last Seshen.

She felt a sense of duty toward the man who rescued her. So, even though she sat alone every day, watching the other children play with each other, wrestling in the dirt, and she wished to join them, she did not. She knew if she tried, they would run away from her. They had done it before. Sometimes they pinned her to the ground and put bugs down her dress.

At seventeen she had come to grips with her life. Sitting atop the hill, staring out over the villages, up to her burned home. It was a scar in the earth, standing out for all to see. She asked herself many times what life would have been like if her home had not been burned down. Would she have had friends? Would her parents have yelled at her for not doing chores or her homework? Would she be anyone special, or just another Seshen child going about their day?

Would she have ever met Shubishi? Would her only encounter with Death be the day he came to claim her soul? Would she have learned as much as she had, been privileged to the freedoms of the life she currently led?

These were questions she asked in her head, and kept them there.

There was no need to bother Shubishi with them. He was off exploring, as always. He had a million question in his mind as it was. Even when he taught her, she knew his mind was elsewhere as well. She was a burden to him.

Sitting atop the hill, watching the kingdom that Death told her would become hers one day, she buried the questions and put on a smile.

Death watched her grow. From a frightened child to a figure of grace and beauty. He stayed out of her life as much as possible, wanting her to become a woman worthy of the heritage Seshen on her own. But there were times he could not help himself.

She looked so much like her. Like his first creation. Though it had been generations, thousands of years, he had never forgotten what Seshen looked like.

At the age of twenty-two, Shion looked so much like his first creation that at times he thought it was her.

Her hair was always pinned up on the back of her head, strands of hair falling into her face. Her blue eyes were wide and curious, searching the land for things to learn and people to talk to. Even if the people did not always talk back.

At the age of twenty-four, a year before he would crown her the new queen of the Vilaim, he realized that she was getting older. She was changing every day, both how she acted and how she looked.

He realized that in a blink of an eye, like everyone else, she would die.

Loneliness struck his heart. He pictured the day that Seshen had left him. The day he had lost the first creature to ever pay attention to him flashed in his mind. Burying her. Taking her soul.

One day, he would have to do that to Shion.

To the last of Seshen's kind.

"Shubishi, why do they hate me?" Shion asked at the age of twenty-five. It was hours before her coronation. She was dressed in all white. Her dress reached the ground, train wrapped around her feet for the moment. It pulled in at the waist, skirt loose and light. Her hair was done up with white flowers, head waiting for the crown.

Shubishi was sitting across from her, nose buried in a book. He looked up and cocked his head to one side. She was beautiful. He knew she would never accept a compliment from him, but it was difficult to believe the shaking child he had rescued had blossomed into the beautiful woman standing before him.

She was still innocent. Though she had seen much, she knew so little about the world. About to become queen, she had asked him a question he had hoped to avoid for the rest of her life.

He was not sure how to respond, or if he should. She was not his daughter, and yet he felt like he was responsible for her happiness. He had done his best to keep her as sheltered from the evil in the world as possible.

Was now the time to break that bubble?

Was her bubble already gone?

He placed the book on the bench and stood, smoothing out his clothes. She was not tall. None of the Seshen women were. He towered over her, though she appeared to him larger than life. A young woman ready to take on the mantle of the crown.

He held out an arm for her to take. She reached out and touched the crease of his elbow with delicate hands.

"They do not hate you," he said. "They fear what your ancestors have done."

"I am not my ancestors," Shion protested.

"I am aware."

She removed her hand and turned away. "What if…what if I do not want to become queen?"

Shubishi had a feeling this would come. In recent years, Shion had shown little interest in learning about the world and the people she was going to rule. She spent more time out on her hill, staring at the burned scar of her former home.

There were nights when he heard her cry herself to sleep.

He touched her shoulder. "Little miss, you know as well as I do that if you do not want to be queen, then you do not have to. This is something you must choose for yourself."

But was that true?

"May I have a moment alone?" she asked. He nodded and stepped out of the room.

She thought she was alone. She reached out to the books and touched them with gentle fingers, smiling. They were more of a comfort than anything in the world to her. She loved living within their stories, learning from them, even if she struggled. The harder a book was to read, the better.

She had come to terms with her fate long ago, but what if she did not have to do it? What if she could get away, run free, and never look back? Did she have to become the queen that Death wanted her to be?

Was it really her choice?

Or was it her duty to do as he said?

She was the last Seshen. It was her duty to follow in the footsteps of her people and rule over the Vilaim, was it not? They were the chosen group. Death picked them to be the leaders. Out of all the clans, he choose them, and out of all the people who could have been saved that night, it was her who stood there that day.

Still, she could not help but think that she could run. Run and never look back. She would escape to the swamps. To the mountains. To the plains. She would explore the world and never have to pin up her hair again. Never have to experience the glares and the whispers behind her back.

She could be free.

Her fingers slipped from the books and she turned to exit, to face her fate. Whichever fate she was going to choose.

But he stood there.

She bowed.

"There is no need to bow, Shion," Death said, stepping toward her. She lifted her head, but kept her back bent. "How are you doing?"

"I am…well," she replied.

"They are waiting for you."

"I am aware."

"Yet you hide in here."

"I…." Talking to Death was always strange for her. He did not look at her. He looked at something she could not understand. "I am coming now." She straightened up and clasped her hands in front of her, smiling. Just like she had taught herself. Hide the emotions.

Hide her loneliness.

Death touched her shoulder. "You are the last of the Seshen."

"I know."

"I am very grateful that Shubishi saved you all those years ago. It would have been a tragedy for your people to die out entirely."

"They will one day," she said without thinking. Death's eyes narrowed and she flinched. "I...I mean that it is forbidden for me to have children with member of another clan, and I am the last. One day...one day I too will...die."

She had not given much thought to this. How did one admit that she was going to die one day?

A flare of heat burst in her chest. His hand moved to the top of her head, and he closed his eyes.

She was frozen. Her body exploded with a bittersweet mixture of pain and comfort. It spread from her chest to her legs. They buckled and she collapsed to her knees, hands dropping to her side. She breathed out as the pain abandoned her body, leaving her panting, sweating, and confused.

Different.

She felt different.

Death's hand left her.

"No," he said. "You will not."

Chapter Five

Shion stumbled, shaking, to the temple. She head the voices of the people inside, mind whirring, body cold with sweat. Death was nowhere to be seen.

Something was off. Something was wrong. She could not focus long enough to figure out what. What had Death said before he left? Had she imagined his words, or had he uttered nonsense?

Her entire life, she had been raised as separate from the rest. She had never had friends. She had grown up constantly hearing she was special. She was unique. She was the last Seshen, and one day she would become queen.

Today was the day she would become queen.

Yet she stumbled. All composure gone. The world around her was crisp. Detached. She did not feel like she belonged in the scenery around her. She did not feel like she belonged in her own body.

All of her life. Every minute since the night of the fire. From the time she could remember. She was told she was special.

And she had never believed it.

One thought crossed her mind as she arrived at the open

arena, staring down at all the people, from all three of the Seshen's supporting clans, waiting for her to arrive. Shubishi was at the front, standing next to Death. Atop a pillow was a beautiful crown made of gold and gems. It was not the same crown that had been part of the Seshen's royal family for generation. It was one designed by the Jous, crafted by the Harashim, and perfected by the Narumi.

They had made it especially for her.

One thought crossed her mind: *did Death make me…special?*

Shubishi knew that something was different the moment Shion stepped into the aisle. He had, honestly, expected her to run. He had been prepared to tell Death that they had made a mistake with her and she had fled somewhere that no one could know. Death would know, but would he go after her?

However, she had not fled. She walked down the aisle, head held high, dress fluttering in the breeze. She kneeled before Death and waited for him to put the crown on her head. The words were spoken. She faced her people. They clapped. Some cheered. And she walked, face pale, back out of the temple and was not seen for two days.

Shubishi tracked her through the gardens after the second day of her being absent, and found her sitting alone on a stone bench, back to him.

"Shion?" he called out, stepping lightly so as to not disturb the flowers.

Her soul, he realized, was different. Not so different that it was noticeable at first. Still silver, and still shimmering, it held a new glow to it now. One that he had never seen on anyone in the entire Vilaim race.

"Why did he do it?" she whispered. She held the crown in her hands, rubbing the jewels with her thumb.

Shubishi sat next to her, staring at the crown, and then at the tears streaming down her face. "What are you talking about?" But he knew. With every second her soul grew stronger, clinging to her body in a way that was impossible for those who could die.

She did not say, and he was not going to press her to answer. But the questions continued.

"Why is this something to hate?" he asked, letting out a loud laugh. He remembered the day when Death made him immortal. It was the most glorious, freeing days of his life. No longer was he bound by the constraints of reality.

Yet, Shion cried.

When she said nothing, he asked another question. "How did it happen?"

Her gaze left the crown, and lifted to the flaming sunset. Tears glistened in the light. "He did not ask me."

"What do you mean?"

"He did not tell me. He did not ask me. He placed his hand on my head and my body changed. I felt it. I knew it had changed, and I was different."

"You will adjust to it."

"I do not want to adjust to it. I do not want to be it."

Shubishi fell silent, staring down at the child he had raised. The young woman he had protected. The queen he was to bow before. Why had Death done it? Why had Death gone and taken away Shion's ability to die?

Was he that afraid of being alone?

"It is wrong," she muttered.

"What is?"

"Immortality."

He was taken aback by her statement. He removed his hand

116

from her shoulder and stood with crossed arms. "I quite enjoy it, Young miss. In fact, I am sure there are plenty who would love to take your place. No questions asked."

Her blue eyes were not accusing when they focused on him. They were hollow.

"I do not want this," she whispered. "I did not want to be queen. I do not want to be immortal. How…how did I end up with both? I was not even born to royalty. The only reason Death cares is because I am…."

Because she was the last Seshen.

"Why would I want to be immortal?" she continued. "I already live a life isolated from those around me, and now I must do so for all of eternity? Now I must sit here, separate from everyone else as they scorn my very existence. Now I cannot find peace. Now I cannot bring my people's story to an end. They will forever exist through me, suffering, unable to rest. Does he not see that? Do you not see that?"

Shubishi had no words. He was unsure how to help the young woman in front of him. To explain the beauty of immortality. The powers she would gain over the years. He did not know how to say that her lack of connections was a blessing. It would mean that she had no death to fear.

There was no sadness waiting in her future.

Chapter Six

It was raining. Shion took cover in the temple, staring out into the dark abyss. Her fingers ran over the crown, wanting to throw it down the hill to be lost forever. It had been five years since her coronation. Five years since her immortality.

Shubishi always told her that time passed faster when you did not have to worry about dying. Time was nothing to them anymore. Yet, she could not help but feel the world had slowed to a crawl. Every hour took ages to pass, and she wished for nothing more than to escape the reality that held her.

There were times when she tried to escape. She tried to get away but someone stopped her. A guard, Shubishi, the citizens. They wanted to speak to her, to have her visit their homes.

She wanted to run.

She wished, more than anything, that she had run on that day.

A voice called to her. One she did not recognize. She tilted her head, eyes dazed until they landed on a woman with flaming red hair and blue eyes.

A Siman.

Shion sat up. The crown dropped from her hands and fell to the ground. Neither woman moved to grab it.

The Siman avoided Shion. They did not speak to her, they did not want anything to do with her. Many protested her as queen. Even more protested her as a god. They did not want their oppressors as their leader again.

Shion did not blame them.

"Hello," she greeted with a bow of her head. The woman stood tall and held her head high. Her clothes were white and amber, a gentle combination. Her hair was let loose.

Shion wanted to let hers loose.

"Hello," the woman said. There was no friendliness in her voice. After everything her people went through at the hands of the Seshen, Shion knew there would never be friendliness between the two groups. There was too much damage.

"My name—" Shion began, but the woman held up a hand.

"I know who you are," she said coolly, stepping forward. She stopped inches from Shion, crouched, and picked up the crown. She examined it with narrowed eyes, and then tossed it to the side. "Our queen. A god. Madam Shion."

Shion backed away, tripping over the floor and falling onto the bench. The woman towered over her, smirking. This animosity was different. The Siman avoided her and spoke ill of her people. They never spoke down to her or insulted her personally. This woman hated *her*.

"Who are you?" Shion asked.

"My name is Enya," the woman said with a slight bow. "I am the newest god."

From the time she was a child, Enya knew she wanted to be immortal. She stared with awe, every day, at the man who walked through the streets, unable to die. He was beautiful, a Jous with brown hair slicked back into a ponytail, eyes the color of a stormy sky, always curious and bright.

He spoke to her once. She was crying on the streets, fearing her master's punishment for her failure to bring home enough bread. Her red hair was stained with dirt, face blotchy and bruised. No one noticed her. A Siman crying in the streets was no new thing. They assumed the child was begging for money.

No one noticed her.

Except for him.

His hand touched her shoulder. She jerked her head up and brushed away tears in case it was her master.

It was not.

"Are you all right?" Shubishi asked with a brilliant smile. Enya could only stare. The man chuckled and reached into his pocket. "I know things are rough, but it is important to keep smiling. To remember that there is also good."

He flattened his hand. A simple, golden ring lay in the center.

She stared, jaw dropped, at the item. Others were watching now, listening. It was not every day their god spent attention on a Siman child.

"It is for you," Shubishi said, gesturing. She did not know what to do or say. She took the ring, hands shaking.

He rubbed the top of her hair and then was gone, walking down the street.

Everything for her changed that day.

She went home to an angry master and smiled. She hid the ring in her room, where no one would find it, and every night she stared at it before falling asleep.

He had chosen her. The god had chosen *her*.

She was fifteen when the fires burned everything to the ground. Enya could not hold back her glee. None of the Siman could. They burned candles and sang songs, celebrating their freedom, while at the same time mourning the loss of lives. With the Seshen gone, they were no longer servants. They were a floating class, one that needed to find its place in the world.

They spoke of opening their own businesses, learning to read and write, attending council meetings, and even running for an office position. For the first time in history, the Siman would have a voice, with no Seshen to knock them down.

Enya knew exactly what she wanted to do. The day after the fires, she stepped outside her house and held the ring up to the sky. The sun glinted off the gold, giving her a fire of life. She slipped it onto her finger. It fit perfectly.

Glee overcame her.

She had not seen him in years. He never came to the Siman compound, and whenever he was with the Seshen, it was for tea with the queen. She did no blame him for spending time with the royal family. He had his reasons, and it could not be because he actually liked the Seshen. It was because Death wanted him to. Because Death commanded he do so. She knew that had to be it.

There were no guards to keep her locked in the Siman section. She stepped through the walls and breathed in freedom.

Bliss tickled her skin. Her hair was clean, curly, and the color of blazing fire. Her clothes were ragged, yes, but she knew him better than that. He would not judge her based on her clothes. He had shown her kindness as a child, why would not he now?

She did not hesitate to climb the mountain to his home. The

other Siman did not pay attention to her. Her parents were long gone, and she had no siblings. She had nothing to lose going to him and telling him that she wanted him to teach her. She wanted to learn to read, to write, to study the world, to explore, and to live outside the bounds the Seshen had forced her into her entire life.

The ring was proof that he had chosen her to be his pupil.

When she arrived at the temple atop the hill, her glee vanished.

Horror and fear overcame her. They weighted her legs. She could not move. She could only stare at him kneeling before a small child with vacant eyes.

Vacant *blue* eyes.

Brown hair.

Pale skin.

A Seshen child.

She fled.

Years passed and the child grew. Years passed and Enya learned. Whenever Shubishi and the child came to her home, she tried to catch his attention. She wanted to show him the ring and remind her that *she* was special, but he only had eyes for the Seshen child.

He raised her. He taught her. He did everything for the child that Enya wanted.

She watched from the shadows. She studied everything she could. Read every book she could find. Explored the world outside the city. She focused on the history of her people. She learned about the war and about the alliances. She tried to find any reason why Death would force her people to be slaves to the Seshen.

His reasons and his emotions were unknown then. He told them only to his confidant, Shubishi. Only Shubishi knew the real reasons for the war. The real story behind Halise and Amir.

That did not stop her from trying.

When she finally returned to the city, a changed, confident woman, she decided to do the impossible.

She wanted Shubishi's attention. The ring was not enough. As long as a Seshen was alive and in his care, she would be nothing. There was nothing more important to Death than that girl, just like there was nothing more important to him than the Seshen. And in turn, there was nothing more important to Shubishi.

She wanted to be more important to Shubishi.

He had chosen her first.

And she knew that the only way she could possibly manage that was to elevate herself to a level he could not ignore.

She needed to become immortal.

Confidence consumed her. She knew, just knew, that this was going to work. She had knock the Seshen child out of his mind and become the only one he cared about. She entered the city, ready to claim her stake, to lift her chin and amaze everyone who once looked down on her people.

Only to find them buzzing about their new queen.

Only to learn that their new queen was the Seshen child.

To learn that Death had made her immortal.

Shion. That was her name. Enya had never met the child before, nor had she any plans to. In her mind, Shion would vanish into nothing, while Enya and Shubishi lived together as immortals. She had be his companion, and the Seshen people would vanish into history.

Now, it would never be.

But that did not mean she could not fight.

This would not defeat her. She would not let it defeat her.

Fire ignited in her heart. Confidence and certainty.

While everyone was focused on the new queen, what her immortality would mean, and if it was possible for others to join the ranks of their gods, Enya approached Death.

She approached Death and demanded to become a god.

Death knew nothing of this woman. She was a Siman, but so unimportant to him that he did not know her name. He did not know her story. In a way, he questioned whether this was a good thing of him, as a leader, and as a deity.

"You wish to become a god?" he asked in clarification. She was the first to ask him of this. He had expected it soon, to be honest, but he had a feeling the others were too afraid to approach him with such demanding tenacity.

In a way he admired it.

In another, he despised it.

"I do," the woman said, throwing back her red locks. "And you will do it, because you owe the Siman this."

"I owe no one anything."

He did not like her silent accusation. What happened to the Siman was not of his doing. It was the Seshen's and society's. He merely let everything unfold. He waved her away.

"You have done nothing to deserve such a gift. Leave."

"What did Shion do?"

There was much animosity in the woman's voice when she said Shion's name. Death frowned and turned to her. Shion had done nothing. She existed as the last of the Seshen. To Death, that was enough, and he made the rules.

"Why do you want to become a God?" he asked instead of answering her question.

"To bring power to the Siman."

She was lying.

But he was curious.

No one had the courage to lie to him. No one had the courage to accuse him of anything. He smiled.

"All right. But you must do something for me."

Shion was unsure how to react to Enya's announcement. A new god? Another one? She clenched a fist, wondering if she should congratulate Enya or not. The woman seemed pleased with herself for saying those words. Was she glad for the change? Did she want it?

Instead, Shion stared at the floor, eyes trailing to the crown.

"It is a pleasure to meet you."

Chapter Seven

Shubishi recognized the ring long before he recognized the woman who wore it. He recalled, one day, giving it to a small Siman child who had been crying on the streets. He had wanted to make her stop, as her soul had been stabbing at him as he had passed by. It had been thoughtless. Giving away something that had belonged to someone important to him from so long ago. Casting away the past.

Enya wore it like a trophy.

Shubishi avoided it, and the memories associated with it, whenever he could. He spoke little to her. No matter how much she tried to catch his attention, no matter how many times she begged for his attention, he brushed her off. Her entire worth, her entire everything, was based on his opinion. On Death's opinion. She carried herself with great importance. A God. Someone to be feared and loved.

In reality, she was nothing.

Not because she was Siman, but because deep inside her soul was empty of any self-worth. He wanted her to leave him alone. He wanted her to attach to someone else. Possibly to Shion, who had never had a close friend, and who—as the years passed—grew more and more distant from everyone.

It was not long, though, before Shubishi realized that Enya had no intention of befriending Shion. In fact, the more attention Shubishi gave Shion, the more Enya treated her like a pariah. Speaking in insults veiled as riddles. Teasing Shion for anything she struggled with. Mocking her and her crown.

Shion, already quiet, already shy, withdrew further into herself until eventually she stopped speaking altogether. And Enya went on as if she were winning a war that no one else was fighting. Her confidence grew with each day that Shion remained quiet.

Shubishi did not know if he should interfere. Shion was strong. Quiet, but full of will. He knew that the history between the Siman and the Seshen impacted the way Shion interacted with Enya, but he was not sure how long this would last. And there was only so much he could handle. However, anytime he attempted to address this with Death, the deity pushed him to the side, preoccupied by his own issues.

The Vilaim were asking questions.

See, the world was changing, as all worlds do. The order that Death had managed to keep for generations was slowly dissolving into nothing. No one had questioned Shubishi's rise to Godhood. They had all understood when Death made Shion immortal, even if they did not all agree with it.

But Enya?

She was a nobody. She added nothing to society but unrealistic demands and an obsession with their first God.

The clans began to question the order of the world. They asked for their own Godhood. They demanded to know how Enya was gifted such a privilege while the rest of them had to wait until death claimed them. Then they questioned deeper, more structural issues.

Why were the Narumi so wealthy while the Nimbon continued to suffer? Why were there walls to separate Vilaim from one another? What was the logic of keeping them so separate from one another?

Protests broke out into the streets. They demanded answers. Buildings burned. Children cried. Walls were torn to shreds.

Death did not know how to handle them. He did not know how to quell their anger or dismiss their concerns without revealing too much of himself. Of his plans. And besides, he was getting distracted by something else going on. Something far away from the world of the Vilaim.

But we will get there.

He consulted Shubishi, and only Shubishi, about what he should do. He asked him if he should keep things the way they are, or if things needed to change.

"Change," Shubishi said without hesitation.

"But they have worked for so long."

"From atop this hill, maybe that seems so." Shubishi gestured to the temple in which Death spent most of his time. "But I walk among the Vilaim. Sometimes when they know, sometimes when they do not. I walk among them and I listen to their grievances. The walls, the structure, it is no longer working. Cities are overfilling. Vilaim want to leave. They want to explore the rest of the world, just as Enya had been able to do, and as she boasts about. They feel unloved. Unappreciated. They feel unheard."

Death nodded, unsure how to handle all of these complaints. They felt unheard? They felt unloved?

He did not know how to do either of those things. To listen, nor to love. For he was Death, and Death did not listen to those whose lives were so unimportant. And he was Death. He did not know what it meant to love.

At least, he did not realize he knew.

"What shall I do?" he asked his closest companion.

Shubishi thought long and hard about what needed to be done. And it was his suggestion that began a new era in the lives of the Vilaim. "A council."

"A council?"

"Yes. We give the Vilaim a chance to become immortal. A select few will become Gods and together we will make decisions. One from each of the clans. Already we have Jous, Seshen, and Siman. Now we must find one from each of the other six."

Death mused about this for some time. Days. Weeks. Until finally he returned to Shubishi with a single nod.

Shubishi collected one from each of the clans to bring back to Death. Each one had volunteered. Each one had vowed to keep the interest of their people at heart. Each one became immortal. Three became four. Four became six. Six became eight. And before long, there was only one left who needed to be found.

Together, the council worked through the issues of the Vilaim. They listened to their clan leaders and brought the complaints to meeting after meeting. The protests diminished. The Vilaim were, at least on the surface, satisfied with their lives. They had someone to listen to them and their woes.

Or, some of their woes.

But the world had changed. And with the creation of the council, so had the lives of Shubishi and Shion.

For Shubishi, he was no longer special. He was no longer the only god. He faded into the background, forgotten by the people and disliked by the other gods. They found him unapproachable, were confused by Enya's obsession with him, and did not care that he was the first.

129

Oddly enough, he found he did not mind. They left him alone to his books. They did not question if he failed to appear at meetings. He found interest in science and conducted experiments. He grew interested in the teachings of other clans and read as much as possible in the ways of their lives. To him, this was the most blissful time of his life. Where he could do as he pleased without any expectation.

Shion, however, experienced the opposite.

She tried to please all of the new gods, but they fawned over her. This was the closest they had ever gotten to the queen, and they took advantage of it. They invited her to parties, requested her counsel, and fought over one another to sit by her side during meetings. It did not matter what clan they came from, nor what their history to the Seshen's were. They wanted to be close to the one Death had chosen as queen.

And the more they did this, the more she wanted to escape from it all. She had never liked having the attention on her. She had never liked the chains keeping her from living a life where she got to choose what happened to her. Everything she did was part of a grander plan, and she hated every moment of it.

She had no voice.

No say.

No Vilaim to speak for.

There were days when she did not attend meetings. There were days when she snuck out of the temple, donned in simple clothes and a cloak to hide her face, and she wandered among the people. Staying far away so as not to be noticed. So as not to be questioned. She wandered among the Vilaim and learned so much about them that her heart soared.

So many things fascinated her. Each clan had their own way of living. Despite everyone being in the same compound, they held onto the traditions of the past, and it created a vibrant life. From the Lan's lively markets, stalls run by the women while the men worked behind the scenes, to the Raan's winter festival on the solstice where they burned a large fire, dancing around it with dried flowers in their hair.

She loved watching them, but the more she saw, and the longer the council existed, the sadder she grew. She saw the Vilaim form bonds. Relationships. Friends and lovers. She watched them and she retreated even more, thinking of her own relations.

Shubishi was her father.

Enya hated her.

Everyone else bowed at her feet.

And all she wanted was a friend.

For Death, the creation of the council sparked something in him. He looked at his creations, and at his world, and he found he enjoyed having more immortals living with him. They acted differently around him now that they could not die. It was as though they were no longer afraid, and this pleased him.

It pleased him, and he wanted more. He wanted more friends.

And it was because of this that he ventured out to the Tep's section of the city. He glided through the streets one night, examining the way things were. He had yet to choose a worthy Tep to become a god. He wanted more friends, but they had to be perfect. They had to be the right ones, otherwise it meant nothing.

When he met her.

She walked down the street, arm linked with her father. In her other arm, a basket filled with food. Her long, blond hair was let loose, an uncommon sight among Tep women, and she moved with a grace that could rival his queen. He watched her for some time, curious about why she laughed like the sound of bells, and how she clung to her father, despite being an adult.

It was only when she opened her eyes, her unfocused, gray eyes, that he realized she could not see.

Adelia was born blind. In Tep, and in many of the other clans, it was customary to kill or abandon children born with disabilities. With defects, as they said. But Adelia's parents were different. For they had struggled to have a child of their own, and they were grateful for Adelia's presence.

When the Raan doctor, who had helped them during the birth, offered to take Adelia away, her mother had protested so strongly that she had fallen ill herself. And the doctor offered no more assistance, confused by the strange attachment they had had to an imperfect child.

Her parents needed no help.

They raised their daughter. They taught her language and read her stories. She played with her toys and helped her mother in the kitchen. She grew to love life, just as any child with loving parents and a warm home did. She did not care that she was blind. She did not care that the other children mocked her. That she had no way of learning to read or write. That she was not allowed to learn a trade and bring in money for her family.

She did not care.

Because she was happy. Her parents were happy. They loved her and did not fret over money or materials.

Even when she was deemed unmarriageable, even when others told her she would die alone in darkness, she knew that they were wrong. Because she did not live in darkness. After all, what did she know of black of white? Light or dark?

She knew instead of smells. The warm scent of her mother's fresh bread, the musky smoke wafting in the air when she passed by a market stall selling meat on a stick to young children, and of the fragrance of flowers on a summer breeze. She knew of sounds. Tinkling bells on the dresses of children preparing for dance classes, bantering between a newlywed couple who could not agree on how to furnish their new home, the elderly shuffling their feet, heading off to visit their grandchildren with presents of sweets and new toys they had knitted themselves.

There was nothing lonely about her world.

There was nothing dark about her world.

And then Death made her immortal.

She was walking home with her father, ready to prepare dinner, when someone approached them. They were not a special family. Well known in their neighborhood, but that was not important when it came to the counsel. Adelia's father bowed, and tugged his daughter down with him. She did not know this man. The sound of his voice. The smell of ash and smoke on his skin.

He was new to her.

"My lord," her father said, "whatever brings you to Tep on this fine night?"

It was then Adelia knew who stood in front of them. Death.

Death reached out and touched Adelia's chin, lifting her head to face him. She blinked, eyes dry. "You are blind, my child."

"Yes," she said.

"Do you live a good life?" he asked.

"Oh yes." She stood up straight, unable to contain her smile. "I live the most wonderful life."

"Hm." Death could not comprehend what she was saying. "I have been searching for the final council member," Death admitted. "Someone from Tep."

"Yes," her father said, gripping his daughter's arm tighter. "We are eagerly awaiting your decision, my lord."

"I have made my decision," he said, staring into the vacant eyes of the woman standing before him.

Adelia stepped back. "I am flattered, sir, but why me?"

"I have my reasons," was his answer.

Adelia's father was ecstatic. His daughter, the one who everyone said would go nowhere, a God! He could not believe his ears and in seconds said yes. Adelia tried to protest, not wanting to leave her family or her home, but it was too late.

Right there, Death touched her forehead. She tried to jerk away, but it only takes a second to take away someone's mortality. It only takes a moment to change someone's life forever. And in that second, his cold fingers against her skin turned blazing hot. It spread through her body, lifting her soul, manipulating it, making it sturdier. Stronger.

She choked back a scream and collapsed to her knees.

And then, her eyes burned as what she had always known changed.

A bland sheet of bright nothing.

Confusion filled her.

The sheet morphed and changed. Figures. Specks of *something*.

It hurt. She had to shut her eyes.

Nothingness returned.

But it was not the same.

"What did you do to me?" she asked, opening her eyes. Feet. She knew they were feet. They were different than she had thought. Legs. A torso. A head. A face. Eyes staring at her. She blinked. Hot tears spilled down her cheeks.

"I fixed you," Death said. His lips were turned up. "You were blind. Immortality comes with benefits. One of those being you will never feel illness, and all your wounds will heal. I healed your blindness."

Fixed. As though she were broken.

There were times where she was angry as a child. When the other kids would not let her play with them. When she could not learn to cook with her mom, like her friends did with theirs. When she wanted to stay up late listening to the man across the street play music and her parents said no.

This time blew them away.

She pushed herself to her feet. She stumbled, having to shade her eyes. It was nighttime. They always said nighttime was dark, and that only the bright hurt. So why did this?

"What is wrong, Addie," her father asked, placing a hand on her shoulder. "This is a good thing! Now there is nothing wrong with you."

Her chest ached. Her mind whirred with all the new information she did not know was possible to have. She stood tall, squinting. More tears spilled out of her eyes.

"There was never anything wrong with me."

Adelia was moved from her home to the council's quarters. She struggled with her eyes. Many days she tied cloth around them, thankful for the simple darkness. But her dreams...her dreams were vivid now. She could not escape the fate Death had forced upon her.

And she had lost his favor. She had rejected his gift. She had refused to thank him. She had yelled at him, and he had rejected her. Of course, now that she was immortal, he could not do anything to her. He was not going to create a god and then cast her out. That would cause chaos. Her parents would speak of the incident.

So he ignored her. He put her on the bottom. She was on the council because he let her, and he made sure she was aware of it.

They all did.

And Adelia went to sleep every night wishing she had not gone out that night.

Chapter Eight

O n the day Adelia joined the council, Shion expected her to bow at her feet like the others had. She had heard there was a final council member joining from Tep, but she had not heard that the woman walked with a blindfold. That the woman was forced into this against her will. That she was unhappy with the situation.

When the two met, Adelia pushed passed her and said not a word. And this intrigued Shion. She had experienced indifference before, but never from a council member. Never from someone who had finally gotten this close to her.

Adelia sat alone. She did not look at the others. She kept on her blindfold and refused to speak to anyone. Even when others went up to her and asked her questions, even when she was called upon in meetings, she crossed her hands over her lap and refused to say a word. It made them uncomfortable. It made them whisper about her. About her past. About why Death had chosen her of all people.

It made them wonder if being a God was not the gift they had made it out to be.

All things Shion had been wondering since the day of her

coronation.

But despite listening to what these immortals had to say, and the gossip they spread about Adelia, she did not contribute. For one thing, she did not believe in gossiping about anyone. For another, the last thing she wanted them to know is that she, too, was unhappy with her situation. That she longed for the days when she aged. When she could fall ill. When a year passing meant something because it brought her closer to death.

Their Queen, their God, wanted to die.

And she could not let them know.

Shion soon became obsessed with Adelia. Staring at her from afar. Listening to Adelia from far away. Becoming more and more curious about the woman who never spoke. About the woman who never saw.

When she attempted to ask Shubishi for his help, he brushed her off, or was not in his quarters. She searched for him, but found that often he left the city. He disappeared outside the walls and did not return for weeks. Months. He always had something on his mind, and Shion did no want to add to that.

It was her job, she had decided, to make things right with Adelia. To make her feel welcome. To make her open up and become part of the council. Because as much as Shion hated it, she knew that the others had found life long—and their life was to be very long—friends.

Shion would never have a friend. She had come to accept that. But that did not mean Adelia had to live her life in such a lonely manner.

So, on a warm day, months after Adelia had joined the council, Shion approached her.

They sat alone in the council room. It was after a meeting. An unsuccessful one. Shubishi was not there, Shion was too focused on Adelia to think, and Enya was not budging on the issues of Seshen's old land.

It was a topic everyone thought Shion would be interested in. She was not. It was not her home, and she had few—if any memories at this point—of it. The fire was hundreds of years ago. If Enya wanted to turn it to farmland, Shion was not going to stand in her way.

The others were the ones who did not want to give it up. Even the Narumi agreed it would be insulting to the Seshen's souls to reuse it so soon.

So they ended the meeting early, and Shion approached Adelia.

"Why do you wear the blindfold?" Shion asked.

The minute she asked the question, she realized how brash and rude it sounded. She immediately took it back. As she stuttered around an apology, Adelia faced her with a slight smile. A first. Shion fell quiet as Adelia said her first words since making her first appearance as a God.

"I do not want to see," she said.

Her voice was soft. Sad.

Shion did not understand. She glanced around the room. "But, the world is so beautiful."

"The world is beautiful without vision."

"How?"

This was not a conversation that ended well. Shion could not get it into her mind how a world without sight was beautiful. How Adelia did not need to, or want to, see. And in the end, she decided she never would understand.

But…just because she did not understand did not mean Adelia was not correct. There was much in the world she did not understand. She did not understand why the class system must be, why Shubishi was so obsessed with knowing the world, why they were immortal, why the sun rose in the morning and set at night.

This did not make her ignorant. It did not make her stupid. All it meant is that she might never fully understand, and that did not bother her the way it bothered Shubishi. It was okay that she did not understand Adelia.

After minutes of arguing, Shion breathed in deep and closed her eyes. "I do not understand why you feel the way you do. I am sorry."

Adelia did not say anything for a minute. Then, she reached up and pulled off the blindfold. She shielded her eyes from the light, scrunching them mostly closed. She turned to Shion and opened her gray eyes.

"It is okay that you do not understand," she said, voice low. "I understand your thoughts. I have heard them my entire life. Vilaim felt sorry for me. They explained the world to me to have me understand what it looked like. They would apologize for me not knowing what the world looked like. I do not blame you for being like them. It is all you know. But I ask that, from now on, you do not ask about my eyes."

Her plea was desperate. It was as though she had wanted to say this for a long time.

Shion nodded and left.

Adelia had spent so long not speaking. It felt good. She knew Shion was the queen, but after facing the wrath of Death, she did not feel at all scared to challenge Shion's views. To tell her exactly why she kept her face hidden.

She was not sure why she opened up to Shion and no others in the council. Shion was not the first to ask about her blindfold, and she would not be the last. Maybe it was because out of all the council members, Shion was the only other one who did not speak.

Adelia left the blindfold on the chairs and exited the council room. The light was harsh, attacking her eyes, but soon, they adjusted. She had heard of this before. She had heard others talk about being in a dark room and then stepping outside. It hurt, but only for a minute. And when it grew dark, it was hard to see, but only for a while.

The outside world was green. Adelia knew the color from stories about plants. She was amazed by how different green was. Different shades. No two plants were exactly the same.

A breeze swayed her hair. It was blond. She knew that from learning about the different clans and classes. She sat on the nearest bench.

She had been fighting to show the others that they were wrong. To prove to Death that he had done the wrong thing, but she was tired. It was exhausting being alone. Exhausting not having friends. She missed the friends she once had back in the Tep territory. They did not care that she was blind.

She touched her cheek, just below her eye.

Was it time to give in? Was it time to stop fighting? Shion had become so frustrated trying to understand that she had apologized. An apology Adelia wanted from someone else.

It made her wonder if anyone would understand her pain and her anger.

Was it worth fighting for?

The world was beautiful, she admitted. Even with sight, it was beautiful.

Death hated the anger Adelia pushed onto him. He had done her a favor. He had helped her. Fixed her. Healed her. Was that not what they wanted? What more did they want from him?

For thousands of years, Death took care of the Vilaim. He created them, watched over them, and ferried them after the end of their lives. He acted as a leader, as a deity, and as a mentor to all the Vilaim who asked.

In return? He asked for nothing.

And this is how Adelia reacts when he gives her the greatest gift.

Death left the city. Parts of him stayed behind to ferry the dead, but the main part of him traveled and explored the world outside. Anger compelled him.

It had been so long since he had explored the rest of the world. He visited the abandoned cities and villages left when he forced everyone into the city.

He explored the crevices, finding homes covered in ivy, buried under snow, and inhabited by animals.

He visited the graves set up by each group. They were all different. Some buried full bodies with stones. Others planted trees. Others still spread the ashes, leaving only stone markers to say who was who.

He thought of all the deaths. The deaths he had caused. The deaths he had paid no attention to. The lives that had changed because of his actions. He found whole families, generations, buried together, and he knew he had taken something from them.

He had done everything he could to control their lives. He had created them. Kept them apart. Killed Amir. Stopped the war. Made the Seshen leaders when he never should have.

He had ruined everything.

He left the villages and walked. Through rain, snow, heat, and bitter cold, he walked until the ends of the realm in which he had come to love. He broke through the dimension and found himself surrounded by white.

And he kept walking.

Kept walking until he came across a new realm.

A realm with no life.
A realm of plants and water and rocks.
He found Earth.

Chapter Nine

Ten years passed. Then twenty. Then thirty. Then one hundred. Time became meaningless to Shion. To Adelia. They watched from their council room as the world continued to change before their eyes. One second, the council was fighting about what to do regarding Death's disappearance. They screamed at each other, desperate for someone to tell them what to do. How to live. What to say to the Vilaim who waited on them hand and foot.

At first, Shion asked Shubishi what to do. The Gods all came to her, asking for her guidance, for she was their queen. But she did not want to rule. She did not want to be the one who made these decisions. Besides, she told herself, Shubishi was the one who was closest to Death. He was the first God.

The first immortal.

Shubishi could not care less about the fate of Death. He was off in his own books, performing experiments on children with powers. On Vilaim who were born sick. Who needed cures. He was lost in his own world and cared little for the fate of the Vilaim.

Adelia, meanwhile, was glad of the news that Death had

vanished. She was never one to hide her contempt for Death, and at the council meetings, she finally spoke. She spoke the truth:

"He has abandoned us."

The Gods knew this was true, but they did not want to admit it. They flew into a fury, screaming at Adelia to hold her tongue and not speak of their deity in such a way. And all the while, she smiled and let them, for she knew that they were scared.

Their fear pleased her.

The council plotted together, thinking of ways to get Death to come back to them. Sheep without a shepherd. Fools without a king.

Adelia spoke of another plan, however. She spoke of a time for them to come to true power. Where they could help their Vilaim without the approval of someone who merely walked among them, but was not one of them.

"Let us do nothing," she pleaded. "Let us leave him be. He is fickle and he has never had good intentions at heart."

Of course, she did not know of Death's intentions. She did not understand the way that Death suffered. That was something she would not learn, that Shion nor Shubishi would learn, for a thousand more years.

When the Gods ignored Adelia, she took it upon herself to make change. To go out among the Vilaim and whisper that Death was gone. She spread the rumors. She encouraged the people to break the rules set down by a deity who cared so little about them that he disappeared when things went a different way.

One second, the council was arguing. The next…the next everything changed.

The Vilaim were in shock at their deity having left them. They had never known a life without him. It had been centuries of them living in the city, obeying his laws, remaining perfect and pure. They didn't know what they should do.

Sheep without a shepherd.

Fools without a king.

But as the years passed, they found that life did not change without Death residing in his temple. They still lived. They still died.

But now…now they could break his rules. There was no ruling class. Shion, their queen, seemed so indifferent to them that it was as though she were only another God, not the leader of all the Vilaim.

So they did break the rules.

Not all of them. Warnings of Halise and Amir still spread among them. It was better if they stayed married in their own clans, but there were other rules to break. Brokering friendships among different clans. Moving into different parts of the city where they had formerly not been allowed.

And, in particular, the Vilaim decided that they wanted to leave the city. They wanted to leave the protection of the life that they had so long lived and explore the rest of the world. Reclaim lands that had once belonged to them, that they had only heard about in stories.

They left. Moved in packs, spreading out among the land that so long ago belonged to their ancestors. Some returned to their native land, while others moved to places previously unknown to them. They spread out and lived their lives like the old days. They found books about their culture, followed their traditions on the land they were created, and they flourished.

The Lan and Narumi clans, always close, always questioning the motives of the council and the queen, moved out together, not in a mixed village, but across a massive lake. They were neighbors, and they were friends. They traded what they could and held feasts together, much like the Lan and Narumi clans of the past. They told stories and ate delicious food. Every year the leaders visited the city and paid homage to their queen, and to the council.

They were happy. Time passed.

And this was the world that Tori and Nina were born into.

Nina, always a quiet girl, was born to the leader of the Lan village. Sweet with a disposition said to be perfect for marriage, she loved to care for her younger siblings. The middle of seven, and the second girl, she always helped around the house and wished for a good life with a good husband, just as her mom told her she would have.

Tori could not have been more opposite. Born as the fifth child to a carpenter, and the only girl, she was wild and carefree. She helped her father with his work, even when she was too small to do more than hand him the smallest of supplies. She was certain, absolutely certain, that she never wanted to marry. That she was going to run her village and follow in the footsteps of great Narumi leaders before her. She fought with her brothers and gave her mother a heart attack every time she came home covered in mud.

But, as it is said, opposites attract.

The two were only five when they met at a trading festival. Nina, forgotten by her parents as they wrangled the rest of her siblings, and Tori having run off to play games and eat delicious food. Tori ran into Nina, nearly knocking her to the ground, and the moment the two locked eyes, they knew that they were going to be best friends.

"Wanna see the fish?" Tori asked.

"Uh huh."

"I am gonna catch one!"

"Where is your net?"

"I do not have one."

Tori shoved her hands into the water and pulled out a wriggling, colorful fish. Water splashed everywhere, getting the girls wet. Nina screamed, startling Tori. The fish wriggled out of her hands and landed with a *plop* back into the little pool. Both girls stared at the water, then each other, and burst into a fit of giggles.

The scream had attracted the attention of both parents. They rushed over and pulled the girls apart, Tori with a scolding, Nina with a concerned mother. But they were laughing. Reaching out for each other, asking for names and their parents relaxed. They relaxed, and they spoke to one another.

A carpenter and a village leader are an unlikely pair of friends, but there they were, bonded by their cackling daughters.

It was a friendship that built with every meeting. The two girls were so similar, if not for their looks some would think of them as twins. It did not matter to them that they were not the same color. They were best friends.

And as they grew into teenagers, to Nina, there was something more.

Death wandered Earth. He watched everything grow and change. It fascinated him. It was different than his own realm, but he found he had powers over these creatures as well. He did not name them the way he named the ones back with the Vilaim. They were not Creatures. They were animals. Evolving on their own time. Dying in similar ways, but without a hint of magic.

The blue skies spread out above him. One sun. One moon. A place where the earth turned faster and the animals died sooner. There was something so different, so pure, about this place, that Death wanted to never leave. He wanted to start over. Create life and begin anew without making the same mistakes he had made before.

No immortals. No clans. No emphasis on perfection.

He would stay as their friend from the very beginning, and it would be good. It would be great.

As he was about to step forward, as he was about to create a new life from the earth and from fire, a voice stopped him.

"So this is where you have been, old friend."

Friend. How long had it been since someone called Death this. He stopped what he was doing and faced Shubishi.

"What are you doing here?" Death asked.

"I have come to find you." Shubishi held out a hand. "You vanished, and it has many worried. Adelia is convinced you have abandoned us for something else. I suppose this is true."

Death did not want to hear that name. "Adelia is not the person to ask about my intentions. She has despised me from the beginning."

"She despises you because you took away part of who she is."

"I healed her."

"You took away part of who Shion was too."

"Shion is happy with my choice for her."

"Is she? Or do you want her to be?"

Death glared. "Are you questioning me?"

"Yes." The answer was blunt and obvious. Shubishi had traveled for many years, searching for the place Death had disappeared to. He was aware of the colonies, and was unsure how Death would respond, but he wanted to know. If he knew, then he could go back without any issues.

Though this new realm was fascinating. It held wonders he had not even considered before. New plants, animals, and the possibility for something like a Vilaim.

"I know you are not a fan of Adelia, and you do not approve of Shion's rejection of her roles, but they have free will. What do you expect of them?"

Death expected them to obey him.

Yet he knew they never would. They were free to do as they

pleased.

Shubishi told him of the world and how things had changed in the past few generations. Anger swelled in Death. They had left the city? They were living together?

But was it not better to let them be?

He did not know.

"I will return," he said. "I will return, but under one condition."

Death did return to his original world. The world of the Vilaim. He returned and found that it was different. But in a way, it was happier. Without his influence, without him controlling their every move, the Vilaim had begun to grow and evolve.

And with his return, came his condition. Each clan was to give him someone to become immortal.

Shubishi had agreed to this, though he had never understood why Death wanted more immortals. After the disaster that was Adelia, Shubishi figured that Death would never want to create another immortal again.

But it was what Death had asked of him, and Shubishi would have done anything to bring Death back to their world. For him to bring a sense of order to the council. For Shion to not feel the pressure of being the queen anymore.

And for Enya to be put in her place.

Nina and Tori were nineteen. They heard the decree, and thought nothing of it. It would not affect their lives, they had decided. They would continue on being friends, they would continue on living their happy lives.

Through all of this, Nina had tried to hide her growing feelings for her best friend. At night, she dreamed of Tori in ways she knew was not normal. When she listened to her sisters and brothers speak of those they fancied, she knew it was the same feelings as what she had deep in her heart.

But she said nothing. She had never heard of a woman loving another woman before, and she was too shy, too passive, to rock the boat, as it were. She did not want to cause problems for anyone. Much less for her friend who did not feel the same way.

Tori was, as was her nature, oblivious to all of the goings on with her friend. She was too preoccupied with learning to fight and working her way to become the leader of her village. They had yet to have a woman as a leader, and she was determined to remind them of the strong women of their history. She would do anything to lead her people.

She would do anything to make her best friend happy.

The day Death returned, the news rippled out to the colonies with a fervor. With the news came the decree, the one that Nina and Tori ignored, stating that each clan must give up one of their own to become a God. A new round of immortals to represent the current state of the world. It would be the last round, he had declared, but it would be the most powerful.

It was not until the day that Nina's father called her to his hut that she realized just how much this would impact her life.

"My darling Nina," her father said, "I have requested for Death to come appraise you as the Lan's next God."

Nina, had she not already been sitting, would have sunk to her knees. They shook beneath her. "Father?"

"You are beautiful," he said, stroking her dark skin, "you are patient and kind and wise. Out of all my children, you have always been my favorite. And I believe that if you were to become our god, then things would be better for us. That I will hold Death's favor, and our family will never know suffering."

Nina was stunned into silence.

"He comes in two days," her father said. "Everything will be better once he has come to see how prosperous we are. This time, he will stay with us."

She had no choice.

Once dismissed, she fled to the other side of the lake, running alongside the turbulent waters. At the time, she did not understand that she was the one causing the uproar of the water. She did not know of her powers, just as Tori did not know of her own. The two young girls had never had a need to control the elements around them, but in that moment, her emotions had overtaken everything and her power had lost control.

Yet, she did not know.

She found Tori helping her father build a house for a neighbor and flew into Tori's arms, desperate for comfort.

Desperate for the woman she loved.

"Nina?" Tori asked. "What is wrong?"

Nina sobbed, incoherently babbling about her woes.

Tori held her friend, stroking her hair and whispering that everything was going to be all right. Even when she discovered the reason for Nina's distress, she knew that it was going to be all right. Death would not choose Nina. Death would not separate them from one another.

"It will be all right," Tori explained. "I will make sure of it."

When Death came to see Nina, to appraise her as a god, Tori snuck in. It was only supposed to be Nina's family. No friends, and definitely no Narumis. Tori did not care. She wanted to see, to make sure, that her best friend was not going to become immortal.

Death, however, had decided to go against everything that Nina and Tori had imagined. He saw in her what her father saw in her. The beauty. The grace. The wisdom. And he agreed that she would be the next God.

The moment he agreed, Tori flew from her hiding space into the open. She blocked Nina with her body, and all eyes turned on her. She could swear that Nina's father flared with anger, but in front of her, taking the form of a Lan man, Death watched Tori closely.

"Who are you?" Death asked.

"I am Nina's best friend," Tori said, pounding a hand against her chest. She knew that nothing she said would change Death's mind about Nina. He was famous for doing whatever he wanted, regardless of what anyone thought. But if she could not change his mind about Nina, then maybe she could change his mind about *her*. "If you make Nina a God, then I want to become one as well."

Gasps echoed throughout the room. Nina's eyes widened, and she shook her head. Tori ignored them all.

Death was curious, and that is what mattered.

"Would you be happier to become gods together?" he asked, directing the question at Nina. She nodded, and then flinched, as if expecting Tori to be angry. But she was not angry. She could never be angry at Nina.

That was the day Nina and Tori became gods. One offer, one volunteer.

When it was over, and the girls prepared to leave, Nina grabbed Tori's hands. They were both crying from the change. "What about your dreams? What about becoming the leader?"

Tori shrugged. "Why be a village leader when I can be a god? Besides, it would be no fun without you here."

The two new gods left their villages, unaware of the issues they would face, nor what it really meant to be a god.

Chapter Ten

Death had returned to the Vilaim, but he had never given up on his other world. He watched it from afar, curious about the state of it. Plants grew and died. They changed. Some vanished forever, while others grew up into the sky. Then life formed. It started in the water. Multiple types of little fish. Then larger fish. Then they moved to the land. Then the skies. The plants changed and adapted as the animals ate them. Animals changed and adapted as they killed each other.

This was how his realm had begun, long before he knew where he was or what his purpose was. This was how Earth began, and it pleased him. This really was a place he could start over. It was a home for a new species he could create. Ones like him. Ones who had no influence from him. He would not walk among them. He would let them live their own lives.

A niggling feeling in the back of his mind kept him from going through with his plan.

He had messed with the Vilaim's lives and caused them pain. So he did not want to make the same mistake. And yet…yet he continued to mess with their lives. Continued to lay down the law.

After much consideration he decided that it was okay. They were not the same. He had conditioned the Vilaim to need him. They needed him to be in charge. Why else would Shubishi have gone to find him?

One touch. All it took was one visit and one touch to create the new group. They looked like him, and like the Vilaim, but they were not. They lived in terms of their own world, rather than the Vilaim. They were not created as intelligent as the Vilaim. They were not given language. They were left to their own devices, and he watched as they grew.

Around him, the Vilaim were falling apart. There was a famine coming over the land. Even the higher classes were feeling hunger, and they blamed anyone who was different. They blamed the Gods. They blamed Death. But most of all, they blamed the children with the bright souls. The children with powers.

The Vilaim grew to hate anyone with powers. Even though they had lived normal lives up until that point, they became monsters. Monsters and pariahs.

Death did not intervene.

Eran first realized he had powers at a young age. He had not meant to read the neighbor's memories. Really, he did not know what he had done until after the fact. She had picked him up and he had seen it. He seen her meeting her husband for the first time. Their wedding. Their child being born. More….

When she put him down, he asked her why she spent so much time with her sister's husband.

The next day a man was burned in their town square for having the ability to make the wind blow. He screamed that there was nothing wrong with him, and he could help, and that he was not responsible for the famine. No one believed him.

Watching a man burn alive for a power he was born with scared Eran. He learned quickly not to speak of the things he saw. He kept it to himself, not speaking of it to his parents, his friends, or his siblings.

Not a single soul knew what he really was.

A world away, Lior was not so lucky.

Nimbon suffered the most from the famine. Poor to begin with, the entire class felt the weight of the rations more than any of the others. They were the last to be given food, the council did not take them into account and they were left to starve.

The worst part is they had almost come out of the thievery and poverty left over from their ancestors. They still were not considered equal to the others, but they were learning how to read, moving outside the city to make money, and sending that home.

But when the famine hit, everything changed. It reverted back to the days of their ancestors. Thieves reigned in the city. Children died in the streets from starvation. Adults turned on each other.

The ones with powers were blamed.

One boy in particular felt the brunt of his clan's anger.

Lior did not know anything but the streets. At one point he must have had a family, because he existed, but he did not know who his parents were. He saw other children, starving like him, with siblings. Did he have siblings?

The thing about Lior is his powers were not like Eran's. They were not pictures flashing in his conscience. They were words.

Spoken words lingering in his mind. As a child, he could not tell the difference between the words said aloud, and those said in someone's head.

There were times when someone would think something, and he had respond. People feared him. They stayed away from him whenever possible. He learned how to hide from the people who might want to kill him. He taught himself to stay quiet, no matter what. He did not beg. He stole what he needed. He was willing to never trust anyone.

Then he met Kirstin.

A girl no older than he, she too lived on the streets. She remembered her family, saying that they sold her to a man in town who hoarded all the food. She escaped one night. The streets were more favorable than his home. She never talked about why, and Lior could not discover the reason why.

It was not as though he did not try. He wanted to know what caused her so much pain. She was small, but tough. She fought for herself every day, and he could not imagine what it was. But the thing about Kirstin was, unlike everyone else he had ever met, he could not read her mind.

It was part of what attracted him to her.

As children, the two stayed out of people's way. They stole what they needed and hid in the alleys. They did not talk to the other homeless children. Lior would read their minds and knew they were not out to help others.

It was just the two of them.

But as they grew older, it was more difficult to hide. In particular, it was difficult for Lior to pretend he blended in with the rest of the crowd. It was difficult for him to pretend like his powers did not exist. No longer a child, he could hide them, but people remembered.

It was not every day they met a Vilaim with different colored eyes.

When they realized he had survived childhood, they shunned him. When he walked out in the streets, people gave him a wide berth. The only person who would look him in the eye without flinching was Kirstin.

But while Lior continued to be shunned by the people around him, Kirstin was welcomed into society as a beautiful young woman. Things were a little better money wise. The famine was not over, but the Jous had discovered a way to grow food with limited water and space. So it was no longer unrealistic for a family to support themselves. For a man to want a wife.

Kirstin had many suitors.

She fit well into society, but she never forgot her best friend. She never forgot Lior, and it was he whom she loved.

When Eran turned ten, his little sister was born.

Flora.

A perfect baby. Never cried. Never got sick. Brought happiness to the entire house. She was a child that everyone wanted to meet. The Raan clan was hit hard by the famine, though not nearly to the extent as the Nimbon. Food was scarce, but enough to keep everyone going. The elderly died sooner, and babies did not make it.

But Flora did. She survived. She brought with her good luck. Rumors spread. The sick came by and relished in the good will. Everyone thought it was a miracle.

Eran was not so sure.

He watched carefully as Flora grew. Never growing ill, never coming home with a scratch. A gentle soul. Never fighting, never screaming. Their other siblings—including Eran himself—were terrors as children, but not Flora.

It irritated Eran. He loved his sister, as any big brother should, but he could not shake the feeling that there was something off about her. He wanted to stay away, but she attached to him. His name was her first word. She would toddle after him as she grew, wanting to play. Wanting him to read to her.

He did not want to hurt her. It was not her fault he was unnerved. She was a child. So he let her cling to him.

It was not until she was five that he learned exactly what it was about her.

The fight was not his fault. Or, that is what he always claimed. It was not his fault the other teenage boys thought his father's job was ridiculous. A soldier? There was no need for soldiers. The Vilaim had been at peace for longer than anyone could remember. It was ridiculous for the colonies to create militaries, as though they thought of themselves as separate from the city.

Eran was not sure on his thoughts, but he stood up for his father.

The fight was not his fault.

He stumbled home, bleeding, bruised, and exhausted. He did not want his mother to see him. She was busy enough dealing with the younger children and taking care of the house while also sewing clothes to make ends meet. With his father gone, there was not much else he could do.

Flora found him. She had the uncanny ability to find him no matter where he was. In this case, hiding underneath a tree behind their house. She came out of nowhere and climbed onto his lap. He wanted to scold her, tell her that it was not safe, but she touched his arm and everything went warm.

Her memories flooded him. They were simple and happy. He thought the warmth was from his own powers, but when she let go of him, he realized they were from hers. He looked down at his body and saw all the bruises, the cuts, and the scrapes were gone.

"Flora, did you...how did you do this?"

"Dunno." She rested her head against his chest and played with his hand. "You were hurt. I fixed you." She smiled. "You are all better now."

He was right. She was like him. She had powers, but ones he had never thought were possible. There were plenty of others like him. Others who could do mystical things with their mind. He had met children who could control the five elements, lift objects with their mind, speak to animals, and even nullify others. But never had he heard of someone who could heal.

And apparently, neither had anyone else.

Because a year later a man arrived at their front door with a letter from the great god Shubishi. A letter demanding Flora come to the city.

Chapter Eleven

Back in the city, the council was welcoming their new members. Death had returned. They no longer felt as though he had abandoned them. They were back in his favor. Things would get better. The world would return to the way it was. To most of the council, this was everything they had wanted from their deity, but to Shion, it was a nightmare. She did not want him back. Because when he was back, the expectations on her grew.

And she gave in. She did not fight her future because every time she tried, Death was there, staring at her, waiting for her to be the queen he had always wanted from her. So, she plastered a smile on her face and pretended. She bowed and welcomed the new members of the council as though she cared even a little bit about the growing of the immortals. Somewhere, deep down, she wondered if maybe this would lead to her freedom. With the council growing, there were more voices and she could disappear more.

But, again, whenever she tried Death appeared at her side, taking her arm in his.

She wanted him gone.

She knew he would never disappear, so she accepted her fate. Only she knew it was fake. The smile on her face. She and Adelia were the only ones who knew how unhappy she was. The two were not friends, necessarily. They sat together in council meetings, but they shared not a word. They did not trade secrets or gossip, as friends might have. Shion would read, Adelia would examine the council as arguments broke out, and together they waited for things to change.

And change things did.

The council grew. One by one the members joined and added their own perspectives. Each one grew more and more bold as the years passed, eager to help their people, but getting more and more out of touch with their needs. They did not live among their people. They stayed in their council room and consulted with the wealthy. With the privileged.

Shion was certain they did their best. They did what they could with the resources they had, but immortality comes with a certain level of passiveness. Every immortal started out the same, wanting to help. But it always ended the same, with them drifting away from normality and eventually giving up on caring.

Because what was there to care about when you could not die?

The only God who did not seem to lose her passion for the council was Enya. She stayed as a leader, demanding that the council stay focused. That they do what she wanted, regardless of what anyone else thought. And no one questioned her authority. After all, she was the third God. An Elder God. One of the first to be chosen by Death.

Shion let her lead. Despite Shubishi asking her why. Despite Adelia asking her why. Despite *Death* asking her why. She let Enya behave however she wanted because Shion did not care. She did not have a people to speak for. She did not have a connection to any of the tribes. She had never wanted to be queen. While she plastered a smile on her face and pretended to play a part, she let Enya run the council. So what if Enya was a Siman? So what if Shion was a Seshen?

Did any of it matter anymore? Were they not equals? Were they not both Gods?

Time passed. Time always passed. Enya gained confidence with Shion's withdrawal and Shion continued to stay away. She took solace in her moments alone. Adelia had shown her a way into the rafters, a place where Shion could be alone. No Shubishi. No Death. No Enya. Just her and her books.

It was those moments when she felt like she could be herself. Where she did not have to plaster a smile on her face. Where she could feel her emotions without judgement from anyone. Where she did not have to be the perfect queen that Death had chosen to rule his creations.

It was in these moments she longed for death. Where she wondered if it was possible to take her own life, knowing fully well that it was not. Death had taken that choice from her. She could not be like Halise. She could not escape from the torture that was her life. So, she read. She read alone.

She wanted to be forgotten. If she could not die, then she wanted to never be seen again. To never be asked another question about ruling the Vilaim. She longed to be free from the strangling world in which she lived.

And then she met Tori.

The day that Tori and Nina arrived in the city, it awed them. They had grown up in little villages filled with the same people they saw every day. This place, however, was massive. Vilaim of all shapes and colors filled the streets. New Vilaim. Vilaim they had never met before. Vilaim who watched them in their carriage and bowed as they passed. Both of them knew that this world, this life that they had agreed to enter into, was going to be so different from the world they had left behind.

They held hands as their carriage clattered through the streets. Neither of them said a word. Fear boiled in their stomachs. What had they agreed to? What was going to happen to them now? Tori feared that she had made a mistake and would miss her family more than she had ever thought she would.

Nina feared that Tori would come to hate her.

The temple at the top of the mountain filled the sky, a gorgeous white with columns as thick as three Vilaim. They exited the carriage and stared up at it as the other Gods came out to greet them. One-by-one, their new friends, their new family, exited the building and lined up, all smiles.

Nina found herself silent.

Tori stared up at the council and her eyes landed on the woman standing in the center. The woman with light brown hair and crystal blue eyes. The woman with long flowing robes and a beautiful, golden crown. A woman who commanded the room without doing anything.

A woman who wanted to be anywhere but there.

Tori cocked her head, curious. Queen Shion's eyes darted from the two new Gods to the carriage behind them. Her hands twitched. None of the other Gods noticed Queen Shion's discomfort, but Tori did. Tori, who had always been curious about the last Seshen, noticed that their queen, the woman who was supposed to lead them, did not want to be there.

She had grown up hearing stories of the Seshen. Blood feuds ran deep in the history of the Vilaim. The Narumi told stories of the Seshen. The cruelty. The lack of respect for the lives of any who did not look like them. Of the great war.

Tori did not care about any of that. Because while she had imagined the queen to be a cruel and inhumane being, the woman in front of her, the woman who commanded all the attention in the room with a single step, did not want to be there, and that was curious. She had no life behind her eyes, and Tori found herself wanting to know more about the queen. She wanted to understand why. Why someone who had given up their mortality to forever rule the Vilaim seemed to hate everything about her life.

And as Tori watched Queen Shion, Nina watched Tori. For Nina cared only about her best friend. About the woman she loved. She watched Tori watch the queen, and her stomach tightened. In that moment, she hated Shion. She too had grown up with the stories of the Seshen, and instead of seeing through the coldness for what it was, she saw the cruelty and the haughty demeanor. She saw Tori becoming obsessed, and she did not approve.

When Tori and Shion met, it was in the rafters.

Shion had gone up to read, bidding adieu to Adelia, and found the Narumi woman sitting in her normal spot with arms crossed. It had been months since the two new council members had joined them in the temple, and Shion had become convinced that the two of them were just like the others.

Uninteresting.

Uninterested in the real her.

But there was Tori, sitting alone with her arms crossed, staring out the window in which Shion observed the outside world.

Shion froze.

"So this is where you disappear off to," Tori said, grinning at

Shion.

Shion had no words for the strange woman. She merely backed away, preparing to disappear and find a new place to read. She did not want Tori spreading this information to the other council members. She liked her peace.

"You do not have to run," Tori said. "I am just here to talk to you. I will not tell anyone where you go."

Shion was not sure she believed Tori. Yet, she halted and stared at the Narumi woman. The other Narumi on the council, a man of much older age, had never been friendly to Shion outside of wanting things from her. She knew of their history, probably better than the woman sitting before her. Shion knew that the Narumi and the Seshen had never gotten along, and while Shion no longer considered herself a Seshen, having become too far removed from her people and with no memory of living with them, she knew that things were always tense.

She remembered how much they had protested her becoming queen.

"How can I assist you?" Shion asked.

Tori stood and crossed the rafters, head cocked, arms crossed. "I have been watching you."

Shion bowed her head. "I see."

"And you seem rather lonely."

This startled Shion. She had expected to be called out for her aloofness. For her disinterest in the council's agenda. But never for her loneliness. Even Shubishi, even Adelia, had never mentioned it.

"I…." Shion bowed her head.

"You are the queen," Tori continued. "You have everyone bowing at your feet. You could have any friend in the world. Why is it that you are so lonely?"

Shion did not answer.

"Would you like a friend?"

166

Shion did not answer.

"Are you okay all alone?"

Shion did not answer.

And for many days after this encounter, Shion avoided Tori. She had become so ashamed of herself for letting her loneliness be known to someone. She had not known what Tori was planning when she had decided to confront Shion, but Shion did know that she could not return to the rafters. Tori would ask her more questions. Poke at her insecurities. There was no saying what the Narumi would do to her. Instead, she wandered to the gardens and took solace there.

For days. For weeks.

Shion remained alone.

Until Tori found her again.

"You know, I could be your friend."

Shion stared at the woman, unsure how to respond. Unsure what the Narumi was planning with all of this. Get on her good side? Was she working with Enya? Was this a way to undermine her authority?

Did she care if Tori undermined her authority?

"You are a Narumi," Shion said.

"So?" Tori cocked her head, a smile on her face.

"You hate my people." The words came out stilted. Shion did not know much about her people, besides what Death and Shubishi had told her. She had been so young, so damn young, when they were all killed. She did not think of herself as Seshen, but as something different. They were gone. Disappeared into history. She was the only one keeping their legacy, their memory, alive. And what a job she was doing.

Tori sat on the bench next to Shion and let out a hearty laugh. "All of my life, I have heard stories of the Seshen. I have heard of their arrogance. I have heard of their history. You are right in that my people hate yours, and yet you seem...different than the stories. It makes me wonder how true they are."

"You do not find me arrogant?"

"I find you sad."

"Oh." Shion looked at her book, fingers tracing the words. Sad. Shion was sad. Shion had been sad for years. For as long as she could remember, she had hated her life and everything in it. The only joy in her life came from the books she read in solitude. Stories. Histories. Learning and learning. Trying to understand why she had to live the life she did.

Would...would having a friend make that better? Tori was here, sitting next to her with a smile on her face, offering to become Shion's friend. Did Shion deserve a friend? Could she have someone who did not bow at her feet? Who did not hate her?

"I do not know you well," Tori said. "But I would like to."

And it was these words that brought Shion a hint of life into her eyes. It was these words that opened up her heart. It was slow at first. Just the two of them sitting in the garden, sitting the rafters, talking. Shion showed Tori books. Tori showed Shion how to fight and build and get her hands dirty. Things that Shion had never imagined she would ever do. Things that Shion had not done in the entirety of her life.

Within the year, the two of them were closer than any others on the council.

The Narumi and the Seshen.

Friends at last.

Death took no notice of their friendship. Had he been paying attention, he may have seen his precious last Seshen learn to smile.

Really smile. Learn to laugh. Learn to open up and talk to someone about her feelings. He may have heard the words she said about him. He may have understood her resentment. Her frustration. He may have seen what was coming.

But he did not. Because while he had promised to be attentive to the Vilaim again, Earth grabbed his attention more and more. The creatures who looked like the Vilaim, but were not Vilaim, continued to grow. They adapted to their changing world. They created art and language and bonds. They hunted animals and each other.

They developed magic.

He grew absent. He did not pay attention as a war stirred beneath the surface. He did not notice the anger brewing among his creations. He was more interested in the humans than anything else, watching them from afar, taking their lives when they died. They were perfect, in his eyes. Untouched. Never to be manipulated by his hand.

The Vilaim once again grew restless. He did not pay attention.

He did not pay attention to the one he had asked to keep a promise to him all those years ago. Back when the council was two. Back in the days when there was no Earth. When he did not know of humans.

He should have paid attention.

Eran was only sixteen when he left his home. He carried his little sister with him, whispering to her that everything would be all right. That one day they would see their parents, their siblings, again. His mother had made him promise to protect her. She was only six, her mother kept saying. Only six. What could the god Shubishi want with a child so small? So young? So innocent?

169

Eran did not know the answers to his mother's questions. All he knew is that his terrified little sister clung to him. That she peered out of the carriage with wide, curious eyes and gripped his shirt as though it would explain everything. He found that he was unable to tell her the truth. That she would most likely never leave this city again. This bustling, loud, angry city.

He held her tighter, arms shaking. Fear clenched his stomach. He did not know what was going to happen to either of them. When his father had tasked him, her favorite brother, with protecting her, he had not been able to say no. She was so small. So precious. So mysterious. She needed someone to protect her from those who might want to use her.

Not much was known about their first God. Shubishi did not visit their home. It was unknown how he had heard about Flora's powers. All they did know is that they could not deny him. He was their God. What he wanted, he received.

Shubishi waited for them when they arrived at the temple. He looked not much older than Eran, but Eran knew otherwise. He knew that the man was older than everyone else in the entirety of their world. Even Queen Shion had been born hundreds of years after he had. He was going to be the one who examined Flora. Who experimented with her powers.

And she was but a child.

"Welcome," Shubishi said.

Flora hid behind her brother's legs.

"Sir." Eran bowed, but his limbs shook. He had never met a god before. He had never been in the presence of immortality. Even Death had yet to visit his home, even though he continued to search for the final Gods for the council. One Raan. One Nimbon. Two left. One from his clan, and one from a clan he hoped to never have to run into.

It took some time, but Shubishi carefully coaxed Flora away

from her brother, asking her questions about her powers and her abilities. She told him the truth, as Eran had instructed her to do, and then Shubishi declared, with all the authority in the world:

"She will stay with me. If you would like, you can stay as well. It would make her feel more comfortable."

Eran knew this would be the outcome, and he knew he should not have fought Shubishi on the decision, but he still needed to look out for his little sister. He begged Shubishi to let her have a normal childhood. To go home and be with her family. But Shubishi would not budge.

"I have lived for longer than life itself," Shubishi said. "I know things you do not know, and this child, this little girl, has a power I have never seen before. She has a power that will change everything if we understand how to utilize it."

And then Shubishi examined Eran, eyes glinting. "And you, my friend, seem to have a power as well."

Eran backed away, clenching his fists. He could not fight a God. He knew that. It was obvious to anyone that Shubishi held all the answers to the universe, but how had he known about Eran's powers?

"I...."

"Do not worry," Shubishi said, scooping Flora into his arms and walking away. "I will tell no one of your abilities. That secret is for you to share when you wish. For now, young man, I suggest you get comfortable living in the city. It may be a long while before you leave."

And it was a long while before Eran left. Almost fifteen more years before he left.

But that is getting ahead of the story.

As Eran watched his little sister disappear with Shubishi, he knew that he had to stay to protect her. He had no doubts that Shubishi would treat her with kindness, but he was her older brother. And when he was led to his quarters in the temple, a room with a single bed and a desk, he wrote a letter to his parents explaining that they would not be coming home.

Then he mailed it, sat on his bed, and tried not to let his emotions overcome him.

Lior wanted nothing more than to be with his beloved Kristin for the rest of their lives. When they were alone, when it was just the two of them, he kissed her like there was nothing else in the world that mattered. She would wrap her arms around his neck and whisper how much she loved him. They were perfect for each other. He could not read her mind, and she understood everything about him. She did not fear him. She did not fear his eyes nor his powers.

But…but that could not last forever.

They could not be alone at all times. And other Nimbon took notice of her. Men took notice of her. Her beauty, her gentleness. Her intelligence. When she was around, things settled into peace. She brought hope to the Nimbon. She brought with her the idea that they did not have to be murderers and thieves.

While she loved Lior, and while he loved her, they knew they could not be together. At least, she knew. She knew that even if they loved each other, if her powers negated his, even if they had a history together, he was a pariah.

So, she pulled away, thinking that if she did, she would not break his heart.

But it was difficult to say goodbye to someone who understood her so well. Lior fought against her distance. He appeared in her window at night and she could not tell him no. She could not pull away. Even when the Nimbon convinced her to marry. Even when the date was set.

Lior tried to convince her not to do it. To marry him instead. They could be together forever, just the two of them. But Kristin did not want to live that life. She had grown up in poverty. She had not known the love of a mother or a father. She did not want her own children to live that way. She did not want to marry a pariah.

He could not argue with her. Because he knew it to be true. Even without his powers, even without his lack of money, he was still born with different colored eyes. One green. One blue. And that was considered an omen. He did not want their children to grow up with the stigma that he had.

"You do not have to let me go," she had insisted. "Just…we cannot marry."

But her husband did not approve of Lior's presence. So they met in secret. They met when no one was looking. When no one was paying attention. They met until one day when she did not come.

Lior knew not to search for her, but he could not help it. Over the years, he had gotten better at filtering the voices in his head. At distinguishing them. It would be a long time before he realized that he could project his own voice, but at the moment he was able to silence them.

And silence them he did, until the day she did not show.

He needed to know if she had decided they could not see each other anymore. He needed to know if his most treasured friendship was over, or if he needed to intervene in her kidnapping.

What he found, though, was that she was ill.

She was ill, and she was not going to get better. The Raan doctor could do nothing for her. The mysterious rumblings of a young girl who could heal anything had disappeared many years ago.

Kristin was going to die.

Lior demanded to see her, but her family refused to let him in. She begged them to see him, but her family refused to let her leave her home. They told her that she needed to focus on her family. Her husband.

She told them that Lior was her family.

When she died, the entire community felt her loss, but none more than Lior. Even her husband, who had admired her beauty, but not her, did not feel the pain that Lior felt. And he knew this. Because when she died, he opened up his mind and let everyone's thoughts in. Anything to gain a last moment with her that her family refused to let him have.

They did not let him near her.

They did not let him near the funeral.

They did not let him visit her grave.

She was buried atop a grassy knoll. To be buried next to her husband when he too passed.

It was a place that Lior would never forget.

Anger flooded him. He had not been allowed to marry his love. He understood that. But to be denied her after death as well? To not be able to give her his final wishes? To be removed from her life as though the two of them had not survived childhood together?

It was too much.

In the dark of night, he stole money from the sleeping family and bought passage to the city.

They all feared him. They all hated his powers and his eyes. They hated his heritage and his poverty.

But Death was still looking for a Nimbon to become a God. Death had yet to find someone to add to the council, and Lior... Lior was going to show them all.

Chapter Twelve

As the years passed, Eran found that he loved the city. He heard from his parents now and then, but he had no intention of going back to the village in which he had been born. He had friends here. He could see his sister whenever he wanted. She was growing into a beautiful young woman with the grace of a queen and the kindness of the most gentle flower. Vilaim came from all over to take advantage of her powers, and she let them, never caring how difficult or how horrid. She healed them with a smile on her face, and Eran knew that this was good.

He wanted to stay with her, more than anything. He wanted to make sure she stayed happy and healthy, safe from those who might want to harm her. He worked in the temple, cleaning it at night while the members slept. And with this he observed the council members, wondering about their lives. About their histories. They did not speak to him, and he bowed when they passed. He did not get close.

Still, they fascinated him. They fascinated everyone. An incomplete council. Death had yet to choose the final two representatives from Raan and Nimbon. From the stories Eran heard, he would disappear now and then, always waving off those who wanted the council to become complete.

Eran had yet to meet Death. The mysterious deity who did not seem interested at all in the Vilaim anymore. He heard stories of the deity. Of the greatness. Of the power that exuded from him. But Eran was no one to Death. Most of the council was no one to Death. He spoke to very few of the council members, from what Eran understood. To Shubishi, of course, to Queen Shion, of course, and, to everyone's surprise, the second Narumi council member, Tori.

Even though he had not met Death, Eran met everyone else on the council. Sometimes they remembered he was Flora's older brother, but mostly they ignored him. They had more important things to think about than a janitor cleaning up after them.

To them, he was nothing.

To him, they were everything.

Except for one. One specific God who noticed him when he thought he was invisible.

He was walking in the gardens, taking a break from his daily chores, when she caught his attention. A blond haired Tep God who watched him with curious eyes.

"You are Flora's brother, yes?" Adelia asked, stopping him in his tracks.

He nodded and bowed.

To his surprise, she rolled her eyes. "You do not need to bow, Eran. I may be a God, but I am not better than you or anyone else."

"But Death chose you," Eran said, stuttering over his words. It was the first time a God had addressed him in such an informal matter.

"Death has chosen many," she replied. "And I have not been in his favor for a very long time."

Eran did not know the inner workings of the temple. He

listened, but they kept many secrets. He kept his head bowed, not commenting on Adelia's bluntness until she stood and held out her arm for him to take.

"Will you escort me back to the temple?" she asked.

He hesitated. Because he knew that when they touched, his powers would give him insight into her memories that she did not know he would see. His powers were only growing stronger, and there was nothing he could do about it. No matter how much he fought against the memories that flooded his brain, the dam would break every time. The only one who knew anything about his powers was Shubishi, and the first God had kept his word.

"Well?" Adelia asked, a small smile on her face.

He could not say no to a God. Just as he could not say no to Shubishi taking away his sister, he could not say no to Adelia asking him to escort her.

And when they touched, when his fingers brushed against her skin, his mind was filled with memories. Strange, confusing, memories. Memories from centuries of life. Memories of a world filled with warmth, and yet darkness. Memories Eran had never had the pleasure of experiencing before.

He gasped and dropped her arm.

"You were blind?" he asked.

Startled, she backed away from him. "How…?"

Realizing what he had just revealed, Eran took off in the opposite direction. But ever since that meeting, all he had been able to think about was the way that her life had been before Death had turned her into a God. All of her memories had been laced with happiness and warmth. And the ones after….

Cold.

So cold.

She had hated what Death had done to her, and he had never thought about that before. What would happen if the person did not want the honor of becoming immortal.

Months passed before they met again. Eran spent much of his time with his sister, who rarely left Shubishi's side. She seemed happy enough, though did not speak much of what happened while Eran was not allowed with her. She showed Eran her powers and gave her brother a reason to want to keep staying in the city.

"Are you happy, Flora?" he asked one day.

She smiled at him. "This is the life I know."

"That does not answer my question."

She sighed and ran a hand along the grass by her side. "Brother, this is the life I know. If I were to know another life, I could compare, but I cannot. If I am ever unhappy, it is because of small things, not of big things. Shubishi treats me well. You treat me well. Lady Shion treats me well."

"Lady Shion?" Eran had never comprehended that possibly the queen would know Flora, but that is what happened when the two of them were both close to Shubishi.

"She does not speak much." Flora closed her eyes and let the breeze rustle her hair. "But when she does, she is very kind."

What a life his sister was living. Gifted with the presence of some of the most important people in all of their world because of her powers. Powers she did not seem to understand were so important. Even being around her made him feel full of vitality. The aches from his day vanished, replaced with a smooth warmth.

She had grown more powerful.

But that was to be expected.

So had he.

When he was not with his sister, he was with his friends. But before long, they disinterested him. He kept thinking of the memories that Adelia had unknowingly shared with him. The anger lacing all of those memories. He watched her from afar. He watched his sister age. He let his powers shift and grow. And before long, he had set his sights on something much greater than himself.

Something above and beyond working in the temple and serving the council members.

Nina did not enjoy her role on the council. She did not enjoy her people coming to her asking for favors. She did not like the other Lan God who spent much of his time trying to convince her that they would be perfect as lovers. She did not enjoy spending time apart from her family and friends back home.

She did not like how close Tori and Shion had become.

Deep down, she knew it was ridiculous of her to be jealous of their friendship. Tori was allowed to talk to anyone she wanted. But there was something special between Tori and Shion. Something Nina did not know how to handle.

She never saw Shion so happy as when she was with Tori, and she did not understand at the time it was because Shion had never had a friend. Never had someone who did not care that she was the queen. She had never had someone who would call her out on things she did not understand.

So, yes. Shion was happy with Tori. But there was nothing romantic there. The feelings Shion held for Tori, and Tori for Shion, were not the same as the feelings Nina held for Tori. That she hid and tried to pretend did not exist.

Tori, for her credit, spent as much time with Nina as she did with Shion. Nina would, forever, be her best friend. Nothing would ever separate the two of them. Nothing would ever sour between the two of them. They had been friends since they were five years old. Tori had given up her freedom, had given up her mortality, to be with Nina.

In her mind, that meant something.

In Nina's mind, it was blocked by the jealousy of the time Tori spent with Shion.

And for Shion, things were going better than she had ever experienced before. She had a friend. Someone who was always there for her. Who did not spread gossip about her, and who she could tell her secrets to.

Tori was *her* best friend.

And she did not realize that Nina's ire toward her was because of that.

It was not until one day, when Tori and Nina were sitting together atop a hill, hiding from council duties, that things changed between them.

See, Nina's feelings had grown increasingly since they had become immortal. They were almost impossible to ignore now, and when Tori began talking about Shion, about how close they were, and how she never thought she would ever become friends with the queen of the Vilaim, Nina, in all senses of the word, snapped.

"So you have replaced me!" she exclaimed, standing.

Tori, shocked, shook her head. "What are you talking about? Of course not."

"But you spend all of your time with her," Nina cried. "You talk only about her."

"And when I am with her, I talk of you." Tori's tone was joking. She did not understand Nina's upset behavior. She did not understand why Nina was suddenly crying. "Hey. What is wrong?"

Nina pushed her away. "Ever since we have come here, things have changed. You have become friends with the queen, and you are pushing me away."

"You are the one pushing," Tori said, again with a slight joking tone.

"This is not funny, Tori." Nina turned away from her, wrapping her arms around her body. It was becoming too much for her. Not being home, being ripped from her family…no, sold *by* her family, was weighing down on her. It was because of her that Tori's life goals were gone. It was because of her that everything was wrong.

She did not know how to handle the emotions inside of her.

And when Tori touched her shoulder, she lost control and spun around. She placed her hands on Tori's cheeks and kissed her so quickly and lightly that it was almost like it had never happened.

Except it had.

A mortified Nina bolted.

A stunned Tori stood there with wide eyes as a million memories clicked together for the first time in her entire life. She had never questioned why Nina acted the way she did around Tori. How she got jealous if Tori joked about courting a young man.

Her jealousy of Tori's friendship with Shion.

All of a sudden, everything made sense, and Tori's cheeks flushed with color as she ran after her friend.

The next time he ran into Adelia, Eran knew that he had to apologize for reading her memories. He had not meant to, but he should have refused to see them. He should not have commented on her blindness.

In the weeks that had passed since that moment, he had learned that yes, she had been blind, and she had rejected Death's gift of curing her when he made her immortal. There were stories of how she used to wear a blind fold to keep herself from seeing, and how that eventually stopped when she became close to Queen Shion.

It was a part of her life that he had had no business getting involved in.

But when he saw her again, he found he could not speak. She came toward him, gray eyes trained on him as though her life depended on it. They spoke, quietly. He apologized for commenting on her blindness, and she asked him how he had known.

He lied. He told her that he had heard from someone, and it had occurred to him in the moment.

But the thing was, Adelia could tell when people were lying to her. She had grown to hear the slight change in their tone. The way her parents used to tell her that she was completely normal. The way that the other kids explained that they did not dislike her because she was blind.

How the other council members tried to befriend her when it was clear she had a connection with Lady Shion that the others just could not have.

She wanted to call him out on his lie, but she realized that he was hiding something from her.

She knew of the powers. She herself did not care if someone had powers or not, but she knew of the stigma that came along with them. She understood that Eran's sister had one of the rarest, and possibly most powerful gifts of all time, in her possession and that anything he did was under strict watch. Possibly in a way he did not know.

If it came out that he, too, had a power, there was no saying what would happen to him or his family. And it was possible that Shubishi, as strange and mysterious as he still was to Adelia, would take advantage of this and conduct research on Eran as well.

She did not want that for him.

But he started to interest her, in that moment.

And he started to gain interest in her.

The two spent more and more time together, telling each other stories of their childhoods, exchanging secrets of the temple that the other did not know—though Adelia knew far more than Eran ever could—and soon, without warning, there was something more there.

Something neither one of them could understand.

One night, as the two lay together, in all defiance of everything they had ever been taught, Adelia mentioned that she missed the days when she could not see.

"Yes," she said, "there is beauty in the world. But there was a beauty in not focusing on what was visually there. And I feel...I feel like I am missing a part of me, now that I am no longer blind. I feel like part of my personality, part of my being, is missing."

Eran did not understand, but he did know that she sounded sad. He kissed her. He kissed her deeply and with a passion that Death would find abhorrent if he found out. That anyone on the council would sentence him to death for, if they were to find out.

But Adelia did not sentence him to death, and Death himself was missing again. So what did it matter? Did it matter that they lay naked together? That he kissed her? That when he pulled away from her, he grabbed his shirt and ripped a part of it off and tied it around his eyes.

Adelia laughed. "What are you doing?"

He fumbled with his shirt again and ripped another piece, holding it out to her.

"You used to wear this," he said. "It made you feel like you were holding on to your family and your friends. It was part of your identity, one you have never come to terms with losing."

"How do you know this?" Adelia asked.

He could not see, but he could sense her. Her warmth. Her softness. He touched her skin and rubbed a thumb along her cheek. "I have always known things I should not know."

"Your power," she said.

"You know?"

"Only that you have one."

"I should have told you sooner."

She kissed him. "If I cared, I would not be here."

"I can read your memories."

She kissed him again. "Then read them."

And in that moment, time stopped. Time stopped as Adelia kissed her lover, dropping her blindfold by her side. For she did not need it anymore. At one time, in her life, she may have been blind, but that part of her was long gone. She could try and pretend that she could get it back, but it would never be the same. She would always know what the flowers looked like. She would always know the colors of the sky.

She would always know every feature of her lover's face as she kissed him. As she pushed him to the ground and the two tangled together.

And with her acceptance of herself, with Eran's acceptance of her, who she was before, who she had become when Death had made her immortal, she was able to stop time.

In that moment, Eran knew that he would never want to be without her. That he wanted to be her equal in every sense of the word. He could not leave her. He could not leave his sister.

Death was still searching for a god from Raan.

And he knew it had to be him.

Tori had not seen Nina in days. She had searched for her friend, but could not understand what was going on with her. She eventually took solace in Shion, finding her sitting atop the very same hill that Nina had kissed Tori on.

They sat together in silence for a time, as Tori attempted to put together words that would help her understand what was going on in Nina's mind, to seek guidance from Shion, and to make her world go back to the way it was before.

But there were no good words. There was no way to understand this.

Nor was there a way to understand the blossoming warmth in Tori's gut whenever she thought of her best friend.

"Shion?" Tori asked.

"Hm?"

"Can a woman love another woman?"

It was not something heard of in Lan or Narumi, but maybe Shion, who had lived much longer, knew more of. However, the confusion on her face told Tori all she needed to know.

"I see."

"What happened?" Shion asked.

"Nina kissed me."

Shion knew immediately that it was not as friends. She stared up at the sky and closed her eyes, trying to imagine what it would be like to have someone love her. To have a man or a woman love her. It did not matter to her. She just wanted someone.

But when Tori asked the question again, if a woman could love another woman, Shion had to think about the past. She had never paid much attention to love, honestly. It was not that she had not wanted someone, it was that she still had in her mind that the only Vilaim she could fall in love with was another Seshen.

And what of the Seshen? Were they open to two women being lovers? Had it been a part of the culture at one point, only to disappear? She could not recall. She had never paid too much attention to it.

But there was one thing she knew for certain, and that was if Nina kissed Tori, if Nina showed that kind of interest in her best friend, then there was something there.

"I suppose they can," she said finally with a nod of her head.

185

"But how can you know?"

Shion smiled at her. "Because I know that Nina loves you."

When Tori found Nina, she knew that it was never going to be the same between them. She knew now of Nina's feelings. She knew now of her own.

Nina tried to apologize.

Tori kissed her.

And all the while, Enya watched from far away, curious as to what this development meant for her and her plans.

During all of this, Death was absent. He had not meant to be. He had meant to focus on his Vilaim, but the humans…the creatures from Earth, were far more interesting to him than the politics and the games of the Vilaim. He no longer cared if they remained perfect. If they remained pure. Because he no longer cared about them.

He had promised Shubishi he would come back under the condition that there would be more council members who would eventually take his place forever. Who would keep their clans in check and would manage the rules that he had set down.

He was going to leave them be.

Except he knew he could not leave them be. Because the moment he left, everything fell apart again. There were whispers of another war. Death had yet to choose representatives from the Raan and the Nimbon clans for the council. He had meant to do it, but no matter who Shubishi brought to him, no matter who applied, he did not find them worthy. He still could not get his mind out of the past.

He could not forget Halise and Amir.

He watched over Earth, over his humans, knowing that he had to return.

And so he did. He returned, and the final arc began.

Chapter Thirteen

It only took one touch for Eran and Lior to understand each other perfectly. One touch for Eran to read Lior's memories. And one touch for Lior to read Eran's mind.

In all accounts, it was an inconsequential meeting. Eran out on the streets, running and errand for the council. Lior making his way through the streets of the city. They had not meant to run into each other. It was an accident. Both swear by it. But that accident changed everything for the both of them.

They stared at each other, knowing without a word that Lior wanted to become the Nimbon God. That Eran wanted to become the Raan God. That both of them wanted the same thing but for very different reasons.

Lior knew that Eran was sleeping with a council woman.

Eran knew that Lior wanted revenge on his people.

Lior knew that Eran's sister was the fabled Raan who could heal with a single touch.

Eran knew that Flora could have saved the life of Lior's lover.

It was an unlikely friendship between the two. One with no

secrets. One where both wanted to help the other for very different reasons.

Lior did not hold Eran accountable for Kristin's death. He knew that Eran knew nothing of her, and that Flora had been taken from her home at a young age. And Eran did not blame Lior for wanting to show all of the Nimbon clan that he was better than them in every way. That he did not deserve to be treated the way they had treated him for all those years.

It was the two of them against the word.

And all of this without a single word passing between them.

A plan was formed. A simple, but obvious plan. Death did not know about their powers. Only Adelia knew of Eran's, and she was not going to tell anyone. Even Shubishi, who knew that Eran had powers, did not know what kind.

They could get away with it.

They could get away with tricking Death into making them Gods.

It happened without warning one day. Death, who had been gone for some time, returned, possibly due to the rumblings of unrest in the Nimbon and Raan clans. He returned and vowed that he would find the remaining two gods. He would put an end to the unrest, and things would go back to normal.

Here was the moment.

Eran, having access to the temple, found where Death was staying and together the two confronted him.

"If you have concerns," Death said with a low drawl, "please direct them to the council."

"The council cannot help us," Lior replied. He removed his

head, revealing his different colored eyes and his Nimbon heritage. Death hesitated at the sight of them both.

He was not a stupid being. He made mistakes, but he was not stupid. He knew in an instant what these two men wanted. And he also knew that he could not give it to them. They had come to him. They had not been picked or chosen. They had not proven themselves worthy of becoming Gods.

"Leave," Death instructed. "Leave, do not look back, and do not bother with your request."

Eran had expected this, and he had expected that it would take longer than a few sentences to achieve their goal. He had been around the council long enough to hear stories of Death's ego. Of his impatience with the Vilaim. He knew that this was going to be a struggle.

But Lior did not. For while Eran could read all of Lior's memories, Lior could only read what Eran was thinking in the moment, and only if he focused on him. He missed so much of the nuance, and he grew angry at the immediate dismissal.

"You have waited for far too long picking a representative for Nimbon and Raan," Lior said. "I know how much you despise our clans, but we are still Vilaim. We still need someone to guide us, and why not pick the two of us?"

Death did not bless him with an answer, and Lior grew frustrated. He could read the minds of anyone. But Death was not anyone. Death was a deity, and his brain—if he had a brain—was different than the brains of the Vilaim. His mind worked differently. It was like with Kristin, Lior realized very quickly.

He could not read Death's mind.

"You will not even hear us out?" Lior continued. "What kind of deity are you if you will not listen to your people?"

Again, Death did not respond, but he thought. He considered what Lior had accused him of him. All of this time, he had been wandering off to Earth in search of something new. Creations he had not trifled with. He had hoped, all of this time, that he would be able to leave the Vilaim alone once he had the council, but he knew that it was not to be. They were too reliant on him. They had come to expect his interference.

It was disheartening to him.

It was frustrating to him.

And he grew angry at the pair.

Eran tried to warn Lior not to keep going. He knew of Death's anger from Adelia, but Lior did not.

"You are the reason we have so many issues," Lior continued. "You are the reason we struggle. You are the reason that my people hated me from the very beginning of my life, even though I had done nothing to them. You are the reason my love is dead!"

This was true on many accounts, but Death did not want to hear it. He did not want to be talked back to by two insignificant Vilaim.

Anger.

He had never felt this kind of anger before.

He rounded on Lior and grabbed him, thinking only of taking his life. Of ending it the way that he had ended Amir's.

But that is when it all changed.

That is when Eran grabbed Death, something no one had ever done before. For you see, while Lior could not read Death's thoughts, Eran could read Death's memories. Their powers, while similar, were different. Their powers, while connected, did not hold the same properties.

And Eran saw it all. The creation of Seshen. The bond that Death had with her. The day he had to reap her soul.

He saw it all. The creation of all the other Vilaim. The loneliness in the depths of Death's soul. The way he felt like an outsider with his own people.

Eran saw everything. The memories, thousands upon thousands

of years of memories, flooded his mind, causing him agony. The souls he had reaped. The deaths he had caused. The mistakes he had made.

Amir and Halise.

The promise he had made Enya keep. A promise to grant her godhood if she watched over the people while he went off to find something to make him happy. Finally happy.

And then, memories of Earth. Of the people down there. Of the things that Death had been doing with the magic in that world.

They only touched for a few seconds. That is all it took for Eran to know everything about Death. For Death to realize that he was learning everything about him.

They parted and Death released a living Lior as Eran fell to the ground, head in his hands. He cried out in pain as the memories settled into his own. As he tried to understand the things he had just seen. The emotions he had witnessed. The beauty, the pain, the anger, the guilt.

The guilt.

All these years, learning of their history, of Amir and Halise, no one had realized that Death was the one who had taken Amir's life early. They had always blamed Halise. Always. Her name had never been cleared, even after all of these years, and Eran could not believe what he was witnessing.

And Lior could not either.

For what Eran saw through Death, Lior saw through Eran.

When the pain subsided, there was silence in the temple.

Death could not believe what was happening. All of these years, all of his secrets, they were now in the mind of not one, but two Vilaim. And who was to say who they would tell? Death knew he could only do one thing.

He had to kill them.

But as he reached for Eran, hesitance stopped him.

He remembered the anger in Amir's soul when he had died. He remembered, all too clearly, the fact that Halise had never forgiven him. If he killed Eran and Lior, if he took their souls before it was their time, what consequences would there be this time?

What could Death do to make things worse?

Killing them was not an option. He could not bring himself to do it again. He could not bring himself to break the laws of nature in such a way. He searched their souls, eager to discover when they would die. When their time was up.

And found he could not see it.

Because there was more than one option.

"I will give you immortality," Death said, "but in return, you will never speak of what you saw here today. You will remain silent, and you will follow my every direction. If you do not, then there will be consequences."

Lior could not believe his luck. He was getting what he wanted. He would show the Nimbon the mistake that they had made and he would prove to the world that he was good enough to have had Kristin's love.

Everything he was doing, was for Kristin's love.

Eran, on the other hand, did not feel the same joy as Lior. What he felt was cold shame. Digging into the memories of Death the way that he had. Knowing what he knew. It haunted him. Yes, he was getting what he wanted, but he could not imagine that it would have happened this way. With him not only revealing his powers to Death, but using them on him.

And the things he had learned. The information about Earth and about their history. Eran shuddered at the thought of both, not sure what to make of the situation. There was another dimension out here. One with creatures who looked like the Vilaim, but were not the Vilaim. Humans. Death called them humans. Death took a passive role with them.

Death favored them.

He was supposed to favor the Vilaim.

Technically, Eran never agreed to Death's terms. Lior did, and was made immortal. But Eran was too stunned to agree. And when Death touched him again, giving him more memories, and giving him immortality, Eran knew that he would have to do as Death said if he wanted to protect his sister.

If he wanted to be with Adelia for the rest of their lives.

It was here that Death thought that the pain would end. He had given representation to all of the clans. Two for each, save for the Seshen, and a queen. He had done his duty as their deity, and he was ready for things to go back to the way they had been for a hundred years. Where the Vilaim were satisfied. Where things were going to be all right.

Except nothing was all right.

Shubishi lived his life as if there were no such things as consequences. He could not die. He could not be injured. He was immortal, and he loved every second of his gift. He loved the way that people respected him. He loved the way that people ignored him. He loved the way that he was granted freedoms that he otherwise would never have had.

But deep down, he knew things could not last like this forever.

Shion had found peace for the first time since she was a young child. She had her best friend. She knew her place. She was coming to terms with being the queen and doing her duty. With her happiness rising, she even attended more council meetings and spoke, giving her opinion based on what she saw.

But deep down, she knew things could not last like this forever.

Adelia had come to terms with her new state. She let go of her anger at Death and began to open up others on the council. They were shocked at her new state, and they wondered what had caused it. Who had caused it. But they did not ask questions, and Adelia went on with her life, happy with her new lover and with her place in the world.

But deep down, she knew things could not last like this forever.

Nina could not have been happier. She had thought she had ruined her friendship with Tori when she had kissed her, but instead, they were together. In secret, as the rest of the Vilaim did not approve of their relationship. But they were together, holding hands in secret. Whispering to each other in secret. Kissing and laying naked together at night when they thought no one was watching.

But deep down, she knew things could not last like this forever.

Tori lived life to the fullest. With her girlfriend on her arm and her best friend as the queen, she pushed boundaries and brought new life to the council. She was a rebel. Always a rebel. And she made as many enemies as she did friends. Nina always worried that Tori had given up her dreams, but in reality, Tori was living them out. She was strong. She was bold. She was happy.

But deep down, she knew things could not last like this forever.

Lior had won. When news spread of his becoming a god, the good people of Nimbon came to pay their respects. He was granted access to Kristin's grave, but he did not take it. He needed them to know that he was in charge, and they were not going to try and take that from him again. He was hungry for power. Hungry for revenge. And he was getting what he wanted.

But deep down, he knew things could not last like this forever.

Eran changed the day that he read Death's memories. He grew humbled. He grew softer. More understanding. More afraid of his gift. He could read memories, but what else could he do? Adelia tried to ask him what happened, what had changed with him, but he had no answers for her. For now, he kissed her, he held his seat on the council, and he was allowed greater access to his sister.

And deep down, he hoped things could last like this forever.

All of this brings us to Flora. A sweet child of eighteen. With long, thick hair and perfectly symmetrical features, her green eyes shimmered in light and her smile brought happiness to all who were fortunate enough to fall into her presence. Without her, so many things would have gone wrong.

Because of her, so many things went wrong.

She sat alone in the gardens, playing with the flowers she was so often compared to. She sniffed them. She smiled at the fragrance. She lay on her back and stared at the beautiful, colorful sky, and she wondered when her life would finally change.

Chapter Fourteen

To understand everything, we must go back a few years. Before Eran was made immortal, before Flora turned eighteen. Before Death returned. The Raan became restless. They were known for their medicine, and they recalled the small child who had left them years ago. The small child from a simple family who had the ability to heal.

The small child stolen from them by the god Shubishi.

For, you see, things did not get better for the Raan when Flora left. She cast a net of safety over the entirety of her town, keeping them from getting ill. From dying too young. They had not realized just how powerful she was until her magic began to fade and Vilaim were falling ill once more. Where injuries held their full, potent, potential.

From the time Flora was fifteen, the Raan had been demanding her back.

But Shubishi had refused each and every time. He had found his pet. Someone who followed him around like a puppy and lived on his every word. He could not give her back, no matter what the Raan

197

leaders demanded. Her life was in the temple now, and he would not rip her away from her life again.

Desperate, the Raan went to the other clans, claiming that Shubishi had stolen one of their own for his experiments, and he had done it without their permission. But when the other clans discovered Flora's true powers, they agreed with Shubishi. It would not be fair for her powers to belong to one clan and one clan alone.

They needed to protect her. They needed to make sure that she was available to all the clans, or none at all.

Shubishi kept her safe from everyone. He did not allow anyone but her brother, who had proven himself over the years, and Shion to see her. Not even the other council members were allowed to know Flora.

And this made Flora very lonely.

Flora, over the past fourteen years, had spent much of her time learning. Shubishi was always fascinated with education, being Jous, and Flora found it interesting. She was the one who sat by his side when he read, looking at the words over his shoulder. She was the one who helped him with his experiments and encouraged him to try new things.

She liked being around Shubishi.

But she found herself wishing that she had someone else to talk to, at times. She loved when her brother came to visit, though that was less and less now that he had found someone to bed at night. Lady Shion visited as well, but rarely said a word. Merely observed her and Shubishi quietly before disappearing.

Flora had no friends of her own. She was separate from the rest. She knew that she was different from her peers, but she did not understand why she needed to stay separate. She asked Shubishi on many occasions why this had to be the case, and each time he would respond that the rest of the world wanted to use her.

He wanted to protect her.

And she began to wonder if maybe she needed to be stronger, if the world wanted to use her, when Death arrived in her garden.

She greeted him, like she always did when he visited. It was not often that he came to see her. She was not immortal. She was not special.

What she did not know, however, was the reason Death had come to visit her.

Death was becoming disillusioned with his creations. They wanted more from him than he could give. They demanded more and more. Two representatives was not enough, they claimed. Having a queen was out of date, they cried.

Since when had Death become a slave to his own creations? Since when did he do what they said, and not the other way around? Since when did he not do whatever he damn well pleased?

When word of the Raan's upset about Flora came to him, his frustration grew. They knew nothing of what the real world had to offer them. They lived, protected by his light, and they wanted more. But down on Earth, he witnessed suffering. He witnessed wars he did not partake in. He witnessed brutal acts.

And he compared them. His Vilaim with his humans. He compared the way they worked together. The things they valued.

He was becoming disillusioned with his Vilaim. They were whiny. They were spoiled. They no longer knew of freedom. And it was all his fault, they said. It was all his fault that they were suffering.

He visited Flora that day because he had always seen something in her that he loved: perfection.

A perfect creature with a soft voice and beauty beyond compare. With a gentle soul. With a quick mind. With a curiosity that only came with childhood.

"Do not tell anyone," Death whispered to her as he ran a hand along her cheek. He pulled away. Took her mortality with him. And left her there in the flowers as she stared after him, confused.

Flora felt no different. She had heard stories of what it felt like to become immortal, but she did not feel anything. She knew what Death had done. It was obvious to her that she had changed, but she felt no different.

She rose to her feet, walking with her head held high. He had said not to tell anyone. A direct order from Death. But how could she keep this from her brother? He could read her memories. And what of Lior, the man who could read minds? What of Shubishi, who could see her soul and would know that it had become immortal.

That she was immortal.

But it was not any of them that she had to worry about in the end.

Enya had been quiet for some time in this story. She had gotten what she wanted. She was a God. She was respected. She had gotten reparations for her people and turned the Seshen land into farmland for the Siman. She had changed the power structure of the Vilaim to suit her wants and needs.

She was happy.

But she was not happy. Because there was still something she longed for that was being ripped away from her. And during the thirteen years of Flora being with Shubishi, she had grown more and more angry with the young girl.

She blamed her for Shubishi not paying attention to Enya. She blamed Flora for everything that went wrong with her life, even if she kept it to herself. Even if she did not spread rumors about her or try to get the council to turn on her, like she had with Shion. Her focus had changed from Shion, who no longer relied on Shubishi, to Flora.

She spied on Flora.

She watched her every move.

And she saw Death make her immortal. She witnessed the moment when Death broke all of his own rules and made another Raan immortal. Someone called perfect. Someone who he gave the gift to without having her bargain. Without having a proper reason.

He had done it for no good reason.

And Enya needed to get rid of her somehow.

She needed to get rid of all the ones who would go against her. But she did not know how to do it. She did not know how to get Death to listen to her, as she had to make him a promise in order to convince him to make her immortal.

It was not until she followed him one day that she realized what he was doing when he disappeared.

He was going to another place. A place with humans. A place with magic. A place brand new that he could watch over.

And she knew that this was how she was going to get him.

She hatched a plan that would change everything. That would lead to the Iravata. That would manipulate both worlds into giving her what she wanted: power over the Vilaim, and her enemies gone.

She went to Earth and convinced them that gods were real.

It took little effort. The humans had already created deities in their mind. Each one had a different idea of what God looked like, but Enya gave them a face. Not her own. She did not want her face to be associated with any of this, but it was that of a young Vilaim man with powers who she asked to come with her. In return, she promised him a job in the temple.

But that promise was never to be upheld.

Death discovered Enya's plot, but did not know who had created it. He was on Earth, wandering invisible among the humans when he noticed a change in them. That they were paying less attention to the world around them, and more to a lore about Gods than ever before. When he walked among them as one of their own, he asked what happened and they explained that God had come down to talk to them.

Not just one, for some. Not always male. Just a confirmation that they indeed lived in a world with gods and magic and everything they had known in their stories were true.

Death was furious.

He had not wanted the Vilaim to interfere with Earth. He had not told them about it for a reason. He had not interfered for a reason. And now, these creatures, these humans, had been tainted. Messed with by a Vilaim, by a God, who had known about Earth. Who had known about Death's attachment to Earth.

His first thought was Eran or Lior. But when he confronted them, he knew they were telling the truth about not knowing anything. It was not until Enya came forward with a confession that Death learned the truth.

Or, what he thought was the truth.

Death thought that no Vilaim could lie to him, but Enya had mastered the gift.

"I never thought she would," Enya exclaimed at his feet during a council meeting. "She seems so sweet, but she was angry for... for...." She burst into tears and named Flora as the culprit. Enya explained that Flora was angry for having been made a God, especially in secret, and she had wanted revenge on Death.

Of course, none of this was true. Flora could not have cared less about her godhood. She had lived among them for so long, and she had not changed that much. The idea of never dying had already been an option, thanks to her powers. She could not have ever imagined that she would be turned immortal, but the day it happened, nothing changed for her.

But when asked this, she was too startled to deny it.

Again, Death was enraged. Too many of the Vilaim had squandered his gift, now. He sought out the Vilaim Enya had brought to Earth and demanded he answer for his crimes. But by now, the entirety of the Vilaim had learned about Earth and were curious about it.

Everything changed, once again.

They had learned where their deity disappeared off to. They felt abandoned. Lost. Lonely. They questioned his authority, the authority of the council, and things fell into chaos.

Death knew that he had to do something, once again. He had to intervene and create peace among his Vilaim once more, but he was tired of doing so. He was tired of watching over their every move.

Yet, this was his fault.

He was the one who had made Flora immortal.

He was the one who had made Shubishi immortal.

He was the one who had made Shion immortal.

It had all started with his mistake. Another, large, immense, mistake. It had taken much longer to come about, to raise above the surface and make his life miserable, but it was there, staring him in the face.

He had to act.

Not everyone believed Enya's accusations. Shubishi, for one. Shion for another. Eran for another. And of course, Lior. Lior who could read the lies in Enya's mind, a power she did not realize he had.

He spoke of this to Eran.

Eran spoke of this to Adelia.

Adelia spoke of this to Shion.

Shion spoke of this to Tori, who spoke of it to Nina.

Shubishi did not need to be spoken to. But he knew that the others were whispering. He heard them speak to each other when they did not know he was there.

And for the first time, seven came together to protect the eighth. For the first time, they sat in a room together and spoke, not as council members, but as comrades, come together through circumstance.

Most of them had never spoken to one another. It would be years before the close friendships would bloom between many of them. But they sat together and they discussed Enya and the problems she had caused over the years. The issues she had.

They knew she was lying. Lior explained to them his powers. How he had read her mind as she announced Flora's guilt and realized she was lying. But he could not say anything in the moment because he did not want to reveal his powers to everyone. He did not want people to know, because he thought it might be useful.

All through the debates about what to do, how to reveal Enya's true plans, Shion sat and thought about where all of this started. Enya had been around for so long. The third god. Older than Shion, but never as important in the eyes of Death.

She thought about the hatred Enya had for her. About the ease in which Enya commanded the other council members. There was something more to this plot than framing Flora for going down to Earth.

Shion just did not know what it was.

None of them did.

Flora was held on trial. She tried to explain that she was not angry about being made a God, that she did not have any issues with being immortal. She wanted to be with the Gods. They were her family. Her friends. It was the only life she had ever known.

Death did not believe her.

But then it all went to hell. Because Eran was getting angry at how the council was whispering about his sister. The seven who had come together, knowing Enya was lying, remained quiet, not sure where things were going to go, but Eran could not stop. He needed to act.

When Enya walked down to explain what she knew, again, this time he stood as well. Adelia told him to sit down, not to rush things, but he needed to and he hurried down, wanting to know more than Lior could read. He grabbed Enya's arm, and only a few knew what was going on.

Flora.

The six who had come together to protect her.

And Death.

He recalled quite clearly what it was like to have his memories read, and he knew that something was going on. But he was not sure what Eran was doing. He had read the memories of Death going to Earth. Had he told his sister? Had he lied? Was Enya lying? Was Flora?

He could not tell anymore what was going on, but he intervened before Eran could read enough of Enya's memories. He blasted them away from each other, leaving Eran with only a few jolts.

Memories of Earth. Memories of the time before the Seshen died. Memories of fire.

He did not know what they meant. All he did know was that Enya was hiding something from all of them, and he was determined to figure out what it was. Except...except Death was not having any of this anymore.

Death was convinced that Eran had spilled his secrets and was going to tell everyone about everything.

Death did not jail Flora. He instead jailed her brother for treason.

Chapter Fifteen

"He cannot do this!" Tori exclaimed.

"He has gone mad with power," Adelia agreed.

"He is our deity," Lior added. "If he wants to do something, there is little we can do to stop him."

"Are you sure about that?" Tori climbed onto the table and stared at her new friends. "He picked us to run the Vilaim, and yet he goes off the word of one Vilaim. He goes off the word of someone we can prove is lying. What does he fear? Why does he fear us?"

The others murmured amongst themselves. Shion looked at Shubishi, who had known Death the longest, and asked him in a quiet voice what was going on. What were they missing?

But Shubishi had no words for any of them. He merely watched, knowing that this moment was going to change all of their lives. He knew what Tori was going to say. He knew what the plan was going to be. He knew…he knew…. He knew.

"What are you suggesting?" Adelia asked, the most furious of them all. She knew that Eran would never do anything to hurt anyone. He was too gentle. If he were going to use his powers on

Enya, there was a reason for it, but she did not know how to explain that to Death. She did not even know why Death was so afraid of his powers.

"She is suggesting that we rebel." It was Lior who spoke, with a slight grin on his face. He had promised he would make his people pay, and what better way than to shake up everything they had ever known. To make Death admit to them that he had messed with their lives for far too long.

It would rattle everything.

"Rebel against Death? He is, quite literally, Death. If he wanted to, he could end our lives right here and now."

"He will not," Lior said, and then he explained to them how he and Eran became gods. How Death had wanted to kill him, but had stopped when the guilt of Amir overcame him. "He will not kill us, but there is no saying what he will do if we do this. If we try to get the council to turn against him…."

"They never will," Nina added.

"You do not know that," Adelia said.

"I know more than you do," Nina snapped. "I actually talk to the other members."

"It is worth a shot." Tori stepped in before anyone else could say anything. "If we get them to agree with us that Death has gone too far by jailing Eran with no evidence…after all, if he did that to Eran, what else could he do to us? The council fears losing their power more than anything else. All Death has to do is snap his fingers."

It was true, and they all agreed upon that fact. It would only take a second for Death to take away their power and then what would happen?

"We need to save Eran," Adelia said. "He has done nothing wrong."

"It is Enya who has done the wrong." Tori would not let go of that fact. She had never liked Enya. Never liked the stories that Shion told about her. Never liked how she tried to control the council in such a strong way. It was wrong for someone who cared so little about others to be in charge.

If only the rest of the council saw it that way.

"So, we do this?" Lior asked.

They were all in agreement. Even Shubishi, who had been quiet the entire time, raised his hand when they voted on whether or not they were going to try and convince the council to rebel against Death. They had almost half of the council on their side. Who was to say that they would not succeed?

On the day of Eran's trial, they began their plot. They whispered in the ears of the other council members, all but Enya, of the issues with Death being able to snap his fingers and accuse one of them of treason. How their power was being threatened. Power he had willingly given them, and now he could willingly take away if they had nothing to give him in return.

The whispers broke out as Enya read the claims against Eran. She did it with such glee that all of his friends felt sick. This was what she had wanted all along. She had wanted to disrupt the order of things, but why?

What was her goal?

Only Shubishi knew.

Because she had come to see him, a fact that he had not told the others, and tried to convince him to go along with her plot. After all, she still saw herself special in his eyes, despite centuries of evidence against this. No matter how hard he tried to show her that she was nothing to him, she continued to wear the ring.

She continued to mock him with its presence.

He had not agreed nor disagreed with her proposal. In her mind, he was going to do as she asked.

She did not expect the council to turn against her.

Death did not expect the council to turn against him.

There were arguments. Fighting. Questions being raised that Death did not want asked. But what could he do? Punish them all?

He did the only thing he could think of. He stood forward and answered their questions.

None of the seven had expected him to do this. They thought his pride was too strong, his arrogance too great. But he answered their questions about Earth. About where he had been. About his motives. About why he had put Eran on trial.

It was not going the way that Tori had wanted it to go. She did not want the council to find appeasement in Death's words. She wanted them to rise up. To question everything about the structure of their world. Instead, they were placated. They sat down and nodded.

Until she rose up and asked the one question Death had not been expecting.

"Why did you create the gods?"

It was then he knew that she was the ring leader. He could not answer. He could not admit that he had been lonely. That he had been afraid. That he had needed to keep the Seshen alive. He did not want to admit to any more of his mistakes.

Instead, he turned the questioning on her.

"What makes you so angry?" Death asked. "You who begged me to make you a God."

Tori was stunned into silence. The others broke out in whispers. They had thought that Tori had been chosen to become a God, just like the others had been. They had not known that she had asked. That she had begged.

"Are you all that unhappy with your immortality?" Death asked.

"Yes."

It was one voice, rising above all the others. A voice that made the entire council go silent. A voice that made Enya pale. A voice that made Death want to retreat. To go back in time and fix all the issues he had ever caused for everyone.

Because the queen, Lady Shion, stepped forward from her seat and came to stand next to Eran.

"I am unhappy, being immortal," Shion admitted for the first time since she had cried in Shubishi's arms after her coronation. "I never wanted to live forever. I never wanted to be the queen. I never wanted any of this. This world, this role. It is nothing more than a farce."

One by one, the others who had agreed to the rebellion stepped down. Adelia. Tori. Nina. Lior. Even Flora. They came to stand by Eran and Shion's side, desperate to make a point. To show Death that he had gone too far in their affairs. If he had just stayed out of it, if he had never created the system that he had, if he had let history play out the way it was supposed to, then none of this would have happened.

But it was not the seven of them who broke his heart.

It was not the seven of them who made him regret creating the immortals altogether.

It was when Shubishi, his oldest friend, walked down and took his place by Lady Shion's side that everything went to hell.

"You?" he asked Shubishi.

Shubishi cocked his head and said nothing. He merely smiled. For he did not do this because he thought Death had overstepped. He did not do this because he thought Enya was overreaching, nor that Eran was innocent. All of the reasons that the others had for standing up to Death were meaningless to him.

He did this because it amused him. He did this because he could.

He was curious about the world below them. The planet Earth

and the humans who roamed it. He had grown bored with the Vilaim and their issues. He wanted something new. A new adventure. And why not take this one?

There are no words to describe Death's anger. No words to explain the decision he made next. His queen, his beloved Seshen had betrayed him. She had taken the side of those who wanted to bring him down.

She had scorned his gift

He looked at her brown hair. Her blue eyes.

His friend, the one who had convinced him to break the rules again, had joined the rebels.

Rage built within him and before he knew what he had done, they were gone. All eight of the rebels were gone from the world they had grown up in. Vanished. Not a trace left.

And when they realized they were no longer in the council room, the eight Iravata looked around them. They did not recognize where they were. They did not understand the feelings in their bodies. They did not know why they could not seem to return home.

All they did know is that they were no longer in the realm of the Vilaim. They were on Earth, they realized. They were on Earth and their queen, their beautiful queen, stood in front of them with hair a black as night and eyes as red as blood.

Interlude

The dark room made it impossible for Cody to sleep. He sat on the bed, staring down at the sleeping form of Mia and his mind blazed with a million questions. Every now and then he closed his eyes and tried to let sleep claim him, but whenever he did, images of the story flashed through his mind. Lady Shion with her blue eyes and brown hair. Shubishi, amused and willing to do whatever it took to learn. Flora, innocent and sweet being held on trial for something she didn't do.

And then there was Death. Not a skeleton of a man with a scythe, but a deity who held more power than Cody had ever imagined. He didn't know where the story would take them next. When night had fallen, he'd been too engrossed in the story to notice, but the Iravata had sent them all off to bed, saying they would finish the story when the sun rose. Cody had wanted to protest, but Mia….

He reached out and brushed a lock of hair away from her face. His fingers trailed lightly against her skin, and his stomach lurched at the contact. He withdrew his hand, unable to take his gaze off of her. She'd been so tired. When he'd gone to protest, he'd found he couldn't because she'd grabbed his hand and squeezed it so tightly he'd thought it was going to fall off.

"Let's sleep," she'd said before begging him not to leave her alone.

He didn't blame her for not wanting to sleep alone. For not wanting to *be* alone. The last time anyone had left her alone, Jae had taken her. The last time she'd been alone, it was in that mansion, locked in her replicated room, unable to escape, unable to contact anyone she loved.

And all of it had almost led to her death.

She'd thought she was doing to die. He'd thought she was going to die. If he hadn't had his powers, if he hadn't known what to do, she would have fallen off that roof and died.

He shuddered at the thought and placed his face in his hands, trying to forget the pain in her eyes as he held her, mid-air, by her mist. As he wrapped his arms around her shaking body and tried to calm her down while the fire raged around them. Last winter, Kathleen and Steven had wanted to take Mia away. They hadn't wanted to hurt her, but Jae had. He'd....

Cody scowled and leaned his head back. There was no saying what Jae had been thinking in that moment. Why he'd tried to kill her. Had he known that Cody would be able to save her? According to Mia, he'd called her his angel. She was someone special to him.

But you didn't hurt the people you loved. You didn't hurt the people special to you.

He glanced at Mia again and his expression softened at the gentle, sleeping, look on her face. He couldn't imagine it. A life without Mia. She had appeared like an angel—though he would never call her that after everything she'd been through—and saved him from loneliness. When he'd thought she'd been missing, he'd been willing to tear the world apart to find her. To save her the way she'd saved him.

There was so much he wanted to say to her, now that she wasn't in danger. There were so many words, words he'd been keeping to himself for all these years, not understanding them himself, but also not wanting to make her uncomfortable. Not wanting to step over that line. Because once he did, he knew they couldn't go back. If she didn't feel the same way, they couldn't go back to friends.

He didn't want to be her friend. He loved her. He loved her more than anyone in his life and he wanted her to know that. To know that she was loved. Cared for. That he would do anything to make sure she was safe and happy.

She breathed out and shifted, turning her back to him, and the smile that had made its way to his face faltered. He wasn't amazing with words at the best of times, much less when it came to admitting his feelings for Mia. And besides, right now wasn't the best time for any of that. Mia didn't want to hear that he was in love with her. She wanted to recover from the hell that was the past few days. She wanted to feel safe in her own bed.

She was so emotionally fragile right now. He couldn't…he couldn't shake that even more. It wouldn't be fair to her to do that. Which is why he said nothing. Which is why, when she'd asked him to stay with her while she slept, he did without a single word. He wasn't going to tell her anything about the feelings he held deep in his gut until things settled down.

If things ever settled down.

Mia shifted again, letting out a small noise and Cody tensed, waiting for her to wake up and ask why he was staring at her. But she didn't wake. Her mist stayed gentle and relaxed, and she settled back into a restful sleep, facing him once again. He watched her, unable to take his eyes off her thin frame wrapped in four blankets.

"For the weight," she'd explained.

He didn't understand, but he'd helped her collect blankets anyway, Flora watching them from the doorway. And as he stared at her, his mind wandered back to the Iravata. To their story. Their history. It was so much more complicated than he'd imagined. So many moving parts. It was difficult for them to keep it straight sometimes, and Cody had trouble as well.

But things made more sense. Where they'd come from, how each of them became immortal, and the basics of their relationships to one another. They had all come together to protect Flora and Eran, which didn't surprise Cody. They all seemed so gentle with Flora. Even Shubishi didn't seem to want to upset her in any way. They didn't get much about her, or her relationship with Shubishi, but what they did get was enough for Cody to understand that they all saw her as someone to protect.

A precious flower.

Just like their queen.

Cody shuddered at the thought. Two flowers, each hated by the woman with red hair and blue eyes. Enya. Her motives were not so confusing when compared to Death's, but there was still something massive missing from the story. Something maybe the Iravata weren't telling them. Something maybe they didn't know.

After all, why would Enya come back into their lives? Why would she still be around when she'd gotten what she'd wanted? Why…why…why?

The door to Mia's room opened, pulling Cody out of his thoughts. He glanced at it as Blair slipped through and closed it quietly behind her. They stared at each other for a moment as Mia continued to sleep peacefully next to Cody. Then, without a word, Blair settled into a chair next to the bed, hands clenched together. Shaking.

"Can't sleep?" Cody asked in a low whisper, not wanting to wake Mia.

Blair shook her head. "It's so much information. I can't get my brain to stop. To shut up."

"Yeah, same."

Blair looked up from her hands. At Mia. "I'm glad she's sleeping, though."

"Yeah, same."

Blair let out a breathy, sad chuckle. Her mist, light blue like the sky on a clear winter day, shifted with her mood and Cody couldn't help but ask the question she didn't want to be asked.

"Did Derek really break up with you?" Cody tried not to let any emotion into his voice. From the time they were young, when their mists started dancing together like those of lovers, Cody had feared what a relationship between the two of them would do. They'd tried to hide it. They'd tried to pretend like they weren't immensely attracted to each other, but Cody had been able to tell from the beginning, and all he could think about was how this would affect Mia. How it would make her life miserable if her best friend and her brother started dating.

If they broke up.

But there was something more in Cody's emotions now. He knew that Derek ending their relationship would be hard on Mia, but it would also be incredibly difficult for Blair.

Even now, her mist shifted, darkening as she curled into a ball and pressed her forehead to her knees. A muffled voice said, quietly, "We never should have left him behind."

They both knew that wasn't true. They'd had to leave him behind. Cody had no doubts there was a better way to do it, but they couldn't go back in time. What was done, was done. They had no excuses. Derek knew it was the best choice. Blair knew it was the best choice. They'd *had* to leave him behind.

Derek was stubborn, though, and he didn't want to admit that he would have been a liability. They'd succeeded in their mission. They'd saved Mia. They'd brought her back mostly unharmed. She hadn't died. She was safe now. That was what mattered, but Derek had it in his head that he had to be the hero.

He'd always been that way. Always needing to protect her, even when they were little.

"He'll forgive you," Cody said. "He just needs time."

Blair shook her head. "I don't think so. He was so angry he was quiet. I'd never seen him like that before. He won't touch me. He won't look at me. He won't say anything to me. I want to go back in time to before I decided to take away his energy and just redo it. He would have fallen asleep eventually. We could have waited for that. He...it...it would have been better."

Cody decided Blair didn't need someone to argue this out with her. She was grieving, and he was going to let her. He focused on Mia, who breathed in sharply. A lock of hair fell into her face and Cody brushed it away.

"Things are supposed to be better," Blair muttered. "We saved Mia. We did the impossible. But now she feels unsafe, Derek hates me, and my entire clan doesn't trust me." She paused. "And I don't trust them."

Cody cocked his head, wondering what had happened when Blair went off on her own. She hadn't said anything about the basement. There hadn't been time. But before he could say anything, ask his own questions, Blair spoke again.

"Do you think any of this story matters?"

Cody blinked. "Huh?"

"I just...." Blair sighed. "Why are they telling us all of this? It's so much and we still have more to learn. I'm afraid some of it is lies. That they're trying to manipulate us because they feel like we don't trust them anymore."

"You never trusted them."

"But you and Derek did." She stood and then sat on the edge of the bed, back to Cody. "You two trained with them. You formed friendships with them. You put all of your trust in them. They were supposed to keep Mia safe, and now they're telling us that not only are they not the only immortals, but they have *enemies* who are immortal."

"Well, just one, really," Cody pointed out.

She glared at him and he shrugged.

"I'm scared," she said. "I don't know what other secrets they're keeping, and I don't know what it means for us. Especially Shubishi. He's sketch as hell."

Cody hesitated and stared out the glass sliding doors that let in the moonlight. He also had a feeling that Shubishi was hiding something from them. After all…who was he really? Where did he come from? Why did he gloss over his childhood so much? And the ring? What was with the ring?

His head hurt.

Blair tensed as if getting ready to leave, but Cody slid off the bed and stood in front of her.

"Stay with Mia," he said. "I…I can't sleep in here and I'm exhausted."

Blair cocked her head but didn't fight it. Instead she nodded and Cody left the room, closing the door quietly behind him as Blair crawled into the bed next to Mia.

He stared at the door for a moment, Blair's words rolling around in his mind. She was right. Shubishi was sketch and he was hiding something. But he wasn't sure what. There was a piece of the puzzle missing from the story, and he wasn't sure all of the Iravata knew what it was. If any of them knew.

He shook his head and headed toward his room. He passed Derek's door. His golden mist was awake and sharp, stabbing at Cody's own mist like barbed wire. He ignored it. Derek didn't want his company, and honestly Cody didn't want his at the moment. Instead he turned sharply into the room that Flora had given him and leaned against the door, breathing out. He sunk to the ground, emotions overtaking him.

It was so much.

So. Damn. Much.

And it was only just beginning.

When Mia woke, she was alone. Her arm flung out in the large bed, searching for a warm body she remembered being there when she'd fallen asleep. Or had there been someone? Had it all been a dream? Her heart whipped into a frenzy as she sat up, head on a swivel. In her mind, the dark room was in Jae's mansion. In her mind, she was in that bed, the one that mimicked her own, locked in her replicated room with no way out. No way to contact her family. Her friends.

She fumbled for the lamp on the bedside stand and flicked it on, panting. Light flooded the small room. A room that didn't look like hers.

For a moment, she stared around, blinking to adjust to the light, and she realized it wasn't a dream. She wasn't in Jae's mansion anymore. She was in Shubishi's beach house. She was safe. She was....

She curled into a ball, pulling the heavy blankets over her head as she rocked back and forth.

"I'm okay," she whispered to herself. "I'm okay. It's all okay. It's okay."

She didn't know where Cody had gone. She'd asked him to stay with her because he was the strongest. He was the one who had saved her. The one who had been able to fight against Jae's powers. But he was gone to who knows where, and she was alone. Safe, but alone.

She didn't want to be alone.

The door creaked open and she flinched, gripping her legs with her eyes squeezed shut. She kept reminding herself that she was safe. That it couldn't be Jae walking through that door. It was probably Cody. Yes. It was Cody. It had to be Cody.

"Mia?"

It wasn't Cody's voice. She tensed for a fraction of a moment before relaxing and pulling the blankets away from her head.

Blair stood in the doorway, clad in a pair of pajamas that Flora had produced from somewhere in the house. They looked similar to the ones Mia wore, though with a pattern of seashells instead of flowers. She looked so out of place. Her hair was down, which Mia wasn't used to, and she cocked her head.

"Blair?" Mia's voice shook.

Blair crossed the room and settled on the bed next to Mia. "Sorry, I didn't think you'd wake up. I needed to use the restroom."

Mia's heart slowed to a normal beat and she breathed out, hand still shaking. They hadn't left her alone. She wasn't...she wasn't alone.

"Where's Cody?" Mia asked.

"He needed some sleep," Blair said. "Do you want me to go get him?"

Mia shook her head. No, he needed to sleep. It was ridiculous of her to expect him to stay with her all night. He'd been through a trauma too. Still, she'd hoped he wouldn't leave her. That he would have stayed with her, keeping her safe from the slight possibility that Jae would come after her again.

Shifting, Mia stood up on her knees and wrapped her arms around Blair's neck, still trembling. Tears welled in her eyes. Blair hugged her back.

"It's okay," she said. "You're safe here."

But was that true? And even if it was, they'd have to leave *here* soon. The Iravata couldn't protect her all the time. They'd already proven that. Jae had taken her from under their noses and they hadn't been able to find her for days. The all powerful Iravata hadn't been able to find her. It'd taken Cody and Blair and a lot of luck. If Blair hadn't been a seer, if she hadn't had that connection to the strange necklace, what would have happened?

"What if he comes back?" Mia asked, voice cracking.

"Then we'll kick his ass." Blair squeezed her and then pulled away, hands on Mia's shoulders. "We've done it before."

"He's strong," Mia whimpered.

"He's only one guy." Blair placed a hand on Mia's wet cheek, trying to comfort her. "He didn't try to take you when you were with all of us. He waited and waited until you were alone. But we won't leave you alone again. Someone will always be with you. And if he comes back, then we'll know what we're up against this time. We know his powers. We know who he is. He's not a mystery. We'll do whatever it takes to protect you."

Mia squeezed tears out of her eyes. "Promise?"

"Promise."

Blair couldn't keep that promise. There was only so much she could do. She had her own drama that she was dealing with, having angered her grandmother. There was no way that Blair could protect her forever. Jae was going to find a way into her life, just like he had with Steven and Kathleen. Just like he had in the airport. He'd done it before and he was going to do it again.

"You should get some more sleep," Blair said. "I won't leave again. I'm just as exhausted as you are."

Mia sniffed and wiped away her tears.

The two girls lay down and Mia turned her back on Blair, hoping she wouldn't ask Mia how she felt about the story that the Iravata were telling them. Because she honestly didn't know. The more she listened, the more she found herself sinking deeper into a pit she wanted out of.

She didn't want to know any of this, she'd decided. She'd asked, yes, but that was before she'd found out about who they were. What they'd been hiding. About Enya and Death. She couldn't bring herself to tell anyone that all she could think about was getting out of there forever. To escape from the magical world and never look back.

She wanted a normal life. One where she didn't wake up in a panic. Where she didn't have to fear for her life, or the lives of her friends. She hadn't told any of them this, but sometimes, deep down, she thought that it would be easier if she just didn't exist at all.

She pushed those thoughts out of her mind, however. She knew it wouldn't be easier if she ended her life. She knew she would just cause more trouble for her family and her friends. She knew that Jae wouldn't stop, that the war wouldn't end.

The only thing that would change is she wouldn't be part of it. And really, that would make her more of a coward than anything else.

Aware that Blair was already breathing deeply next to her, she decided that when they left this place, after they heard the last part of the story, that she was going to pretend like none of it had happened. She would go back to school. Back to her normal life.

Because she wasn't part of this. She didn't have magic. She wasn't special.

So why should she be involved at all?

Earth

Chapter One

Shubishi blinked, staring at the sky above him. Blue. A beautiful, crystal blue. Nothing like the skies of home. He tried to sit up, but his body would not obey him. It would not do as he commanded, and so he lay there, taking stock of every limb. His fingers twitched against his will, coming to life bit by bit. His ears picked up sounds. The gurgling of water. The twitter of birds dotting the sky.

The screaming.

He closed his eyes and reached out with his power, but even that would not listen to him. For the first time since he was young—and that was a very long time ago—he could not feel the souls of those around him. It did not panic him, however. He did not know what Death had done to him, but he knew it would not be permanent. It would take time for his body to respond. For his powers to return to his grasp. Already, he was able to control when his fingers twitched. He was able to curl his hand into a fist. To lift his arm from the hard ground beneath him.

The screaming grew louder.

Adelia?

He recognized her voice. He recognized many voices but there were fewer than he expected. Even staring up at the blue sky, even missing the color of his home, he had guessed that the council would be in an uproar.

The council was not there.

He pushed himself into a sitting position, staring around him. Beneath his hands, he crushed emerald green grass, and all around his body, blades danced in a light breeze. He breathed in. It even smelled different here. He'd been once before, searching for Death, but he'd never paid much attention to the minutia that made Earth so different. There was something on the air. Murky. Dense.

His legs trembled as he clambered to his feet. They were on a cliff. The eight of them. Beyond the cliff, a gentle river flowed by, fish leaping out in search of food. He cocked his head, neck creaking, and a groan left his lips.

"Where are we?"

They were the first words he could make out through the screaming. His eyes flickered to Adelia and Eran. Eran was comforting her, holding her in his arms as she cried. Then they flickered to Nina who was crouched on the ground next to Tori and ranting something in the language of her village, which Shubishi had yet to learn. Tori responded to her in kind, and the two scrambled to their feet, examining their surroundings. Next to them, Flora was in tears, apologizing over and over for whatever had happened to them. And Lior stood with his head in his hands, most likely overwhelmed by all the screaming internal voices.

As Shubishi's body came back under his command, and the colors of souls reappeared, he noticed that he felt different. It wasn't the most fantastical change, but it was there. A slight tinge to his soul. A slight tinge to everyone's soul. Whatever Death had done to them, it was more than just sending the to Earth. He focused on the other dimensions, just like he had when searching for Death, but found he couldn't leave this one. He was locked in place. Stuck forever on Earth.

Death could take your soul.

Death could create life.

Death could remove mortality.

He was a fantastical being, but this…this was something else.

"We should not have done anything!" Nina snapped at all of them. Maybe at none of them.

"He was going to punish Eran for something he had not done," Tori countered. "We had to do *something*."

"He is the living embodiment of *death*." Nina wrapped her arms around her body. Next to them, the peaceful river turned turbulent, waves splashing up the sides of the cliff. Nina took no notice. "We should not have challenged him. We have been abandoned. Lost. We know nothing about this place. Are we still immortal? I feel different. I feel wrong."

Shubishi wanted to explain that whatever Death had done to them, it hadn't been taking away their immortality, but before he could, his gaze landed on the last of them. The one who had changed the most out of all of them. With her black hair and red eyes, Shion stumbled to the edge of the cliff and stared out over the rushing waters. No one else took notice of her at first. They didn't pay attention to the way she stood up straight, her beautiful robes swaying in the wind, examining her hands.

Shubishi did. He watched her reach up to the silver crown atop her head and remove it. He watched the smile curl across her lips. He watched her soul, black as night, shift and shimmer as she used her newfound powers. The others did not notice until the crown shattered into a million pieces.

They went silent, startled by the sudden explosion of metal and gems.

"…Lady Shion?" Tori dared asked.

Shion did not answer. She reached up once more and one-by-one, pulled the pins out of her black hair. It fell to her waist, thick and wavy. Her pinned up, always perfect hair, swayed in the breeze and she closed her eyes. Her smile widened as she breathed in the murky air.

And then she laughed. Bells ringing out in the air. An undignified chortle that widened Shubishi's eyes. Shubishi had not heard her laugh. Ever. Even when she was a small child, she remained sullen and awkwardly calm, traumatized by the death of her people, bullied by her peers. She did not laugh. She did not grin with all of her teeth. She did not throw back her head and shake it, letting the locks of her beautiful hair swish back and forth.

"Has she gone mad?" Lior asked in a low voice. Adelia hushed him, but the question lingered on Shubishi's mind when Shion grabbed at her robes and stripped them off. They fell to the grass in a puddle and she stretched her bare arms out, clothed only in her undergarments.

The seven stared at her, some with dropped jaws, all with wide eyes.

"What are you doing?" Adelia sputtered out.

Still, Shion said nothing. More laughter burst from her lips and she ran, trampling grass, arms and legs a blur before she reached the edge off the cliff and leaped.

"SHION!"

Shubishi wasn't sure exactly who yelled, but he was not one of the voices. He merely stared at the place where she'd once stood and listened for the splash from her entering the river.

"Does she know how to swim?" Tori asked, whirling on Shubishi. He shook his head and she cursed. Tori struggled out of her clothes and dove in after Shion.

Shubishi didn't think. He ran down the hill toward the bank of the river and waited, panting, while Tori helped Shion to the river's edge. She was still laughing, water spilling from her mouth. Tori dragged her onto the shore, breathing heavily, and then glared at Shion.

"Stop laughing!" Tori smacked her on the arm. "This is not funny. We have been cast out. You have been cursed. All of us have been. We cannot go home. Why are you *still laughing*?"

Shion wiped water off her face and smiled at each of them.

"Do you not see?" she asked in a breathy voice. "I am free. I am…I am finally…finally free."

Realization dawned on Shubishi. For so long, some longer than others, they'd been contained. Rules governed their lives. Ones that Death had created without rhyme or reason. Rules that had made them all miserable in one way or another. They'd fought to keep peace among Vilaim who looked for some reason to be unhappy. Who threatened war over the smallest things. They had been part of the system that had oppressed them, and in the process, had oppressed those underneath them. Those who hadn't been lucky—or unlucky—enough to become immortal.

Shion had taken the brunt of it. For her entire life, she'd lived as a queen she'd never wanted to become. Trained to be perfect. Never a hair out of place.

Free.

She was free.

They were all free.

Standing at the edge of the river, the eight of them realized that the chains binding them had shattered. Death had tried to punish them, but instead he'd done them all a favor. They were free here. They didn't have to bend to his will. They didn't have to pretend to be happy on the council.

This moment didn't need to be negative. They didn't need to feel sorrow. Their tears dried up and smiles broke out among them.

None of them knew what was going to happen from here on

out. There were no rules to govern them. No council to demand their energy and attention. Nothing to keep them bound. They could have the relationships they wanted. The friendships they wanted. They could smile and laugh. They could say whatever pleased them.

Shubishi bowed his head. He may not have known what was going to happen to them from now on, but he did know that it was going to be an adventure.

Chapter Two

There are some things that are meant to be. Some things that are not meant to be. Some things that are in flux. There are incidents that bring out confusion. Some that bring about peace. There are times when events change without warnings. When you lose a friend. When you lose a lover. When you give up everything to stop a war you didn't know blazed on around you. Or maybe you are aware, but have conveniently turned a blind eye to the terror and frustration. To the death. The destruction.

We have told you much in this story, but at its core this is not a story of how the Iravata gained and lost their power. This is not a story of the war between the mage clans and the immortals. This is not the story of pain and suffering, of a grand scheme put into place long before most of us were born. We've told the story of Amir and Halise. The story of the Narumi and the Seshen. The story of the Gods.

We've told the story of us.

There are many stories we could tell you now of our time on Earth. Some you may know from the clans. Some you have grown up hearing, or have heard in the years since you discovered magic and the clans. Some of these stories would be so familiar to you, that you could recite them in your sleep.

The one we are about to tell, few know. And out of those who do, only some know the true story. Some of us do not know the full story. There are only some events we can recount. Some points of view we cannot relay.

This, here, that we are about to tell, is the story of a queen and a priest.

For nothing else matters. We could tell the story of everyone learning and practicing their powers. We could explain how the Iravata came about their name and their status. How they gained power and lost power all in the span of a few lifetimes. How they hid from humans for centuries, learning their language and their culture in order to blend in with those who most fit the physical appearances that match our own. How they traveled. Saw the world. Explored its beauty. Discovered powers unlike any they'd ever experienced back in their home.

Maybe another day. Maybe another time. Maybe when things are not so dire.

Those stories do not matter. They are filler, parts of our lives that mean little to us in the grand scheme of things. They are bedtime stories that we remember at times and forget at others.

The story of the queen and the priest, however, we have seared into our minds forever. Because this story is how we lost our dear friend. How we lost a war we never wanted to fight.

And how it came to be again.

This story is that of our lady, Queen Shion, and the mage priest Niran. How they met. How they became friends. How they fell in love.

How he betrayed everything their love stood for.

It all began a thousand years after the Iravata first stood on

Earth. After they'd explored their powers. After they'd explored the world and found their place in it. They had their name. They had their happiness. When a little boy made a flower for a beautiful woman with eyes as red as the king's rubies.

Chapter Three

Shion did not think much of the day when it happened. She lounged by the Mekong River, though it had other names at that time, and bathed in the heat of the sun. It'd been centuries since she and the other Iravata had come to Earth. Centuries since that day by the river when she'd destroyed her crown and realized her freedom. In that time, she'd grown accustomed to the ways of Earth. To the ways of humans. They were beautiful creatures, she'd decided. Simple, their own imaginations guiding them. They had their own histories, though those histories had yet to connect the way they do now.

She liked this simplicity. Following their desire for food and to survive, humans did not yet have the complications of the Vilaim. They would get there, she was sure, and get there they did, but for now it was simple. The mages lived separate with their magic and their stories, and the normal people, those without magic, did the same with different stories and troubles.

She was in some of those stories. A red-eyed demon who brought with her misfortune. Misunderstood ramblings of people who didn't understand immortality or the powers she possessed. Some may have hated the way they looked, but Shion did not. Every time she caught her reflection, sometimes in a mirror, sometimes in water, she smiled at her appearance. Her red eyes. Her pitch black hair, so dark that light disappeared into it. They were not a reminder of her curse—though she did not quite understand what her curse was—but instead a reminder of her freedom.

No longer did she look like a Seshen. No longer did Death have his obsession. She was no longer contained or isolated from her peers. There were no expectations of her to act a certain way.

She was no longer the queen of the Vilaim.

For the first time in her very long life, she was doing what she wanted when she wanted. She did not concern herself with the troubles of the world except for what interested her. Listening to stories by the firelight, hidden in shadows. Eating what food she desired in that moment. Learning any language she found beautiful. Speaking only when she wanted.

She did not have many friends on Earth. Only the Iravata, but that was enough. Shion had never been the most social of Vilaim, and that didn't change after her freedom. But now she didn't have to make excuses for her solitude, for her friends had lives of their own. A whole world to travel and explore. When she saw them, she was grateful, excited, pleased. When they left, she smiled too.

It was paradise.

On that day, a thousand years after their expulsion, Shion did not think much of the meeting. When she saw the little boy by the river. He was small in stature, even for a boy of that age in that time. He was thin from poverty, or maybe from neglect. She did not know, and she did not question it. Instead she cocked her head and watched him watch her, eyes wide from shock.

There was nothing particularly spectacular about the child except for one thing. One very important thing.

He had magic.

That was not uncommon in this part of the world. In any part of the world, really. Mages lived everywhere, but what was odd was that she was not near a mage tribe. Shion had come to the non-magical side of the river, desperate for a moment where no one would find her.

Except this little boy had. This small, thin, tanned, powerful little boy.

She stood, walking with the grace of a thousand queens, and crossed the field toward the little boy. He trembled, stone flower nestled in the grass at his feet. She crouched before him and lifted it, holding it out to him. He did not take it.

"This is beautiful," she said in his language.

The boy must have heard stories about her. He did not speak, but he did not run either. He stood, head bowed with trembling hands. A normal response from humans when they saw her. But there was something different about the boy. The way that he *did not* run from her.

"May I keep this?" Shion asked. He had created it from magic. A beautiful lotus flower carved so intricately and delicately that Shion thought it might have once been real.

The boy nodded, gaze still stuck to the ground.

Shion could not stop her smile. "Do you fear me?"

Again, he nodded, though this time accompanied with a step back. She didn't blame him, nor take offense to his fear. She had heard some of the stories told about her and her people, particularly the ones that mothers told to their children to keep them safe. Stories of monsters who came to take their souls if they were not careful.

She let out a soft laugh. She could not take a soul no matter how hard she tried. Shubishi might have been able to, but even he said that he never would. She trusted him. That he would not do anything to purposefully hurt the innocent humans they lived among.

Standing, she turned to return to her place by the river, but the little boy reached out and grabbed her skirt with one tiny hand. She paused and faced again him.

"Yes?"

"Are you a demon?" he asked in a quavering voice.

She cocked her head, crouching. Humans certainly thought she was a demon. An evil monster come from the depths of hell, and each had their own version of hell, to haunt them. Again, she didn't blame them. After all, no one had red eyes but those who came from evil, right?

"I am not a demon," she said.

"What are you?" His voice was barely above a whisper.

"Hm...." She did not know how to answer him. She was no longer a God, no longer a Vilaim. Some called her and her friends the Iravata, the immortals, but sometimes she wondered if that name fit either. Yes, they were immortal, but there was something wrong about the name. Something so distant. Tori laughed when she had learned of the name and said she would claim it. Shion was not so sure.

Instead of calling herself an Iravata, instead of giving the boy a name to hate, she held out the flower. It was small in her palm. A little stone lotus.

"I am a flower," she said. There was truth to her words. In some languages, that's what her name had come to mean, and in her history, Death had created her people from flowers.

"A flower?" he asked.

"Yes. Beautiful. Full of life. And very fragile." She wrapped her fingers around the stone flower and held it to her chest. "I am not someone to fear. I am merely a flower surviving in a world that she did not come from."

In her ear, she heard Adelia tell her not to expose so much to a human, but he was just a child.

The boy nodded. "A flower."

Shouts sounded in the distance. A frightened voice calling for someone. Shion smiled. "I think someone is looking for you."

"It's just my mom," he said, frowning.

Shion did not know of mothers. She had barely any memories of her own, and the last one turned her dreams into nightmares. She closed her eyes for a moment and let the memory of fire and smoke overtake her for a moment. When she opened her eyes, the boy still stood there, staring at her.

"What is your name?" she asked, not wanting to speak of mothers.

He shook his head. "I can't tell you."

She understood. "All right. Then I shall call you...Niran."

"Niran?" he scrunched up his nose. "That's a silly name."

"Maybe. But it is the name I give you."

There was another shout and he half-turned. "I gotta go. Mom sounds mad."

She nodded and he took off. She clutched the flower to her chest, staring after him, and a light laugh escaped her lips. While she knew she would never see the boy again, she knew she would remember this day. She would remember the flower. It was inconsequential. A simple meeting that would not change her. Still, it was not every day that she met someone who did not fear her enough to run.

Niran.

Standing, she turned back toward the river, she knew he would be someone of importance someday. She just did not know how important.

Chapter Four

That meeting was inconsequential for Shion. A fond memory that did not impact her life. She kept the flower, putting it in her home where it collected dust. She did not forget, but it was something that made her smile, rather than decide her future. She did not even tell her friends about it. What would they say? That she needed to be more careful? He was a child. Just a child.

But for Niran, that moment changed his life.

Niran had always known of his magic. Had his mother not been busy with the farm and chasing his many older siblings, then she may have also noticed, but Niran's life was filled with poverty. With children to help on the farm. With adults who went to sleep at night and did not have the energy to pay attention to all of the minutia of the kids' lives. He was the youngest. His older sisters raised him more than his mother, though he never minded. They were busy with their own lives, and he…and he knew from a very young age that his magic was something to hide.

His sisters knew there was something off with him, but they never guessed the reason. He was aloof. Always running off into the woods. But they didn't know about his magic. He kept it hidden, having heard all of his life the stories of people across the river. His people, his village, hated them. They made the other side of the river seem unapproachable. Dangerous. A place where children had their souls stolen from them if they gave their true name.

Then he met the woman by the river. He'd known immediately that she was dangerous. He'd heard the stories of the woman with red eyes. The demon. He'd thought that she would steal his soul or his magic, and then his sisters would cry. But she did not. She'd crouched before him and gave him a name. She'd called herself a flower and had told him that she was fragile.

He'd believed her.

In that moment, he'd believed that she was not as harsh as the stories told. He'd known, deep down, that she was someone to protect. She glided when she walked. Her voice was soft and gentle. Her eyes, while an odd color, did not hold any malice or anger. She'd seen him use his magic and she'd accepted him. She'd wrapped her smooth, pale hands around the flower and held it to her chest like it was the most magical and mystical thing in the world.

She was the first person besides himself that he'd ever met with magic. No one in his village practiced the ancient art. He hadn't known for sure that was true until he'd met her and felt the energy swirling beneath her skin. It drew him toward her, it made her appealing to him. He wanted to know more about her.

He hadn't gotten her name. She hadn't offered, and he'd been too scared to ask her for it. But she'd given him a name. Niran. Everlasting. A strange name. Not anything like the ones his family called him by.

It was a name he clung to.

When the others called him by other nicknames, he grew angry and demanded they call him "Niran." He never explained why. He never told anyone about the meeting by the river, but he insisted, and they listened. Before long, Niran *was* his name. It was the name he wanted to be known as. It was the name he felt most comfortable with. It became his identity.

It wasn't an obsession, he told himself. As he grew older, as he grew stronger both physically and with his magic, he told himself it wasn't an obsession. The dreams he had about her. The amount of times he thought of her. Of the beauty and grace in which she held herself. Of the way her voice seemed to shake when she'd called herself fragile. He remembered it all and he thought about it daily. He knew, absolutely knew, that he needed to find her. He needed to know her name.

She was across the river. That much was clear, but he wasn't sure how to get there. There were no boats that crossed the river. Everyone in his village was too afraid, and he was too cautious to ask. But his village, his family, it was too small for him. He did not feel at home there. And as he aged into a teenager, to a young man of eighteen, he realized that he needed to leave.

He taught himself to read and write. He taught himself the script of neighboring empires. The languages. The cultures. Whenever travelers came to the village, he hounded them to teach him. Maybe it was his magic, or maybe it was something about his eagerness, but all of them agreed.

His mother fretted. His sisters told him to stop looking beyond the farm and focus on his family.

But he couldn't. Because he needed to know who the woman with red eyes was.

At eighteen he left home. He traveled far and wide, growing as a person. And it was through these travels that he learned her name. He learned what she was. The red-eyed demon. The queen of the Iravata.

Lady Shion.

When he returned, two years later, a man of twenty, he knew it was time to cross the river.

For two years, he traveled the world, meeting people like him. Those who hid their secret from all who could not see the powers within them. But he could. He was always able to seek out the people who had powers, and from them he learned about the world of mages. It was extensive, larger than he'd ever imagined. People with magic were everywhere, and some were more powerful than others. He gathered, from conversations about his own magic, that he was particularly powerful, and that pleased him.

If he was particularly powerful, it meant that he would be able to protect her. His flower.

He practiced his magic. Growing stronger and stronger. Honing his skills until he knew it was time to cross the river. To find her. The queen of the Iravata. Lady Shion. The woman he knew he needed to see again, at least once.

He returned to his village a new man. A changed man. He was no longer the shy little boy who used to run into the forest to practice his magic and hide from his bullying older brothers, but instead a confident young man who knew where he belonged in this world. His sisters cried when they saw him, happy to have him back in the village. He did not tell them that he was leaving again.

The last night at home, he attended a wedding. It was his brother's wedding, one with festivities and excitement. It was a simple ceremony. Everything about their lives was simple, and he was not a simple man. He had greater things in his destiny. He knew that. He *felt* it, deep within his soul.

On the night of the party, everyone danced and music played

and people drank the alcohol they had been saving for this moment. Niran watched them from afar, unable to join in to the festivities. His mind was elsewhere. Wandering across the river. Before long, he found himself sneaking away from the party, toward the river. Toward the cliff where he had first met Lady Shion. He knew she would not be there. It was not like her to meddle in the affairs of mortals. With a party as loud as his brother's wedding, she would avoid the cliff.

But he was not going to look for her there. He was going to cross the river.

He stood on the banks of the river, trying to comprehend what life would be like on the other side. Where he would not have to hide his magic. Where he could be whatever he wanted to be. He didn't know if the others would accept him, but why would they not? He was like them. He belonged with them. They would give him everything he'd ever wanted.

Before he could step into the water, a voice called out to him. He turned, smiling at his older sister. She stood in the shadows of the trees with crossed arms. She was beautiful. The most beautiful of his sisters. He was surprised she hadn't found someone to marry, though he knew she would eventually. When the time was right for her.

She asked him if he was leaving. He could not answer her, and she crossed the clearing to stand next to him. "Do you think you'll ever return?"

Niran sighed. "I don't think so. This isn't where I belong."

"I know." She stared out at the river, watching the fish jump for the flies dancing atop the smooth water. "You've never belonged here. Even as a little boy you were always hiding from the rest of us."

In that moment, it wasn't clear to Niran if she knew of his magic or not. When he looked at her carefully, he noticed a spark hiding beneath the normality. It wasn't anything amazing. No, it wouldn't move mountains or dry up oceans, but it was there. A hint of magic deep within her soul.

They didn't speak of it. He didn't ask her if she knew about him or about her own powers. Instead, he bid her adieu and she went back to the party. He focused on the river again, knowing that this would be the last time he ever saw his older sister. For the rest of his life, he wondered what would happen to her. What she would say if she knew what he was planning to do. Not just cross the river, but find *her.*

Cautiously, he stepped into the water. His foot sunk beneath the surface, mud filling his toes. He grinned and took another step. Then another. And another. The water came up to his knees and he breathed in the musky smell of the Mekong River. He could swim across. He was an excellent swimmer. But, he realized that he didn't need to exhaust himself like that. The river was large. The moonlight shone down on him, and a smile crossed his face.

This time when he stepped, he lifted his foot above the water. Warmth spread to his toes and he placed it down on top of the surface, as though he were stepping on a stair. With great strength, he lifted himself atop the water, magic dancing from the tips of his fingers to the heels of his feet.

Magic. He'd never used his magic in such a way before. But he understood, and had understood for a long time now, that anything was possible if he could just imagine it. Magic was malleable. Magic was creative. He did not need to fear it anymore than he needed to fear those on the other side of the river.

With a whoop, he sprinted across the river, barefoot and excited. His heart raced, beating in his ears and he jumped in the air now and then. His lungs ached. His legs protested. But he continued, running under the light of the moon, until he reached the barrier keeping those without magic away.

He did not hesitate for even a second.

The world around him shifted. It was slight. A shimmer of color dancing on the trees. A slight orange tint to the moon. All around him, magic coated everything. The forest, the river, the grass, shimmered with energy.

Laughter spilled out.

For the first time in his life, despite all of his travels, despite all of his attempts to connect with his siblings, with his parents, he felt like he finally belonged somewhere. This wasn't a place with mages who hid among the humans. This was a place where he could be himself. Where he could use his magic without fear. He had only been on this side of the river for a few seconds. A minute. But it welcomed him, drawing him in closer and closer until he couldn't help but turn his back on his non-magical family forever.

The community accepted Niran instantly. They found him out by the river that same night and he showed them his powers. He explained that he was born to a non-magical family and was raised in their ways, but he'd taught himself magic. He told them stories of the places he'd gone to and the people he'd met who lived like he had these past twenty years.

They fawned over him. A mage from across the river. A young man with powers unlike any they'd seen before. Someone with green eyes. He didn't know, when he'd crossed the river, that they had been waiting for him since he was a small child. They'd heard a prophecy about him, brought to them from a seer who had crossed the oceans to see them: one day he would come to them and he would bring with him an era of peace.

When they told him this, he laughed. He didn't believe in

prophecies, and even if he did, he wasn't there to be their savior. They were merely a stepping stone for him. A chance to find the real reason he wanted to cross the river.

Still, he went along with what they wanted from him. They trained him in his magic. They sent him off to the priesthood. He didn't fight them. He may have been ready to cross the river, but if he wanted to protect Lady Shion, then he needed to become stronger. There was so much to learn about the world and he wanted to know as much as possible before he found her.

All he wanted out of life was to find her again. He wanted to show her how powerful he'd become. To thank her for giving him a name. To thank her for giving him a purpose in life.

He wanted, more than anything, to create another flower for her. This time, it wouldn't be made out of stone, but out of thin air. From his magic. He would give it to her and promise to protect her from the world for as long as he lived. It was his duty. His destiny.

He just knew it.

A year after he'd crossed the river, he was ready. Twenty-one and the strongest mage in the entire village, he knew it was time. He could have waited longer. He could have finished his training with the priesthood, but it was the right time. Something—someone— deep in the woods called to him. His friends warned him not to follow the voice. They told him stories of her wickedness and of her tricks.

He believed none of them.

Instead he wandered into the woods, telling no one where he was going, and followed the feeling. He followed the voice. He followed his instincts. He followed the magic trailing along the forest floor, knowing he would not stop searching for her until the day he died.

It didn't take him long to find her.

Shion sat on the edge of the river, dipping her feet into the cool water with closed eyes. The sun beat down on her face, warming her, causing sweat to drip down the back of her neck. She kicked her feet, splashing the water as the beautiful, colorful sky above her reminded her of home.

Well, her old home.

Earth had been home for so long now that she did not think much of the realm of the Iravata. It was her history, but not her future, and she was grateful every day that she had told Death the truth. Life had been so peaceful since that moment. Tori and Nina were off traveling together, wanting to explore more of the world now that humanity had grown and changed. Adelia, Lior, and Eran had gone to the tallest mountain on Earth in an attempt to climb it. Flora, kept close by Shubishi, went about healing humans in their sleep. And Shion was content. She knew she could live like this forever. Always happy. Always peaceful. She did not have a reason to hate the world and she actually looked forward to how the world would change.

She was free. From the grips of her past. From the pressure of being a Seshen. From the chains of Death.

Honestly, she never thought that things would change.

Until the day that a man approached her. Even with her eyes closed, she knew he walked up to her. She could sense his magic, sense that he was a powerful mage. She tensed, ready to flee. The last thing she wanted was for the peace between the mages and the Iravata to break. They did not speak, but the two groups had come to an understanding: the Iravata stayed out of their lives, and the mages did not try to hunt them.

But before she could flee, he called out to her, asking a question she was not expecting.

"Are you Lady Shion?"

The mages knew her name, but they rarely called her by it. When they met, they called her the queen or nothing at all. Startled, she turned to face the man, pushing herself to her feet in the same motion. It was a young man, no older than twenty or twenty-one. He wore the robes of a mage priest, though he did not look like he was comfortable in them. And there was something else about him...something about his jawline. Something about his eyes. It was familiar to her.

She hesitated. "Who are you?"

He bowed. "My name is Niran. I've come to make a request of you."

Niran. Niran. Niran. She knew that name. It was a memory from years ago, not a long time in the grand scheme of things, but long for a human. She had given a little boy that name, wanting to make him smile and feel at ease with her. She had wanted him to feel like he belonged somewhere as a mage growing up with non-magical folk.

"You made the flower," she said. It sat at home atop a shelf, gathering dust. Every now and then, before she went to sleep, she stared at it and wondered what had happened to the little boy who had made it for her. She had not realized so much time had passed since he was a child.

He smiled. A grin? "You remember."

"It is not often a child does not run from me screaming." She meant no harshness by this, but her words made Niran flinch and bow once more.

"Your eyes?" he asked in a low voice.

"Yes." Her eyes. Her aura. Her demeanor. It was too much for even the oldest of humans, much less children who were taught to be cautious of everything. Who had yet to experience the world and so everything was terrifying and new. She did not understand why his tone was so apologetic. What did he have to apologize for? She held her head high. "What is your request of me?"

He stood straight and took a step toward her, closing the distance between them. "I want to spend my time by your side."

She blinked. "You…what?"

He reached out and took her hand. She jerked it back. No one touched her without her permission. She was the queen. She was an Iravata. People ran from her. They did not take her hand.

"I want to spend my time by your side," Niran repeated.

"Why?" Shion asked. Mages did not want to spend time by her side. They wanted her gone from their lives. They feared her.

He stepped even closer, forcing her a step back. "You gave me my name."

Their eyes locked. Ruby red and jade green. He did not look away. Even the other Iravata looked away from her red eyes, reminded of their curse. But he did not. He held her gaze and smiled. She did not understand his motives. She was not sure why he wanted to spend time with her, but she decided that it was not going to hurt her. He was a human. He would die soon anyway.

Maybe it was a mistake. Maybe she should have thought harder about what she was letting him do. But the next time he reached out to take her hand, she let him.

Chapter Five

She did not realize what was going on at first. Because at first it was simple gestures. Flowers left for her at their meeting spot when she was too late. A display of magic in the middle of the night with beautiful colors dancing in the sky. Stories about his life. About the mage community that she did not dare visit herself. At first, she found his affections tedious. She did not understand what they were, or why he was doing all of this. No one had ever treated her this way before.

Before long, she found she liked the sound of his voice. She liked the way he kissed the back of her hand. She liked being with him.

The other Iravata did not approve of their friendship. They avoided humans whenever possible, sticking together as the only immortals on Earth. Humans were too different from them. They did not understand what it took to be immortal. To have the powers that the Iravata have. They had a bond that no one could break, having survived together for so long. Shubishi compared it to having a pet. Something to love for a short time, but not to get too attached to because eventually they would die.

Shion did not agree.

She'd always found humans interesting, but none had ever wanted to get close to her before Niran. She had found her peace, but there was always something missing from her life. Something she had never been able to put her finger on. At least, not until she met Niran. Not until he gave her flowers and put on shows for her and taught her language and culture. Not until they had spent so much time together, that she knew all of his stories. That being with him brought her a joy she had never imagined she would ever feel.

To him, she was not the queen of the Iravata. She was not the queen of the Vilaim. She was a woman. A red-eyed, black-haired woman who was more than just a crown.

Maybe that is why she fell for him. Maybe it was the way he smiled. Maybe it was the gentle way he held her hand as he led her through the jungle. How he would ask her about her day. About her friends in family. The way he took an interest in her. Not the crown, not her immortality or her position. But her. It reminded her of the day Tori broke through the shell and became her friend, but this was different. Her heart did not pound when she was with Tori. Her cheeks did not flush when Tori appeared at her side.

She did not understand what was happening. But before long, she realized that she felt something for him that she had never felt before.

Love.

She loved the mage priest from across the river.

It happened gradually. She would visit him once a week. Then twice. Three times. Four. Five. Six. Every day. She sought him out, wanting to be by his side. Wanting to hear his voice and hold his hand. It was a sweet year, one where they spent most of their time together. When he was not training, when she was not visiting her friends, they were together, exploring the world. With her magic, Shion took him everywhere. Everywhere he could not go by himself. Everywhere he had wanted to go all of his life. He saw so much, and her heart thumped in her ears when he smiled at her.

He was so young, and yet he seemed so old, as though he had lived a thousand lifetimes before. He had so much wisdom and so much love for the world. For her.

"You are going to get in trouble one of these days," Tori said. Her warning was lost on Shion, who merely smiled at her before returning to her preparations. An outing with Niran. It was the second this week that they had planned to travel to a new part of the world. One with snow.

Niran had never seen snow before.

"This man wants something from you, does he not?" Tori asked.

"Just my time," Shion hummed.

"That is what worries me." Tori sat on Shion's bed, holding the stone flower between her fingers. A fire blazed in the middle of the hut Shion called her home, her walls covered in art she had collected from all around the world. This world had not invented bound books yet, which she dearly missed, but she displayed as best as she could scrolls with poetry and written stories.

Shion sighed and brushed a comb through her hair. "Why does that worry you?"

"Because he is a human, and humans are only interested in what makes them happy. They are like the Vilaim in that way."

"So, you are telling me I cannot be friends with a human because he is like a Vilaim?" Shion rolled her eyes.

"Are you only friends?" Tori asked.

Shion hesitated for a second too long before saying, "Of course."

256

Tori did not believe her. "You know, I thought the same thing before Nina kissed me. I was convinced we were only friends, blind to her feelings. Blind to my own. Are you sure you do not love him? That he does not love you?"

"This is different," Shion protested, though her heart fluttered. "You two had known each other your entire lives. She has loved you from the time you were young. Niran and I are friends."

Still, Tori did not believe her. She dropped the subject, but remained worried for her friend. Shion had no experience with love or lovers. She had lived her entire life separated from everyone. She was susceptible to being tricked due to her innocence. Her lack of relationships throughout her life. Even with the other Iravata, her curse and her training as a queen made her stand above them. They may speak informally with her, but at the end of the day, they respected her in a way that they did not each other.

Once a queen, always a queen.

But, Tori figured, they had been through worse. Death had kicked them out of their home. He had cast them away to a foreign realm with different rules and new powers. They had adjusted to Earth. Whatever happened with Shion and this human mage, it would be over soon enough. A human's lifetime was not long enough for her to be concerned about. Unless…unless Shion fell in love and decided she wanted to have children.

Tori was not sure how that would work. It would make sense. Shion had always been alone. The last of her kind. If she wanted to have children…what would that entail? Was it even possible? What would that create? As far as Tori knew, no Vilaim, no God, had procreated with a human. That scared her, and she was not even sure why.

But Shion was not thinking of those things. She bid her friend goodbye and headed out into the jungle, tracing Niran's magic. It did not matter to her what Tori thought. It did not matter to her what the future held. She thought little of the consequences of her actions. She was in love. And she thought of little besides being by Niran's side.

Niran used his magic to shield her. He changed her eyes to brown. Her hair to shine with the same color. He dragged her away from their meeting spot and toward the mage village. Her nerves tingled her fingertips, but she let him take her anyway.

It was not like they could do anything to her, she had decided when he had proposed this idea. It was not like they could hurt her if they found out who she really was. And Niran was powerful. Powerful enough to hide her true features. The ones she had come to accept as her—the real her.

"They'll never notice us," Niran said with a confidence Shion wished she had.

"They'll never know who you are," he continued. "To them, you are a visiting mage. Come for the festival."

The festival. Niran had not stopped speaking of the festival for weeks. He was so excited to show her some of his culture. Not as an observer, but a participant. The culture was new to him as well, but he wasn't about to let her know how much that terrified him. It was part of why he wanted to show her. He wanted her to *experience* the joy and happiness that he experienced being with people like him. There was only so much he could explain to her, especially since he hadn't grown up with it. These people, the humans, were so different from her, but at the same time they were so similar. If she only looked like them, she could feel the joy. The happiness.

Shion laughed as they entered into the mages territory. A world with a sky the color of the rainbow. It reminded Shion of home.

The festival was bright. Alive. Torches were lit and the heavy beat of drums carried out a rhythm of dancing. And people did dance. They moved their limbs in beautiful waves, connecting with other humans, only to break away.

Shion hesitated. She did not know their dances. She only knew her own. But Niran pulled her into the crowd. The thumping of the drums matched her heartbeat and she breathed out as he spun her around. Another burst of laughter.

No one paid them any attention. As Niran had said, they thought she was a mage from another clan who had managed to travel all the way here. They thought of her and Niran as close friends. They did not know.

And she danced with him. She spun around, letting her loose hair fly, her skirt dance with the movement of her legs, and she allowed the drums to guide her. The drums, and Niran's hands touching her body with gentle, yet firm, expressions of dance.

Once they finished dancing, when the music stopped and the food was served, she could not stop speaking of the exhilaration. She could not stop her smile. The warmth in her stomach. For no one here knew who she was. They did not bow to her. They did not address her as a queen.

They saw her as their equal. And that had always been what she had wanted out of life.

Adelia and Eran came to visit her, having traveled for months on their own to various parts of the world where they fit in much easier. But they returned one day, visiting Shion in her home with gifts from across the world.

They spoke of their travels. Of this place with humans who

spoke very different languages and had very different customs. They encouraged Shion to go with them next time, to see how the world had changed since the first time they had explored the earth. But Shion could not go with them. Because she had already made plans. Important plans with Niran.

"Who is this Niran? Tori mentioned something about him. A human?" Adelia's questioning was too obvious. Shion knew they were there to try and convince her to stop spending time in the human's presence. That he would be bad for her. That this would lead to things none of them wanted.

Shion ignored their concerns.

"He is my friend," she admitted. "He shows me things that I could not see otherwise. You should have seen me, hidden among the mages during one of their festivals!"

Eran and Adelia exchanged glances, but they did not interfere. They offered again for Shion to come with them, but she turned them down. She invited them to stay with her, but they had to go. When they asked if they could meet Niran, she became nervous. If they met him, if he saw how they treated her....

Would he stop treating her like an equal and start treating her like a queen?

This time he took her to the base of a mountain. It was one she had been to before, but it looked new through his eyes. And it looked new to him through hers. They climbed, laughing and talking, showing each other little things the other might not have noticed.

Shion explained to him how the mountain looked before humans had moved onto it. And Niran explained to her the beauty of the temples and the shrines. She did not fight him. He didn't fight her. They worked together to climb to the top, and once they had, they watched the setting sun together.

"It is beautiful here," Shion said. "In my home, the setting sun looks different. It is not quite so…orange."

"Orange, and pink," he commented. "With some red and yellow."

She laughed. "Always so specific."

He beamed at her. She did not notice, focused too much on the scenery before her.

"My friends are worried about this friendship," she admitted to him when they had been sitting for quite some time.

Niran nodded and took her hand, pressing a light kiss to the back of it. Color rushed into her cheeks, and she looked away.

"I should meet them," he said. "They will see that we have a friendship that nothing can break."

But Shion did not think that would be so. She knew that once her friends met him, they would find all the reasons in the world to make sure that the two of them stayed separate. They disapproved of human interaction. Of becoming friends with them.

Shion did not want to hear from them about it. Not again.

"They will seek you out one day," Shion said. "When that day comes, I suggest that you run as fast as you can."

"You think I can't handle them?" He stood and waved his hand, bringing about a jolt of lighting from the clear sky. "I am the most powerful mage. I can take care of myself."

She was impressed by his show of power, but it was nothing, she knew, to the powers that she and her friends held. Niran had no idea what was coming for him when he finally met with the Iravata. He hardly knew of the powers that she, herself, possessed.

She never wanted to show him.

He sat back down and the two continued to talk, sitting just a little bit closer than before.

261

When Shubishi and Flora came to visit her, Shion knew what they were going to say before the words came out. The two of them had been exploring the coldest reaches of the earth, looking for signs of life to study. Now, they were sitting in her living room, without her having invited them in, and she told them straight out that she was friends with Niran.

Shubishi said nothing. He merely smiled and nodded.

On this particular day, Niran had planned something. He hadn't told Shion, he hadn't told his friends back at the mage camp. In fact, that mages still did not know that he rendezvoused with the queen of their enemy. They were unaware of how gentle she was. How kind and caring. They thought she brought death with her wherever she went. They were convinced that her friends were filled with misfortune, and it was easy for that misfortune to transfer to their bodies.

Niran didn't try and correct them. He knew little about the others, save for what Shion had told him during their conversations. She'd kept them separate from him for two years, and no matter how much he pushed, she wouldn't budge on that matter.

He hoped that this would change things.

He sensed her coming from a ways away. The way her magic mixed with the air was unmistakable. There was something so gentle, and yet so haunting about it. She'd seen so much in her long life, and yet….

Niran knew she longed to see more. To experience more. Which is why when she arrived at their meeting spot, and greeted her with a question.

She was not expecting it. Or maybe she had been. Maybe she'd been waiting for him to ask her this question for many moons now.

"Shion," he said, taking her soft hands, "do you love me?"

It was so brash. So quick. So unlike him. His hands were shaking. And Shion wondered if she had been waiting for him to ask this question, and for how long.

Did she love him, though? Did she feel for him what Tori and Nina felt for each other? Adelia and Eran? The love she had seen between Vilaim all of her life. Between the humans who married. What was love? How did one know they were in love, and how did one know when it was a relationship of convenience?

How could she possibly know of love when she had no experience with it in her past?

She thought briefly to what Death would say if he knew that she was thinking of these questions with a human. With someone who was not of Seshen birth. What would he say if he knew that she was no longer pure?

But he had changed her, had he not? He had taken away her eye color, her hair color, and he had sent her to Earth. He had removed all of her duties and severed the tie she had with her home.

What did it matter what he thought?

Niran took Shion's hands and pulled her closer. They stood on the edge of the river, the grass tickling their toes.

"I have loved you for so long," he said. "The way you dance. The way you speak. The way you sing and laugh and walk. Everything about you is perfect. You, as you are." He brushed hair out of her face. His fingers left tingles on her skin.

"I am not human," she reminded him. "I am cursed. I will never be able to give you the life that you want."

"You don't know the life that I want," he whispered, leaning in closer.

Her eyes fluttered closed. Never, in her long life, had she felt the turn in her stomach. Never, in her long life, had she let anyone get as close as Niran.

Never, in her long life, had she let someone kiss her. She did not understand the feelings behind it. She did not understand why it was so gentle and soft. She did not understand why she didn't pull away.

There was so much she did not understand, but she pushed those thoughts away and let him kiss her. She kissed him back. The two stood at the river's edge and broke a million laws of the universe.

When he pulled away, caressing her cheek, she smiled at him.

Happiness, she decided. "This is what happiness is, isn't it?"

He merely kissed her again.

During all of this time, Enya had been quiet. Yes, Enya. The woman who had gotten them sent to earth. The woman who had made it clear to anyone, once the Iravata disappeared, that she was in charge now. They listened to her. They did as she said.

But she was never happy with her position in life. Because every day of her reign, she looked at the ring on her finger and knew that Shion had taken something from her. Shubishi. The one she knew was supposed to be hers. The reason she had become immortal in the first place.

Shubishi was the reason for all of her ambition. The reason she was able to do what she wanted to do.

And he was on earth. Far away, never able to return.

But she could go to him.

And go to him she did. For hundreds of years, she made secret trips to him, promising to return him home if he would only comply to her wishes. If only he would give up his connection to Shion and pledge his loyalty to her.

But he refused. Each time she visited him, he refused her advances. He refused her offers. He did not want to return home. He had learned all he could about the Vilaim and the world they lived in. This one, Earth, was far more interesting.

Shion was far more interesting.

Enya understood this. He never tried to hide it. So, she did the only thing she could think to do. She stalked Shion. Watched her from afar. Got to know her habits and her friends. She watched her fall in love with the human being, and she knew that this was what she could use against her.

Enya knew, from that very moment, that she could get Shubishi to come with her. If only she could get rid of Shion.

And so, she hatched a plan.

Chapter Six

Shion was at home when the fires started. She did not know what was happening at first. The poem she was reading had caught her attention, written in such beautiful characters that she was fascinated. Niran had been teaching her this language from the place they called the middle country, and she loved every moment of it. But then she smelled smoke. But then she felt the heat.

Confused, she bolted from her bed and burst out into the jungle. Flames licked up the trees, consuming them in a circle around her home. She froze. There were fires now and then in the jungle, but never like this. Never so harsh and burning so bright. They were not normal fires.

That is when she heard the screaming. The angry mages appearing from the fire, holding up spears and staffs, their magic swirling in the air.

She should have run the minute she saw the fire, but memories consumed her. Memories of fire. Never ending fire. Heat so blazing it burned her lungs. A hand reaching from the flames to take her. Her eyes widened and she sunk to her knees, head in her hands as a scream attempted to burst from her throat. There was no sound, but she felt it in her soul. The fear. The anger. The chanting and beating drums of the mages.

Without thinking, she fled. The mages had assumed she could only run, but they did not know all of her powers. She disappeared from her home. Her beautiful, well-hidden home, and appeared far away. Half a world away on the small island in the middle of the pacific that Nina and Tori called their home.

She was in tears.

Nina and Tori found her outside, wrapped up in her arms, shaking. Both women dashed to her side, wanting to comfort her. It took a while to calm her down. To get coherent words out of her. Nina brought with her a cup of clear water from the waterfall at the center of their island. Tori held Shion and whispered that she was okay now. She was safe.

They were all safe.

But Shion did not think they were. How had the mages found her home? It was deep in the jungle and Adelia's magic protected it. Her own magic protected it. The only way anyone could have found it would be if she had shown it to them.

"What happened?" Tori asked once Shion had stopped sobbing.

"Fire," Shion said. "They lit everything on fire. My home. My collections. They are all gone." There was no time to save anything. Not even the stone flower Niran had made for her. All of her prizes, all of her collections, all of her poems and scrolls. The art. It was gone.

"That bastard!" Tori stood. "I am going to end him."

"No!" Shion grabbed her hand. "It was not Niran. He did not know where I lived. I always met him elsewhere. I never brought him to my home."

Even though they were lovers, even though he was her friend, she had never been willing to give up her safety. Her privacy. He knew she lived somewhere in the jungle, but she had never shown him where, afraid that someone might follow them. Afraid that the mages would discover where she lived.

"Come inside," Nina said in a gentle voice. "Drink some water. You are safe here."

They were not safe there. It did not take long for them to realize that there were mages on the island. The island protected by Adelia's magic. By Tori and Nina's magic. The mages should not have been able to get there, even if they had learned of the location. But they were. They marched along the beach toward the house. A different clan than the one that had attacked Shion. These mages were native to the surrounding islands. Ones that Nina and Tori had observed but never interacted with, afraid of a misunderstanding.

"How did they find us?" Tori asked.

"I do not know, but we should flee," Nina said.

Before the mages could set their home on fire, though they held torches in their hands, the three women disappeared from the island and appeared in the snowy, abandoned wasteland of the far south. No human would follow them there. In her mind, Shion let the others know where they were and before long, all eight of the Iravata were standing around in a circle, shivering.

"What is going on!" Tori screamed.

"I do not know," Adelia said.

"Why are they attacking us?"

"Something must have changed," Nina added. "They have always hated us. Always feared us, though we have done nothing to them."

"What changed?"

"I do not know."

"We have to do something to make it stop."

"They cannot harm us."

"They can make our lives miserable here, just like they were back home."

"If we just wait, they will die and we can go back to normal. Humans do not live for very long."

"I do not think that will happen! They were chanting for our heads. Their fear and hatred will spread through the generations. We will never be safe again."

"Then what do you suggest?"

Shion stood next to the arguing Iravata, legs trembling. They were safe, she kept telling herself. She could not die. She could not be burned up like her mother had been. All of her people had been. And yet she could not help but feel the fear. It was something she had never had to face before. Her own mortality. She had been so young when Death had made her immortal and it was not something she had had to worry about since.

But those moments still haunted her. The fire still haunted her.

She stared out across the icy plains and considered how this could have happened. Had Niran somehow found her home? Had he betrayed her? Their love? Had he really been using her?

As her friends continued to argue, she turned and walked away. None of them noticed her leave, all still angry and frustrated, and she continued on, disappearing to her home. The mages were gone now, and her house was nothing more than a pile of ashes. The only thing that remained was the stone lotus sitting in the center, untouched.

Anger burned in her stomach. She turned heel and stormed into the jungle. Away from her home. Away from the destroyed, dead trees. She rushed to their meeting spot. Any minute now she was supposed to meet Niran there, and she knew she had to confront him. He *would* tell her what happened, even if it ruined everything. Even if she lost her temper with him.

He was late. He was never late.

She waited for hours for him, sitting with the patience of an immortal. She did not need to eat or sleep. All she needed was to wait. Time was on her side here.

When he arrived, she stood and stared at him. He stared at her. She did not speak, but she did not have to. Because he knew what was wrong.

It wasn't until he left his hut for the day that Niran realized there was something wrong. He'd woken up like every day, ready to do his priest chores, to practice his magic, and to meet with Shion. She was everything to him. A bright light in a dark world. Without her, he didn't know what he would do with himself. She was the reason he got up in the morning, and the reason he fell asleep with a smile.

He'd thought, up until that day, that he would grow old loving her. That nothing would ever break the two of them apart. He loved her more than life itself.

But the moment he stepped outside his hut, he knew something had changed. There were whispers on the streets. People avoided eye contact with one another. Niran stopped in his tracks and watched the other mages prepare for…something.

"What's happening?" Niran asked a friend.

"It's the queen of the Iravata," he said in a low whisper. "She has brought death to our village."

Niran's brow furrowed. "Who died?"

"Our leader!" His friend clenched his fists and stared toward the gathering mages.

Niran knew that it could not have been Shion. She was too gentle of a soul to hurt anyone, much less bring death to someone as important as the leader of the mage village. But he kept his mouth shut, not wanting to give away that he knew Shion.

His friend continued. "A mysterious figure came to the village this morning after we found him dead. She said that the queen of the Iravata had been plotting to overthrow our village for years, now, and this was only the beginning. She gave us a way to find her. She said to follow the signs."

"The signs?"

"She didn't clarify. But an hour ago, the trackers picked up a mysterious energy. One he'd felt before but couldn't place."

Niran's stomach settled into his gut. He had changed the way Shion looked, but he couldn't change her magic. The tracker recognized her energy because she'd been here before. He bit the inside of his lip, not wanting to speak out. To tell them that they shouldn't do anything. That she was too dangerous to hunt.

But they believed that she'd killed their leader. This mysterious woman, whoever she was, had convinced them of the impossible. Shion would never harm anyone.

Shion wouldn't.

"We're going to find her," his friend said. "We're going to chase her out of or territory once and for all. She will no longer bring death to our doorsteps. Once we find her, and erase her from existence, we will do the same with her friends. All eight of them. The woman said there were eight of them."

"They're immortal," Niran said, voice weak. "There's nothing we can do to them."

His friend shook his head. "The stranger told us there *is* a way. But she's waiting for the right person to give it to."

In their talks, Shion had mentioned Enya. A woman who hated her for something her parents and grandparents and great grandparents had done. Niran didn't make the connection right then, but the memory of Shion talking about *someone* who hated her flickered in his mind and he knew that he needed to get out of there and find her. He needed to make sure she was safe. That she was all right. He needed to warn her.

The Iravata didn't want to harm anyone. They wanted to exist in the world and never worry about persecution or rules that kept them oppressed. They wanted freedom, same as anyone on Earth.

So, who was causing them trouble? And why? Why would someone care enough to do this?

He excused himself from his friends and left, needing to find her. But he didn't get very far before the mages gathered together and marched off to burn her home to the ground.

He explained all of this to Shion while she sat on the rock, staring at him with cold eyes. He was late, he explained, because he had been searching for her. It was not until he felt her energy here that he knew she had come back from hiding. He knew how it looked. For the first time in her life, she had let someone get this close to her, and now the mages were attacking her and her friends. He pleaded with her to believe him.

And the thing was, she did.

He had never given her a reason to doubt him, and she had never believed it was him to begin with. Her anger shifted. It was no longer directed at him, but instead at herself for giving in to the idea that he was behind this coordinated attack.

The coolness disappeared from behind her eyes and she stared into the jungle, hoping that the mages would not search for her here.

"Who is this mysterious woman," she wondered aloud.

"I don't know." He took her hands and pulled her to her feet, gripping them tightly. "But I will find out and I will put a stop to this."

He did not put a stop to it.

It only got worse.

No matter where any of the Iravata went, the mages found them. They hunted the Iravata down and attempted to kill them in every way they could think of. Often, normal humans were caught in the crosshairs and many died. The Iravata tried to hide, but it did not matter. Somehow, in some way, the mages could track them now. The only solace they took was that they could not die, but the mages eventually would. They would eventually forget about the Iravata.

The Iravata just needed to run.

For two long years, the Iravata ran. The mages fought. The Iravata had nowhere to hide. At one point, they'd captured Adelia and tormented her, trying to get information out of her about the whereabouts of the queen. Asking her how she could die.

Tori saved her in a blaze of frustration and glory. But that only made things worse. The mages found their dead kin and banded together. No longer were they separate clans, but one large group bound together by a common hatred of the immortals. Of the queen with the red eyes.

During all of this, Niran tried to convince the mages to return to peace. There was nothing any of them could do to the immortals, and there was no proof that they had caused the disasters or the deaths. But as it is with war, the blood had stained their eyes and made them blind to the logic behind Niran's words. They continued their hunt, desperate to rid the world of the Gray Spirits.

During this year, Shion did not feel safe being with Niran. She did not want the mages to discover their relationship and make things worse for everyone. If they did not listen to him now, how would they feel if they knew that he'd bedded the queen?

For a year they met scarcely and always in secret.

Until one day when it was too much for her to handle.

Chapter Seven

Thing did not happen suddenly. They built up over a period of months. A short time in the Iravata's life, but no less important. Shion's frustration did not happen suddenly. Her anger built over time until it was all unleashed. Enya had not planned on this. She had not planned on things going her way at all. She had honestly thought more of the humans. She had not realized they would be so easy to manipulate. So quick to anger.

But she did not mind. The more damage they did, the less she had to do. All she needed now was for one of the Iravata to snap. For Niran to lose his trust in Shion and the Iravata he had been fighting so hard for the past few years.

And that day happened. And when that day happened, everything fell to pieces. The bonds fell apart. The lovers split. The earth changed forever.

Shion sat in one of the mage temples. She knew that they would not look for her there. They were convinced that she and her friends were incapable of entering their holy sites, and they all took advantage of that, hiding when they could.

They were exhausted. Physically they were as healthy as ever, but mentally they were drained. Constantly being chased. Constantly being in danger. Never being able to escape the world they had never wanted to come to in the first place.

It was the first time any of them had wanted to go home.

At least there, they were respected. Or, had been respected. But they had ruined that, and now their paradise here was ruined. Nothing they did would ever be enough.

That was, until the mages sent out a message. One for all to hear.

Give us the queen and we'll leave you alone.

It was about her again. Everything always came back to her. It did not matter how she tried to run from it, she would always be the queen. They would always want her, not the others. They wanted to know how to kill her. To keep her away from her friends.

Give us the queen and we'll leave you alone.

She didn't want to go to them, but she knew she had little choice. She couldn't see her friends suffer anymore.

The door creaked open.

She panicked.

Had they found her? Did they know that she and her friends could enter their safe haven?

Without thinking, she attacked. A tightly wound spring waiting for danger. Luckily for her, and for Niran, she missed, but she did not calm down when she saw it was him. All these years he had been insisting that he was on her side, but was that true?

"Go away!" she screamed at him.

"Shion," he muttered, stepping forward. "I'm here to help. I think I might know a way to get the mages off your back."

"No." She backed away, nearly knocking over the altar. "You are not helping, you are hurting. They must be finding us through you. They must be!"

This was the first time she had snapped this at him, but he was not shocked to hear it. He wouldn't have trusted her either after this long. But he knew the truth. He knew that he spent day after day trying to convince the mages to let the war go. It was getting to the point where they no longer trusted him. Him and his power. They wanted to use it for their own means but he didn't want to let them. He refused to let them.

"My love," he said, voice pleading. "Please, listen to me. If you disappear–"

"I should not have to disappear!" Her scream echoed in the temple, and with it, the building shook. Shion breathed out, staring at her trembling hands. She'd never, not since arriving on Earth, tried out the full use of her powers. But here they were. Coming out. Her anger. Her curse.

"Shion...."

"Go away!" Her magic exploded out of her, knocking Niran out of the temple. It crumbled around her, missing her by mere centimeters. Part of her immortality, she assumed. Part of her curse.

Her curse to live on this earth and never be happy. Anytime she tried to find happiness, something got in the way. When she made a friend, that friend was used against her. When she tried to make a life here, when she had fallen in love, her family was in danger.

No matter what she did, no matter how far she ran, she would not be able to be happy.

She fled.

Niran stared at the crumbling temple, shocked by the power of his lover. He'd thought he was powerful. He'd thought he was the strongest mage in all of existence. But Shion outclassed him. She hadn't even tried. And he'd felt her magic. It had been so little of it destroying the temple, knocking him out. To her, it was no different than lifting a finger.

She was dangerous. He'd known this, but he'd never thought she would use that power on him. On anyone. But here she was, destroying one of the finest temples in all of the land, leaving him bleeding and bruised outside.

"I told you."

It was a voice Niran didn't know. He jumped to his feet and spun around, coming face to face with a pair of blue eyes. A swirl of red hair. Cheeks pink like the petals of cherry blossoms. Niran froze and stared at her, stunned by her beauty and her rarity.

"I told all of you," the woman said, stepping around Niran. "The queen is dangerous. She and her friends have caused so much havoc across the world. It is amazing, really, that you cannot see through her act."

This was the woman who had been telling the mages where to go. But why did she show herself to him now? She'd never done that before. She'd appeared in front of every other member of the mage clan except for him.

Unless....

"You're not a mage," Niran noticed.

The woman chuckled. "Why no. I am not. I am something better than a mage. Something better than an Iravata."

She walked past him, touching his shoulder with long, slender fingers. "I, my little Niran, am a god."

Niran couldn't help his snort of derision. "I don't believe in gods."

"You believe in magic," the woman said, continuing to circle him. "You see magic. You see the immortals. You know that things outside of your world exist. Why not gods? Why are we impossible, when everything else is possible?"

Niran didn't know what to say. Her logic made sense, and that made him uncomfortable.

"My name is Enya," the woman said. She stopped in front of him and held out a hand. He wasn't sure what she wanted him to do with it, so he ignored it and stepped away from her. He recognized the name from Shion's stories. It all came back to him. The things this woman had done to hurt Shion. The hatred she held for her.

"You're the one who has been hurting Shion," he said. "Why?"

"*I* am not hurting her," Enya said. "She is hurting herself. It is her curse, you see."

"Her curse?"

"The red eyes? The black hair?" Enya tapped her cheek. "Her eyes used to be like mine, you see. And her hair was brown like the soft dirt beneath our feet. But she made a mistake. She angered the wrong person and now she lives, cursed. Her power will only grow, and it will only continue to bring misery to the people around her."

Enya sighed. "It is a sad fate, really. I wish something else for her, but the only way to make things right is to end her life."

Niran watched as Enya walked away from him, toward the jungle. He hesitated, but followed, wanting to know more. Before today, he might not have believed Enya, but he'd seen what Shion could do. He'd seen the shock on her face when it happened.

She didn't know what was happening to her. And that scared him.

When they reached a stone in the middle of a clearing, Enya sat down and held out her hands. In them rested a leather sheathed knife with a bamboo handle.

"This can kill her," Enya said.

"She's immortal."

"It will work." A twinkle flashed through Enya's eyes. "Trust me, young Niran. I know what I'm doing."

And she did. The knife could, in fact, kill an immortal. It was infused with so much magic, so much anger, and so much pain, that

278

it could destroy any soul it came in contact with. Not just kill the person, but destroy every aspect of their soul.

A way to kill an immortal.

"Take it," Enya said. "I have been waiting for someone who will use it. Who can get close enough to the queen. And that person is you."

"But why?" Niran asked. "I can't kill her. She is—"

"Dangerous," Enya said, voice growing tight. "I know how you feel about her. I've been watching the two of you. Falling in love with a demon…you could not have known better, but I needed you to see it for yourself. I needed you to see how dangerous she could become."

Niran wasn't sure he believed Enya, but he knew that if he didn't take the knife, someone else would. He reached out and snatched it from her hands. The magic of it melded with his hand and he gasped.

"Good boy," Enya said. "I know that it will be difficult, but it is the right thing to do."

And then she disappeared.

Niran stood there, quietly, and tried to understand what just happened. Why a God had visited him. Why she cared what happened with Shion. There was so much to the story he did not have. An entire history of life that led up to the moment she gave him the knife.

And he knew almost none of it.

Shion gasped for air between sobs. She had lost control of her powers. She had never, in her entire life, lost control of her powers. She had not even realized she had them, to be perfectly honest.

She did not know what to do. She hid away in another temple, sobbing in the corner when a voice called out to her. A gentle, sweet, familiar voice.

"Lady Shion," Enya said, appearing out of thin air.

Shion's stomach dropped. Had she been behind all of this?

"Enya." Shion wiped away her tears. She stood and faced the woman who had caused all that fuss years ago. Who had slipped in unnoticed. Who must have known what was going. If she did not, why had she appeared?

"It has been a long time, my queen," Enya said with a bow. "I was wondering what had happened to you and your...friends."

"Why are you here?" Shion asked. "Go back to the Vilaim. Be their leader. Just leave me alone."

"Ah, but you see, I cannot." She stepped forward until she was on the same step as Shion. "Because I have grown interested in this world, and I know that you and your existence will, in time, taint it. Just as you had tainted our world."

"I did not taint our world," Shion protested. But deep down, she wondered if that was true. The Seshen people had caused all the problems in the world. The social classes. The slavery. The wars. It was because of her people. Her existence could have made everything worse, and she never would have known.

Enya shrugged. "If you say so. But you are tainting this one. You are making things worse for everyone here, including your... friends."

Shion grimaced. "There is nothing I can do about that. I exist. I have no control over that. If it had been up to me, I would have died a very long time ago."

"But it is up to you now," Enya whispered.

Shion froze. What did she mean? Had she found a way to die? A way to never deal with this world again?

"There is a knife," Enya said, backing away. "I've given it to the most powerful mage in the world. In his hands, he should be able to end your life. The life you never wanted. The life that is causing everyone trouble."

"But—"

"No buts," Enya interrupted. "Just sweet relief. When he confronts you, I suggest going along with what he wants. Which is to end your life. To end this war. Because if he kills you, then the mages will be satisfied. They will leave the rest of your friends alone."

"How do you know any of this?" Shion asked.

"Because I am smart." Enya turned to her. "Because I know things. Because I have always been deserving of being a god, and you never have been. I pay attention. I care about our people. You just wanted to die. Now you have your chance. Do not squander it."

And then she disappeared.

Shion sank to her knees again, uncertain. She did not realize how much she had gotten lost in her thoughts, trying to understand what Enya had said and what it meant for her, until Tori shook her back into the real world.

"Shion!" Tori screamed.

Shion blinked and stared up at her friend.

"What is going on?" Tori asked. "Why are you just sitting here? We cannot stay still for too long. Already the mages are on their way. They caught wind that we can enter their temples."

"No," Shion whispered. It was Enya doing all of this, she knew it. It was not Niran. It was Enya. But Enya had given Niran the knife, and he…of all the people in the world, he was the only one she had begun to trust outside of her seven immortals.

"We have to go," Tori said, but Shion did not budge.

"I have to give myself up," Shion said.

Tori froze. "What?"

"I have to do it." There was no other option. This was not going to end. Enya was not going to let it end. "It will not be bad. You will all learn to live without me. But you will live and in peace. They will not bother you anymore."

Tori scoffed. "You are talking nonsense."

"I am not." Shion's determination grew with each passing second. Let them find her. Let them see who she was.

"Shion, I am not going to let you give yourself up to them." Tori grabbed Shion's arm tightly. "I love you too much to put you through that. Adelia...Adelia still has not recovered, and there is no saying that she will anytime soon. They are ruthless. They are monsters."

"To them *we* are monsters."

"But we are not." Tori was pleading.

Shion had made up her mind. "I am going to do it. To protect all of you."

"I will not let you."

"You cannot stop me."

"I can try my best!" Tori summoned plants from the ground. "I will take you wherever I have to go. We will disappear. They will not be able to find us. Soon they will forget and we can go on with our lives. We can disappear."

"You can disappear!" Shion snapped. "I cannot. Do you not see my eyes? No matter where you go on this earth, no one will have red eyes. No one back home had red eyes either. I am a freak, Tori. I cannot escape. But I can do this."

"No!" Tori grabbed Shion by the arms. "Please, be rational."

"I am being rational!" Shion ripped herself from Tori's arms. "I am dangerous. I am unstable. I am unsafe."

"No you are not!"

"Yes, I am!" The words flew out with the magic. Unlike before, when she'd merely knocked Niran out of the temple, her magic cut through Tori like knives through butter. Tori gasped and flew back, hitting the wall and crumpling to the ground.

Blood splattered on Shion's body. Her face. Her hands. Her clothes. She stared down at them, only to hear a scream. She looked up. Nina, in tears, stood over her lover.

"Nina," Shion gasped.

"You monster!" Nina snapped. She had never liked Shion as the others did. She had always found her strange and alienating. "You demon. What did you do? How could you have done this?"

Trembling, Shion stepped back. Another step. Another. Another. Until she was racing out the back, Nina screaming after her.

And for the second time that night, she fled.

Chapter Nine

Her feet matched the rhythmic thump of her heart. Thick underbrush nicked her bare soles, laying out a trail of blood in her wake. Every one of her muscles screamed for her to abandon the flight. Her throat stung with iron, pulsing with each breath.

Logic begged her to stop.

Fear propelled her forward.

A root caught her ankle, wrapping around her bare skin with a vicious grip. Yelping, she plowed into the soil. Branches nicked at her porcelain skin. After spitting out a mouthful of dirt, paralysis consumed her limbs. It trapped her to the ground, black hair splayed around her head. Every breath came with a wheeze. Each thump of her heart pounded against her temple.

There was nothing left except to lay there and wait. She had committed the greatest sin. Anger had consumed her and forced her into violence.

Fate had arrived to punish her.

Her life was going to end.

She closed her eyes and listened. The forests she had called home for decades welcomed her into the silence of the night. The only sound was a rumbling current from nearby. It caught her attention.

Water.

She wanted to see water one last time.

Pushing herself to her knees, she inhaled a deep musk. All she could manage was a crawl. Her weak, shaking fingers dug into the ground and pulled her forward. Inch by inch she crawled, thinking of only the river. Water was the purest source of life, something to give her hope.

She hauled herself to her feet, strength returning for one last moment of regality. Back straight, head forward, she continued, holding onto trees to keep from stumbling. The moon was her source of light. It mocked her, taunting every sin she had committed from high up on its throne of stars.

"You failed," it jeered. *"Your family suffers. The war continues."*

The river was black. During the day, it was brown and gray, matching the mud beneath. At times, when the sun hit right, it shone a bright blue. Warm colors. Friendly.

Black was empty. Black was cold. It was everything people hated. What she feared.

She let go of the last tree and moved into the chilled water. When her knees brushed the water's surface, she halted. Her joints relished in the relief from muggy heat. The water cleansed her of her fear and anger. It washed away anxiety. It brought a moment of clarity. She reached down into the river and scrubbed her dirt stained hands until her porcelain skin was clean.

With the dirt came blood, tainting the river with its foul history.

The sight tugged forward a long ago abandoned emotion. Dry sobs racked her body. She squeezed her crimson eyes tight and wrapped her arms around her chest. Weakness was the last thing she could allow. Her family needed strength. They needed their drowning queen.

It wasn't until a warm energy pricked at her supernatural senses that she looked up from the water. Swirling power nicked at her back, begging her to turn and face destiny.

He stood on the bank of the river. His black hair was covered by a straw hat, beneath which a pair of green eyes watched her quietly. Violet robes cloaked his body, signifying his position in the mage's court. A priest. The highest rank.

Shion stared at the man she had called her lover and tears spilled from her eyes. "She gave it to you."

Niran nodded. He pulled out the knife and unsheathed it, letting the moonlight reflect off the blade. Markings on it, ancient markings, glowed a light blue. "I don't know what to do, Shion. Are you...are you evil?"

"No," Shion said. "I am not evil. I...." She thought back to the way she had hurt her friend. How she had hurt Niran. "I do not know what is wrong with me."

"Would the world be better off without you?" he asked. "Is Enya right?"

Shion could not answer him. Because she did not know.

"I could kill you with this," Niran said. "Is that what you want? I know you never wanted immortality. I know you've longed to not live. I know this. I know you. I *know you.*"

And he did know her. He knew her better than anyone ever had. She had shared things with him she had never shared with anyone else in her entire life. He was her confidant. He was her lover. He was Niran, the man who she'd fallen in love with, despite being the last Seshen. Despite being cursed.

She could never be happy.

Niran crossed the way and placed a hand on her cheek, brushing hair away from her eyes.

"I don't want you to die," he whispered.

"You gave me a reason to live," she replied.

He breathed out and returned the knife to its sheath.

"But I am dangerous," Shion said. "And maybe…maybe I am not meant to exist anymore. Maybe I am here only to bring pain and suffering to the people around me." Tears welled in her eyes. "It is okay. You can do it. I know it is the right thing."

She was determined.

He backed away, backing onto the bank of the river. He reached into the folds of his robes again, but didn't pull out the knife. Instead, he bowed his head and began chanting. Shion did not recognize the language, which was abnormal for her.

What she did recognize, however, was a spell. She glanced down at the water at her feet as it rose into the air. She felt the seal before she saw it. It hardened her feet and she knew he wasn't going to kill her.

She reached out a hand, wanting to beg him to change his mind, to end her life, but he didn't respond to it. She pulled it back to her chest and bowed her head. A single tear ran down her cheek, and as darkness overcame her, she whispered, "I am sorry."

Chapter Nine

They found her in the morning light. The Iravata arrived at the sight of her sealed body, and they wailed.

Tori, healed by her immortality and Flora, fell to her knees and screamed in anger.

Nina, feeling guilty for what she had called Shion, sobbed and hugged her wife.

Adelia, still broken from her torture, let a single tear drip down her face, while Eran held her and tried to hold back his own tears.

Flora was too shocked to react.

Lior reached forward and touched the stone cheek of their queen, wanting to read her thoughts.

Finding nothing.

And Shubishi bowed his head. For he had known this would happen. He had known there was nothing any of them could do to stop it. And he had regretted not doing something about Enya when he had possibly had a chance. Taken her offer. Done something to stop this.

Even though he knew it would have meant nothing.

"I will kill him," Tori said. "I will kill Niran. His blood is mine."

But before they could do anything with Niran, they had to bury their queen in hopes that one day, somehow, they would find a way to unseal her. That they would find a way to get their friend back.

When Niran returned to the mage village, his stomach turned at the weight of what he'd done. Sealed away the queen. Stopped the war, but at what cost? He hadn't killed her. He knew that Enya would be angry with him for not doing as she asked, but he couldn't do it.

He couldn't kill the one he loved. No matter how much she begged for it. No matter how many times she told him it was for the best, he couldn't kill the one he loved.

But she was gone now. Forever sealed in stone.

"What happened?" one of the mages asked.

"Did you kill her?"

"Can we see the knife?"

Word had spread. He had not spread it. Enya must have.

He was brought in front of the mage council. His eyes dead. His soul wanting to escape. There was no life in his words when he said, "She is gone. The war is over. The Iravata will never harm us again."

They had never harmed them to begin with.

But the mages didn't care about truth. They only cared about the fantasy they'd created. They cheered for the death of the queen, not realizing that she was still alive. They didn't know that she'd been sealed away. They called Niran a hero. They offered to make him the leader of the clan. They said that his name would live forever in infamy.

He couldn't take it anymore.

He ran from the crowd, needing space. Needing to get away from the praise he didn't deserve. He'd taken the cowards way out. He knew that. They didn't.

But Enya did.

"Why did you not kill her?" Enya asked.

Niran looked at her and shook his head. "I couldn't do it. This works just as well. No one will know she's sealed. Peace will overcome everything."

Enya's anger grew. "That was not part of the plan."

"Plan?" Niran's eyes grew. "What plan?"

Enya laughed. "Oh, little Niran. You really know nothing about the world. You parade around thinking that you are the most intelligent, most powerful being in existence, but there is so much you don't know. So much you *cannot* know."

"What are you talking about?"

"You owe me," Enya said. "You broke a deal, and now you owe me."

Niran shook his head and backed away from Enya. She'd tricked him. She…she was the one who had spread the rumors. She was the one who had any stakes in this. Shion…Shion had talked about Enya. The two of them knew each other. He hadn't seen this before. He hadn't realized.

He'd been tricked.

He didn't know what Enya wanted from him, but something in the back of his mind told him it wasn't a good thing. It wasn't going to go well. She wasn't going to stop until she got what she wanted, and while he didn't understand what that was, he knew it wasn't going to go well if she got it.

"No," he said, backing away from her. "I owe you nothing."

Fury raged in her eyes. "You will do as I say."

"No."

"Niran!"

She reached for him. He was faster. He blocked her with his magic, sending her spinning away. She cried out when she hit a tree and collapsed to the ground. Meanwhile, he pulled out the knife and unsheathed it.

This could kill an immortal. That's what Enya had said. But he knew that he didn't stand a chance against her. He'd caught her off guard, but if she had half the power that Shion held, then he stood no chance. He wasn't going to be able to get out of this.

"I'm sorry," he muttered. He unsheathed the knife. Enya screamed at him to stop, and then he plunged the knife into his heart.

From far away, Shubishi watched all of this happen.

For he knew it would.

He watched as Niran argued with Enya. As he thrust the knife into his chest. As his soul fought against the power of the knife. As instead of disappearing, it split into two. One gold and one white.

And he watched Enya try to take the knife.

He watched the knife reject her.

He watched her scream in frustration.

He watched her walk away.

He watched it all and said nothing. He did nothing. His friends did not know he was there. No one knew he was there. He stepped forward and picked up the knife, staring at the bloody blade before wiping it clean on his pants. He sheathed it. He placed it in the folds of his robes.

And then, he looked up into the eyes of Death, there to take Niran's soul. The soul that had disappeared into the night sky.

The two stared at each other. Death invisible to all. Shubishi invisible to all.

To all but each other.

They stared at each other, and then Shubishi turned and walked away.

Interlude

Interlude

"After that, we disappeared," Adelia said.

Mia looked up from her hands, tears in her dead eyes. She didn't know why she was crying. It wasn't her story. It had nothing to do with her.

Except, when she looked at Lady Shion, she knew exactly why she was crying.

She knew that she felt sympathy for the queen. She blinked back tears and held back her hand which wanted to take Lady Shion's. Nothing she did could help the poor woman after losing everything to Enya.

Enya. The woman with red hair and blue eyes. The woman who had plotted Lady Shion's death and for what? Why was she so obsessed? It couldn't just be because of a ring, could it?

"We didn't know what to do without her. Most of us had never lived in a world without our queen, so we disappeared. We went on with our lives, pretending to be normal humans. We formed bonds and made connections. Then, we disappeared before anyone could realize we were immortal. And we've been living like that ever since."

"At least," Tori added, "until last fall."

Last fall, when everything had changed for everyone. Mia glanced at Derek who caught her eye. He was also crying, and Mia wondered if it was the part of him that was Niran. He'd just heard the story of how he'd betrayed the woman he loved and killed himself to save everyone. She couldn't imagine how hard that must have been for him. She reached out and took his hand, squeezing it tight. He squeezed back and they both faced the Iravata again.

They were spread out, all in different positions. Lady Shion and Shubishi sat in front of them on the stiff love seat, while Adelia, Lior, and Eran stood behind them, none of them making eye contact with the teens. Tori leaned against the armrest, arms crossed with Nina leaning her head on her shoulder. They must have never told this story before.

Mia...felt sorry for them. She'd never felt sorry for them before.

"So, what do we do?" Cody asked, breaking the silence. No one looked at him. "Derek said he saw Enya, right? That's who the red-haired woman was?"

"We believe so," Lior said. "Eran has scanned Derek's memories and she matched his own. We hadn't realized how involved she was in Lady Shion's sealing until you broke the spell and we heard the other side of the story. If we'd known, we might not have stayed so quiet for so many years."

"I wouldn't have," Tori snapped. "I would have hunted that bitch down and destroyed her if I'd known."

Lady Shion placed a hand on Tori's arm and shook her head, but Tori merely snorted and a scowl broke out on her face.

"Anyway," Lior continued, "we think that Enya's been behind everything."

"What about Jae?" Mia asked the question in such a soft voice she wasn't sure that anyone had heard her at first. Just at the sound of his name, her body tensed, and Derek gripped her hand tighter.

He didn't push calming emotions onto her, but part of her wished he would. That he'd take away any choice she had and just let her calm down. She was still too frightened to ask him for help, but maybe...someday....

The Iravata all exchanged glances until Shubishi finally said, "He's connected to Enya."

Mia blinked. Without warning, her mind exploded with theories. Some were nonsense, but one stuck with her. Who Jae was. Who he'd talked about in his journals. Why he hated the Iravata so much. How he was connected to Enya, the woman from Lady Shion's nightmares.

Mia gasped, her stomach turning until she wanted to throw up.

"Oh my god," she whispered. "He's...he's her son."

No wonder he was so powerful. He wasn't a Natara. He was a Vilaim. And the son of a God.

When Shubishi nodded, confirming all of her suspicions, Mia stood. She let go of Derek's hand and he didn't fight her on it before she dashed out of the room. She heard footsteps behind her, and Blair calling out her name, but she ignored everyone, desperate to read the journals again. She arrived at her room and threw open the bag she'd stolen from Jae.

It was empty.

"Where are the journals?" she asked, spinning around. "I need to read the journals. Where are they?"

"You'll get them back," Shubishi said. "But we need them for now. We need to learn as much as we can about Jae in order to protect you children."

Mia's knees gave out and she sat on the bed, staring at Shubishi, too afraid to challenge him. The last time she'd done that...well it hadn't exactly gone well.

Her friends and her brother joined her on the bed, all tense and waiting for more explanation, but none came.

Finally, Derek cleared his throat. "Why didn't Enya do anything to me? I'm Niran's reincarnation, right? She had me right there. Why didn't she hurt me or take the knife?"

"We do not know." Shion's voice was quiet and haunting. "We do not know what she wanted from you or why, but we are certain she is determined to reclaim the knife. She wants power. She wants to prove…something. And she is going to use her son to get it."

Mia's gaze landed on Cody. They hadn't told the Iravata that Cody was Jae's half brother. It was clear that Enya was not Cody's mother, but would she come after him too? Would she do something to hurt Cody? Use him the way she was using Jae?

Mia shuddered and leaned her head on Cody's shoulder. He wrapped an arm around her shoulders, trembling. He must have been wondering the same thing.

"For now," Adelia said, "I think it's time to get back to reality. If I recall correctly, you have parents who have questions."

Mia breathed in sharply. She didn't know how she was going to explain any of this to her parents. But at least she'd have Derek to help her. And finally, *finally*, they wouldn't have to keep these secrets from their parents. They could be open about what was going on in their lives.

Adelia was right.

They needed to get back.

Everyone left the room one-by-one, until it was just Mia and Derek sitting on the bed. She closed her eyes and tried to imagine what life would be like now.

After being kidnapped.

After hearing the story of the Iravata. When she opened her eyes, for a second she was back in the room in Jae's mansion. Afraid and lonely. Never knowing if she was going to survive to the next day.

Derek squeezed her hand.

"It's okay," he said. "You're okay now."

Mia nodded, and together the two sat in silence while the moon rose into the sky behind them, bringing with it night, and an uncertain future.

Epilogue

Shubishi walked, barefoot, through the house. His footsteps were muffled by the socks encasing his feet. Joyous voices echoed around him, coming from down the hall. It was a one-story house. Old-fashioned and beautiful. It had probably been in the family for a hundred years, if not longer. Generations. Such was the way of wealth, but he didn't care about the history of the house. Not tonight, anyway. There would be time to learn of it later when he'd laid the seeds.

He touched the wooden walls, examining the paintings on the walls. Some were forgeries, and he chuckled at those. Others were real, and he marveled at their exquisite beauty. He wondered, briefly, how much the family knew was real. He knew they were not in touch with the secrets of the world, but were they foolish enough to believe that all the art they bought was real?

Shaking his head, he continued on. This was not why he was here tonight.

He passed by the room with the family. An elderly man and woman sat with their backs to him while three others, much younger, raised glasses of *baijiu* and lit cigars. He watched them for a moment, reveling in their excitement and celebration. They would not see him, even if he stepped into the room and stood under the brightest light. He knew why they were celebrating, but it still fascinated him. He knew everything about them, if he was being honest. He'd been watching them for some time.

But he wasn't being honest. Not with them, and not with the other Iravata. They knew some of the story, but not all of it. Not the small details that Shubishi had kept from them about before. Before he was immortal and before he'd approached Death.

He wanted to keep it that way.

With a smile, he headed away from the celebrating adults and continued through the house to a room where the noise wouldn't reach. He stood in the doorway, watching a woman, still thick from childbirth, sing a sweet lullaby in Thai to two bassinets in front of her. She didn't know he was there.

He didn't want her to know he was there.

"Sleep well," the woman whispered in Thai. "I love you, my sweets."

She backed away quietly from the sleeping babies. Shubishi stepped aside, letting her pass him. There were dark circles under her eyes, and her hair was oily from labor and lack of time to shower and sleep. Still, she smiled. A smile only a mother could have for her new babies. With a sigh, she headed back to the party where her husband and in-laws waited for her to continue the celebration. She didn't have long before the twins would wake.

Shubishi didn't have long.

He slipped into the nursery and closed the door behind him. It closed with a small *click*, and he revealed himself to the room. He was alone, other than the two sleeping souls. He wandered over to them, wanting a look. Wanting to make sure it was real. He hadn't been hallucinating or imagining it. Staring down at the squished newborns, swaddled with little hats, he smiled at them.

At their souls.

One gold.

One white.

To Be Continued in...

A

HOLLOW

SECRET

Acknowledgements

This was probably the most difficult book to write for many reasons. For one, it's an entirely different style of writing. It's eight people, all from a different world, telling the history of their world. Of their lives. Originally, I had this book in first person, a different chapter for each of the eight (though at the time it was nine), Iravata. But that caused its own problems, and I ended up deciding that I was going to write it like this. In third person omniscient. Because for some reason, I like to make my life more difficult.

But the other reason it was so difficult to write is because I knew, absolutely knew, that it was going to be contentious. It's a break from the main story, but it's important to the main story. Some suggested I weave it through the other books, but that would A) make the other books so much longer and B) make me cut out some of the most important parts. This is over 70,000 words of history that explains everything and shows so much of where these characters come from. It also moves the story forward and sets up book four in ways I wasn't expecting. It's important, and it was important that I got it right.

Anyway, onto the actual acknowledgements.

Karen, of course, who made me excited about this book again when she compared it to The Silmarillion. You are 90% of the reason this book exists, and why I managed to finish the first drafts of the series. You are the best and I love you so much.

Aunt Lorin, of course. You push me to expand my reading and to look at books in a way I'd never thought of before. Because of you, I was able to tackle the complications in this book and have fun writing it. All those books you gave me and had me read helped so much in the process of writing this book. Also, I learned how to use "had" from you. I'm still learning, and I'm not perfect, but I'm so much better. No need to make that red "HAD" stamp now!

Not to forget my other critique partners, Kathleen and Ashley. I love you both so much, and appreciate all the times you've listened to me rant about this book and help me through all the rough patches I went through while writing it. It's been a difficult couple of years, and you both are amazing.

In the same vein, Jen and Nani. You two are so busy with school, so I appreciate all the time you've taken to help me with this book and with my own insecurities about it. Love you both.

To Jules, who worked so hard to bring this beautiful new cover into the world and managed to shift through my complicated explanations and moods and timelines to create something so freaking beautiful!

And finally, Cas. You've been amazing all the time every day. There when I need you, helping me with my graphics and my website, and just overall being an amazing friend. You are fantastic, and I appreciate everything you do for me.

I love all of you, and everyone who has gotten this far with me. I'm grateful for everyone and hope you're enjoying this series as much as I've enjoyed writing it!

About the Author

A Colorado native, Linn Coldiron spends her time reading, writing, and studying languages. Her love of language and culture has led her to live a peripatetic life filled with inspiration from all over the world.